The
JOHNNY MOPED
Files

Tourists

C R Johnson

Grosvenor House
Publishing Limited

All rights reserved
Copyright © C R Johnson, 2025

The right of C R Johnson to be identified as the author of this
work has been asserted in accordance with Section 78
of the Copyright, Designs and Patents Act 1988

The book cover is copyright to C R Johnson
Cover image copyright to Lena_graphics, courtesy of Shutterstock

This book is published by
Grosvenor House Publishing Ltd
Link House
140 The Broadway, Tolworth, Surrey, KT6 7HT.
www.grosvenorhousepublishing.co.uk

This book is sold subject to the conditions that it shall not, by way of
trade or otherwise, be lent, resold, hired out or otherwise circulated
without the author's or publisher's prior consent in any form of
binding or cover other than that in which it is published and
without a similar condition including this condition being
imposed on the subsequent purchaser.

This book is a work of fiction. Any resemblance to
people or events, past or present, is purely coincidental.

A CIP record for this book
is available from the British Library

ISBN 978-1-83615-143-2

Other Titles

Book One
The Curious Reappearance of Sir Isaac Newton

Book Two
The Impossible Bream

Book Three
The Man who believes people to be good

Chapter one

Sir Isaac turned to Yesuah and the two women, Mary and Martha. He smiled benevolently, reassuringly; time travel could be an unsettling and bewildering experience for those not used to it.

"So, where would you like to go?" he asked pleasantly. "Or more pertinently, when?"

"Why did you leave Johnny behind?" Mary asked.

"It's complicated. Now, in which period of history—"

"Have you left Johnny there to die?" Martha accused.

"No, well possibly. I don't know. There are many vagaries of time of which I simply do not have the patience to explain. Now, please, where do you want to go? And when?" Sir Isaac's goodwill was rapidly fading.

"France," Yesuah whispered as he sat up, then faltered further.

"Glad to see you feeling better old chap. France?"

Yesuah pulled a long-necked instrument from under the seat that he'd rested uncomfortably upon. "What is this for?"

"The lute? A harmonic device for creating order from chaos. Please don't strum it or heaven knows what you'll cause. Now, where?"

Yesuah carefully placed the lute down then handled Galileo's telescope. "What's this?"

Sir Isaac sighed. "Please leave things alone. And be careful with that. It allows you to see things usually hidden. Why France?"

"Something Johnny said. I always thought I would like to see Greece, but that is past. We have to look towards the future."

Sir Isaac nodded and reached for the metronome.

"We have to go back for him. There's room," Mary, the younger, brighter woman explained.

"Johnny Moped's future is out of my hands, I'm afraid. You don't interfere with Death. At least not if you know what's good for you. Now, are you sure about France?" Sir Isaac wasn't convinced and watched patiently as Yesuah manipulated the telescope. "You look through the other end."

Yesuah swung it around. "The French freed the slaves, abolished the royal family, changed the government. Things I've been fighting for all my life."

"And equal rights for women," Martha, the older, darker woman added.

"Well, yes initially, but then not really. People become complacent, you know, and then find the people they've put in power become, well, people in power." Sir Isaac shook his head as he looked thoughtfully at the young man. "I did consider you."

"You did? For what?"

"However, I see you've a lot to learn, young Yesuah, and I haven't the time nor patience to mentor you." Sir Isaac calmed himself. "Now, I do have other things to do."

"Are women subordinate to men in France?" Martha asked.

"I don't think so. They even had Madame Guillotine cutting off those aristocratic heads. I assumed she was largely figurative… until I met her." Sir Isaac shivered.

"Good."

Sir Isaac sighed. Handing over the time machine to someone couldn't come soon enough, yet a note of caution stopped him. Johnny Moped wasn't ready for the responsibility and would probably refuse it; Deianira wanted it too much. He supposed it would be up to him to deal with the meteor two thousand years in the future, or perhaps he already had. It was difficult to be certain of anything.

He had to warn Johnny Moped to evade the aliens that seemed ever intent on capturing them for whatever nefarious purposes the Starachians had. He shivered at the thought of their glowing, probing fingers.

But mostly he just felt so overwhelmingly old. And tired. This was one loose end he had to tie up before retiring. There were so many more.

"After things have calmed down a bit, after the revolution you understand, it's tolerable. Certainly not before. I met him, Napoleon. Had terribly inflamed haemorrhoids. Gave him some suppositories. Too late by then. He lost at Waterloo. So, France it is." Sir Isaac turned his attention to the metronome once again.

"Professor, do you think you have room for one more?" Yesuah asked.

"I have already tried to explain..." Sir Isaac wearily began once again. "Now I have to concentrate, so if you please."

"No. Yeltsin." Yesuah smiled as he held the telescope to his eye. "Protection. I've a feeling I'm going to need it. Ah, Professor. What are all these others doing here? Why couldn't I see them before?"

Sir Isaac didn't need to see. He knew who they were and wanted nothing to do with them. "The worst form of parasitic life," he stated. "Tourists."

"Tourists?"

"Vultures come to pick over the corpse of what passes for entertainment for those with far too much time and money on their hands."

"What do you mean?" Yesuah passed the telescope to Martha and Mary.

"The super rich visit various hellholes throughout history, then manipulate and gamble on the outcomes for pleasure."

"Why?" Martha asked, horrified. "They came to see Yesuah crucified?"

"Oh yes, made a picnic of it, too. One of the most famous scenes to visit – at least in this solar system. See that big vessel in the sky? That's a Starliner. They pay a fortune for the privilege, though thanks to you and Johnny, not entirely what they were expecting."

"How does it just hang there in the sky?" Yesuah asked.

"Gravomagnetics. Now…" Sir Isaac turned his attention to the metronome and focussed. "…if you please."

"And pick up Yeltsin, Professor."

Sir Isaac took a deep calming breath. He had at his disposal the unlimited resources of a device unique in the Universe, and he was being used as a taxi. Sometimes he despaired. Well, most of the time, really. Yet another reason to hand on this responsibility.

He'd probably be blamed for this, too, just like everything else.

"Someone should do something about those tourists," Martha stated.

Sir Isaac agreed. "But not me. I'll leave a message for my successor. And good luck to him."

"You said you considered me. For this? As your successor?" Yesuah asked.

"Yes, you still have much to learn about the human condition, I'm afraid," Sir Isaac replied. "Too trusting by far. I made that mistake with Mal Salik."

"Who? Can't I come with you?" Yesuah asked. "And learn?"

"No, sorry. This is a solitary pursuit. And you wouldn't like it. Australia is unforgiving at this time of year. It might take me a while to find it. Been buried for millions of years."

"Professor, what are those?"

Sir Isaac looked to where glittering spinning tops appeared in the sky. They had to leave now. The Starachians were here. With a curt, definite nod, Sir Isaac turned to the metronome and fixed his thoughts on post-revolutionary France.

Chapter two

Johnny Moped frowned into the shadows. It had been several weeks since Death had attempted to put the 'fun' back in funeral. At least, that had been his plan. A plan which hadn't been entirely successful. And Johnny had played a part in that disappointment.

He'd lain awake since, fearful and anxious, until he realised there would be nothing he could do if Death returned. He hadn't yet, for which Johnny was grateful, though he had a feeling they would meet soon enough. Hopefully, not before his time. He hoped to extend his life through diet and exercise, which was currently under review.

He finished his Scotch egg and idly watched the TV, enjoying the sense of relief and peace after his trials at the stadium. A peace that was short lived.

"Could you do that later? Please?" he asked Alka.

She turned and frowned at him. Alka was usually brusque and rude, but after his refusal to pay for her cousin's coach fare from Slovakia and marry her, Alka had turned bad mannered and ill-tempered and refused to speak to him at all. She frequently glared at him when she answered her phone, shouting and swearing in his general direction, making it clear that whatever troubled her cousin was entirely his fault.

"The increasing conflict between Israel and Palestine has escalated into a full-scale war that sees the Palestinian people being forcedly removed from Gaza." On-screen, a sad procession of unhappy people trudged through rubble and barbed wire to a refugee camp that looked like a prison. "International support is to be withdrawn and the UN to begin a peacekeeping mission with the formation of a buffer zone."

Johnny looked away from the dreadful scenes of carnage and wondered why such horror always had to be. His thoughts were suddenly interrupted by a name he had hoped never to hear again.

"I am here with Hercules, who retained his world wrestling crown earlier this week after the surprise tag team spectacular on the island of Crete where he, Bernard, and Cerberus faced the Minotaur, Hydra, and Harpies. The fans want to know, will there be a rematch?" A fake-tanned, loud, white-toothed man thrust a microphone at an imperiously bearded muscled one.

Johnny shook his head. There simply was no escape.

"No rematch. I am here to announce my retirement from wrestling and leave the title open." Hercules unloaded the many large sparkly belts from his larger person. He swung his head back and swished his hair, snorted like a horse and gazed off into the distance, which was hard to do being in a studio.

"Many have tried to leave wrestling before you. Most have returned. When will you be making a comeback?" The presenter flashed his white teeth, also very much like a horse.

"I will be pursuing my film career and launching my own range of healthy foods and drink," Hercules persisted. He raised a can of Minotaur, crushed it in his fist, and threw it away. Hercules then displayed a can of Hercules with his grinning face on the front as he stood there flexing his biceps.

"Eat well, exercise, and you could become like me."

"So, we say goodbye to our champion and ask, after the tag team spectacular, who was the mysterious stranger who finally vanquished the Hydra? And will Death return to the wrestling ring? Who can stand against his 'kiss of death'?"

Alka walked in front of the TV and busily vacuumed a square inch for several minutes until Johnny returned his attention to the paperwork on his desk. His perennial problems returned and settled upon him like a backpack: the lack of funds, the lack of clients, and the cold damp greyness of Manchester.

"In other news, the civilian space flights funded by the world's billionaires have vanished without a trace." Johnny turned away from news concerning the wealthy and privileged.

He'd been putting this off for a week but finally had to face his fears. Admin. He opened a file folder labelled 'The Curious Disappearance of Sir Isaac Newton', crossed out the 'dis' and added 're'. He also added his notes to the file, stamped CLOSED and PAID, and placed it hanging in his recently decluttered bottom drawer.

It hung there alone, forlorn... but not for long.

File two contained little in the way of notes, apart from a brief account of his even briefer adventures in Vladivostok. After some thought he labelled it 'Missing Passengers/ Penguins' and added this to his bottom drawer. He would not add his personal events with the Undead but would forever fondly remember the canals and subtly suggest to Julia that was where his future lay. Though after the events with Lazarus, his sister wasn't returning his calls.

How she could blame him for that Johnny had no idea.

On second thoughts, his subjective experiences with the Undead were entirely relevant, and he re-titled file two

'The Impossible Bream' after his not-stepfather's restaurant and the titanic alien fish. He wondered if he'd ever see his mother again, and whether he even wanted to. He stamped CLOSED, but he had not as yet been paid. After fiddling with the little rubber letters, he re-stamped PENDING.

Johnny smiled at his £2.50 stationary purchase. A rubber stamper. Such a small thing yet it gave an enormous sense of well-being just being able to stamp things into finality.

File three gave him more pause for thought. Old Joe, Death, Yesuah, Sir Hieronymus and Hercules, and assorted monsters. Who had actually hired him? And to do what? It was unclear, and the conclusion more so. Had Death actually achieved his aim of putting the 'fun' back into funeral? Judging by the media reports, no.

There was always a media backlash, and the Liberal left-wingers weren't happy – not to mention the Undead. They had even started rioting again, stating Death was unrepresentative of their aims, and the living simply couldn't lump them – the dead and undead objectives and adjectives – all together.

Johnny looked up to see Alka staring at him.

"Mora has nowhere to live. She has been evicted. Living on the streets."

"I'm sorry, but that really has nothing to do with me."

Old Joe had achieved his goal of getting his latest version of biblical events in the public eye, but even interest in that was waning. So, what to name his third case?

He walked the large coin over his knuckles and palmed it, so it appeared in his other hand. How much was this gold coin, given to him by old Joe, worth? He had no idea but knew a man who would, though Mal would be unlikely to give a true and honest valuation.

Mal never paid if he could avoid it, and if handing over cash looked unavoidable then a swift stiletto usually did the trick.

Joe *had* paid, but the case had been unspecific at best. Johnny had found Yesuah and prevented a certain series of events from unfolding or possibly not, even probably made things worse. So, Death and Hercules aside, case number three revolved around his time in BCE Jerusalem.

Johnny smiled at the memory of the man who you couldn't help but smile along with. 'The Man who believes people to be good.' Johnny added his copious notes to the file and stamped CLOSED and PAID, then added this to his bottom drawer.

"Tea?" he asked himself. Admin done; Johnny felt relieved. Peace and quiet had returned, as Alka bustled her cleaning things out of the door. He glanced at the clock. At first Alka had been thorough and professional, spending an hour cleaning his offices and flat.

This had gradually waned to forty-five minutes, with minimal cleaning and much cajoling for coffee. Now, after his refusal to marry and pay for transport, Alka spent a harried half hour moving dust around and sighing loudly before she left.

Even this was not enough to persuade Julia to replace her or to have no cleaning company at all. Should *he* clean? Johnny briefly entertained this idea then dismissed such a drastic course of action. How could he persuade Julia to let him sell the house and buy a narrow boat and become the first totally water-borne investigator, navigating the ancient waterways of England, solving crime and investigating the extraordinary?

This was an attractive and wonderful thought, so absolutely would not happen. Happiness was not the life of

Johnny Moped. He slumped, locked his administrated files away, pocketed the key, and tried a smile. He thought of Yesuah, and his smile became genuine.

"Let us see what awaits," he announced to no-one in particular. But you never knew; Death might be listening, a sentient machine, or even his time-travelling doppelgänger.

Momentarily happy, or at least not entirely unhappy, he followed Alka down the stairs, watching her struggle with the trolley of cleaning materials she now rarely used and the truculent little Hoover that managed to trip her with its long and windy hose. The fridge in the hallway did not make this process any easier.

"Let me help," Johnny offered, but was rebuffed with a shake of her head.

"Please, Alka. This is silly. I made you a coffee."

He had. It still sat where he'd placed it on the dusty mantelpiece. And would remain there until Alka removed it. There were many unspoken battles of wills currently escalating in the house, the defrosting of the freezer the main bone of contention. His capitulation over the coffee just the most recent ceasefire.

"Mora will die there."

"This has nothing to do with…" Johnny began but stopped, appalled, when he saw tears in Alka's eyes. He took a deep breath and smiled at the memory of Yesuah once again. Johnny knew exactly what Yesuah would have done.

"How much?" The words were out before he could choke them back.

"How much what?"

"How much do you need for coach fare?"

"£65." Alka sniffed.

Surprised, Johnny shrugged. "Why didn't you say so? I thought it would be more like two or three hundred.

'Course I'll lend you the money. Lend," he added, then prompted, "Loan." Just to be absolutely clear that nothing could be lost in translation. "With interest."

"For single. She won't be returning." Alka sniffed. "She has nowhere to stay here."

"Your cousin is not staying with me," Johnny stated firmly, as an alarming premonition rose before him like an unnerving shark before a swimmer.

"You have empty rooms."

"No."

"You could rent out room and Mora will get job. There is always cleaning work," Alka pressed. "Care work. You need woman to take care of you. A wife."

"No." He hesitated then reluctantly opened his wallet and ironed five twenties into Alka's hand. He felt a brief spasm of doubt knife across his chest at his generosity and barely restrained himself from grabbing back the money. Yesuah had brought a cheery and expensive change to his life.

"Now will you cheer up?"

"No."

"And clean properly?"

"She can rent out room?"

Johnny slumped and walked outside, taking a lungful of fumes from the congested traffic, mindful of Cyborgs, flying horses, or old wandering Jewish men. He hoped the gold coin Joe had paid him with was worth a few quid. He was down to his last couple of hundred, if he could ignore the insistent pile of bills that always threatened to overwhelm him. If he couldn't, he was several thousand overdrawn. If karma was working, he'd done Alka a good deed, so he hoped he'd seen the last of his odd doppelganger, Hieronymus Calmly.

His thoughts led him to the café opposite and the extortionate prices. He absolutely wouldn't be buying an extravagantly priced beverage from here. Cake? Forget it. They didn't even do tea.

Johnny watched Alka drive away in a cloud of exhaust gases and rattly car things that should be positively connected to her vehicle but barely clung on like baby koalas on their mother's back.

That too had been an unwelcome experience, kicking off these unwelcome baffling cases. He even gave Alka a happy little wave, smiling at the peace to come. Then his smile dropped as he saw a shabby campervan stumble down the street like an unwelcome drunken sea creature unused to roads. It parked beside him with a screech of brakes.

The engine cut out, then restarted, then cut out once again. The beached walrus shuddered as it gradually subsided with many rattlings and wheezings of its own. The driver's door groaned open as a smiling Sir Hieronymus Calmly doffed his new hat and nodded a greeting.

"Johnny Moped. Just the man. Got a minute?"

Chapter three

Johnny sat opposite Hieronymus and glanced around the sparsely populated interior. Johnny hated to admit it, but the place was clean, enticing, and he would indeed have liked to spend time here. Oak benches and willow woven chairs sat at interestingly tatty tables, intriguing memorabilia on the walls beckoned, bookcases full of invitingly obscure titles awaited inspection. Flyers for various community events pinned to a noticeboard.

Hieronymus read a flyer for a choir and jumble sales. Whooshes of steam and seductive smells of baking and coffee assailed them like exotic promises.

"The aesthetics are quite pleasing," Johnny admitted. "And no, before you ask, I will not be engaging with you in a preposterous adventure. You also need to find a better method of locomotion."

"All designed to make a person spend their time and money, of course. This would have been indeed the case, except for the prohibitive prices," Hieronymus deflected as they waited.

"Are you free in an investigative sense?"

"No." Johnny became immediately suspicious. "At the risk of repeating myself, I have no wish to become entangled in more time-travelling, god nonsense."

"Yes? Oh, you again." Susan, the impatient waitress, stood in front of them. "Who's this, your brother?"

"No," Johnny began.

"Yes," Hieronymus replied and smiled.

"Who are you two supposed to be? Sexually unsuccessful bounders from a bygone age? Fancy dress, is it?"

"Pardon?" Johnny spluttered.

"Now, my good woman, tea please. For two. With a selection of cakes and picky things."

"We don't do tea. And I'm not a waitress."

"I don't believe you." Hieronymus recoiled at her glare. "Tea is universal. What then would you recommend for two weary travellers?"

"Oh my God. You're not a writer, are you? Have to use a dozen words when one will do?" Susan pointed to the sign that stated: 'NO WRITERS. NO LOITERING. NO LOITERING WRITERS. By Order of Management.'

"I suppose *you* consider yourself a barista?"

"Do I look like a solicitor?" Susan asked.

"Barista? Never mind. Sorry," Johnny apologised hastily at her frown.

"You do have the look of someone who is used to soliciting," Hieronymus added.

Johnny shook his head, embarrassed, but this thankfully passed Susan by.

"*Coffee* shop. Take it or leave it."

Hieronymus sat back, surprised. "You have an unusual sales technique. However, you are to be applauded on your aggressive style. I am pleased that you are not 'passionate' about your profession."

"Well, who would be making bloody coffee?"

"Who indeed. Are you related to Mal Salik, by any chance? Is he in? We have an appointment."

"*We* have?" Johnny asked, surprised.

"Of course. I thought you headed this way for that very purpose. After our business is concluded, I have a proposition for you." Hieronymus removed and then placed a Panama hat on the table and took off his coat. Johnny was startled to see he'd parted his hair in the middle and now wore tweeds like the 1920s were back in fashion.

Susan's initial estimation had been correct.

"Brylcreem?" Johnny asked, as he peered closer. Infuriated, he couldn't ignore the transformation before him any longer. "Is that a moustache? And an accompanying goatee beard?"

"It is in the first tentative stages, however it will, I feel, lend me an air of authority. It is necessary we differ, otherwise people will talk," Hieronymus explained, as he reflexively stroked his bristling chin. "You seem to be making no efforts in that direction."

Johnny only possessed three sets of identical items of clothing, bought when a store was going out of business: black suit, white – at least, once-white – shirts, loafers with accompanying pork pie hat, and fish-tailed parka. An ensemble that required no thought or effort at all. And he absolutely did not suit any form of facial hairiness as Judea had proven.

"Sartorially speaking…" Johnny began and stopped. He had to admit Hieronymus did resemble a well-heeled individual; a visiting Victorian professor who had become lost in the 21st century. "Why tweed?"

"It lends itself to solidity and a certain confidence," Hieronymus replied.

"Does it? And the bow tie?"

"Intellect and a touch of self-irony, don't you agree?"

Reluctantly Johnny agreed. "The goatee does lend itself to a whimsical effect. But a monocle?"

"Indeed."

"Why are you here to see Mal? Do you owe him money?" Johnny asked. "That is nothing to do with me. I wish I could help but…"

"Do you?" Hieronymus sat back, surprised.

"No," Johnny admitted, immediately suspicious. "Why are you here?"

"I have certain questions about Mal, his heritage, and future plans. He is somehow entangled in the current troubles. Also, he will give us the money we need."

"We need? *We*? And whatever 'this' is, is no entanglement of mine. Sorry. Did you say Mal? Give money?" Johnny felt the amusement reach his face. "*Bonne chance.*"

"*Certainement.*"

"He's in back. I'll ask," Susan interrupted, frowning at them. "Are you going to buy anything or just loiter?"

"We are his guests." Hieronymus yawned and stretched.

"Weary?" Johnny asked.

"Don't ask. Had a few loose ends to tie up. Of yours. I lit the fuses in the temple; bit of confusion over the dates. I may have been a few decades out, but too bad. And all that home-made explosive did was to put a large crack in one wall anyway. Ah well, never mind, eh? All done and dusted." Hieronymus smiled and whistled a little tune, taking an interest in the specials board.

"And Lazarus?" Johnny asked guiltily. He'd tried, with varying success, to forget.

"Ah yes. Him, too." Hieronymus nodded but didn't elaborate. "What's a ciabatta? A tea-drinking cricketer?"

"Did you find a dead body to replace him with?"

"No, I opened the tomb and let him out. Quite mad, you know. Going on about travelling to the future. I suppose he'll join the rest of the madmen and prophets wandering around in the desert. Quite a popular pastime in Palestine then. I fancy the carrot cake. With walnuts." Hieronymus pursed his lips as he scanned the laminated menu.

"So, there is no dead body to account for Yesuah either? Death won't be happy."

"Good for the brain. Mood boosting, too, walnuts."

"So, you haven't replaced the bodies?" Johnny persisted as dread stole over him.

"How would I go about finding a corpse with a passing resemblance to a middle-aged man from two thousand years ago who lived in the Middle East? And a Frappuccino, whatever that is. Do you know?"

"No, and I don't want to." Johnny shivered and glanced around for Death.

"Have I upset you, my good man?"

"If there is no body in the tomb, then all that I went through will have been for nothing."

"Ah. Yes. I have considered this, which is why we find ourselves here. That, however, is the least of our problems." Hieronymus drummed his fingers on the oak table as the machines steamed and whooshed.

"We? Our? There is no we. I am not returning to Jerusalem with a corpse." Johnny shivered at the memory of that horrible place.

"I did not realise being unreasonable was in our character."

"Unreasonable?" Johnny spluttered.

"I cannot manage on my own. I had hoped you'd view this as a partnership. Perhaps cinnamon sprinkles?" Hieronymus mused as he tapped the menu. "Your treat?"

"Good god, no."

"No?"

"No," Johnny added firmly. "On both accounts."

"Perhaps you're right. The choco-frothy top it is."

"Mal says to come on through." Susan pointed to a door marked 'OFFICE', next to the toilets.

Chapter four

After a brief struggle at the door, as to who went first, they followed her through and squinted into the dim interior. Mal liked to conduct his shady business in shadow, but they could just make out his wispy grey beard and piercing eyes under his kippah. His hands moved under many rings, like bejewelled spiders.

There was a venomous laugh. Mal always looked like he expected to be in receipt of terrible news. He did not look physically well; someone had painted a sepia portrait of him and dressed it in his clothes. He lit a cigar from a dancing flame in the palm of his hand. A master of illusion and distraction.

"So, here you are again. The authors of my downfall, here to repay their debt." Mal smiled with gold teeth and offered a theatrical cough. The air rapidly became heavy with thick cigar smoke that also acted as veils.

"He looks much worse since last I saw him," Johnny whispered to Hieronymus, then turned to the cigar smoke. "You gave me the map to Isabella."

The resting actor/manager appeared to be in his Fagin period, with a passing reference to Gandalf. Behind him rested his unlit elaborate candlestick, scrolls, and several tombstones which he never seemed to be without. And his treasure chest.

"Another favour you owe me for," Mal grated. "Usually, to look upon my face means death. How I've fallen."

"Well, it is hoped we can do something beneficial for you," Hieronymus offered, as Mal gestured to two leather chairs facing him. The only illumination came from a jeweller's circular light in front of Mal that only dimly illuminated his cluttered desk.

"How is the coffee business?" Hieronymus asked. "Better than the religion game?"

Mal shook his head sadly. "Woeful. How is the time-travelling business?"

Hieronymus just smiled as Susan returned with a tray of refreshments, reluctantly distributing them.

"I sincerely hope these drinks are complimentary," Hieronymus added, as Susan departed.

Johnny fervently hoped so, too.

"Maybe." Mal smiled his shark-like smile. "Depending upon how our business turns out, my busy little prophets. Have you come to rewrite that which was written?"

"Pardon?" Hieronymus and Johnny shrugged at each other.

"I see. So, my little scribblers, what have you for me?"

Hieronymus gestured for Johnny to start. If Mal Salik was fazed by two identical men seated in front him, he gave no sign. Johnny reached for the coin Old Joe had given him and passed it over.

Quick as a magician, Mal had his jeweller's eyepiece fitted and peered intently at it. He pressed it with a sharp taloned fingernail.

"Ah." Mal feigned disinterest but placed it on his side of the desk. "Old, tarnished, dubious provenance, worthless lead, gold plated."

Johnny smiled and reached forward. "So, you're not interested?"

Mal leant forward and smiled, then placed his hand over the coin which vanished. He sat back and steepled his fingers. Johnny was watching for this move and couldn't decide if the coin was in Mal's other hand or up his sleeve. The old trickster had lost none of his touch. Mal Salik was a master of misdirection.

Hieronymus slurped his coffee and took a huge, noisy bite out of his cake.

"I'll give you two hundred pounds," Mal offered, as Hieronymus coughed and almost lost his cake into Johnny's face.

"Then we'll take our business elsewhere," he spluttered.

Mal magically produced the coin once more and held it under the light. "Grapes on one side and a tree on the other. Have you translated it?"

"No," Johnny admitted.

Mal smiled. "It says 'Year One of the Redemption of Israel'. I wonder where you got this. And why it's now come to me."

"Wonder away," Hieronymus replied.

"Five hundred, and that's my final offer." Mal nodded, suddenly serious.

Before Johnny could accept, Hieronymus jumped in. "Five *thousand,* and there is another small matter to take into consideration."

"A penny more and I'll be cutting my own throat." Mal leant back as the coin disappeared into his hand. "And this small matter?"

Johnny was staggered at Mal's capitulation. He must really want something very badly from them. Which was very, very bad news indeed.

"Ah, well, there's no easy way to say this." Hieronymus shrugged. "I need a dead body. Male, middle-aged, Middle Eastern descent."

Mal didn't bat an eye. "When?"

"As soon as," Hieronymus replied. "Preferably crucified. With a beard. Have I missed anything?" Hieronymus asked Johnny.

"Two bodies would be better. I don't want anyone murdered. Just, you know, natural causes," Johnny added. Despite his best efforts to distance himself from this business, he was being drawn in like a hooked fish.

Mal sat back and folded his arms. This was never a good sign. The negotiation ball was definitely back in his court, but Hieronymus tried a googly to confuse metaphors.

"Five thousand for the coin, cash," they both heard Mal's sharp intake of breath at this, "and two, not murdered, bodies," Hieronymus finished.

"Deal." Mal leant forward and smiled.

"Pardon?" Johnny and Hieronymus looked at each other in flustered confusion.

"A deal?" Business negotiations with Mal Salik were never this straightforward. They had barely passed from the brusquely informal, never mind the threat of physical violence.

"On one condition," Mal added.

"Ah." Johnny felt a fluttering in the pit of his stomach and checked for a recently applied stiletto blade. This would not be good.

"You take me to a time and place of my choosing. It appears I have to return." Mal rubbed the coin thoughtfully as it once again magically reappeared. "Before it's too late."

Hieronymus sat bolt upright. "No, never. A time machine, if there was such a device, is not to be used as a... a... taxi service," he ended lamely.

"Then no deal," Mal ended with finality and placed the coin back on the table. "£50 for the coffee and cake. Each."

"There is no need to insult us," Hieronymus blustered.

A thin sliver of stainless steel did then materialise in Mal's hands. He used the blade to pick at his nails and waited, staring at them silently like a large anaconda. Mal flicked out his tongue that Johnny was distressed to see forked in the middle.

"Why not?" Johnny asked.

"So, you admit you do possess a time machine?" Mal smiled.

Hieronymus shook his head at Johnny. "If you remember, I told you I do the thinking. I will also add, the talking."

"Sorry." Johnny slumped back and took a bite of his cake. "This really is delicious, the coffee, too. But £50?"

"London prices," Mal replied.

Johnny felt he needn't add they were in Manchester.

Hieronymus drummed his fingers on the arms of the chair. "One way. To a destination of *my* choosing. And you help me with unloading the bodies, seeing as my colleague is unwilling, despite this being his case."

Mal nodded slowly as he considered, then he smiled, spat on his hand and offered it to Hieronymus who reciprocated. They shook.

"Now, my dears, any other business?" Mal grinned his golden smile at them.

"Just one. Why?" Hieronymus asked. "Why do you want to go to the past?"

Mal lit a cigar and gazed levelly at them and then at his body. "It's dying. Cancer. I would like to see the golden age of my people before it's too late."

"Your people?"

"Sorry to hear that," Hieronymus added, frowning at Johnny's insensitivity.

Mal waved their concerns away. He squinted at them through the heavy smoke, took a deep drag from his cigar and coughed.

Johnny looked at Hieronymus and shrugged. What possible harm could it do? They watched Mal unroll notes from an elastic banded roll, count then hand them over to Johnny, who handled them like hot potatoes. You never knew with Mal; they could simply vanish at any moment.

"These seem genuine." Surprised, Johnny shrugged at Hieronymus, who turned to Mal.

"How long?" Hieronymus asked, trying to be sensitive.

"Weeks, months at best. Depends." Mal nodded. "The tide is turning against us, not that it was ever with us, but with this current war we have reached the end."

"I don't understand…" Johnny began.

Mal held up his hand in which once again a small flame danced. "I don't want your apologies or sympathy. Just give me a few days to get my affairs in order. And a few bodies. I'll be in touch."

Chapter five

Johnny reluctantly invited Hieronymus to his offices and, after a brief struggle as to who sat behind the desk, they settled into a strained, companionable silence.

"You know Mal is an inveterate liar," Johnny began, as he proprietorially arranged things around his desk. "And an accomplished magician."

"It is his stock-in-trade," Hieronymus agreed, and moved several things back to where they'd previously been.

"Would he lie about something like that?" Johnny asked. "These are no longer your offices. Leave them there."

Hieronymus waved away his concern. "The deal is done. There is no going back. We will find out soon enough."

"Find out what?"

"History will show us his hand in affairs. Even if Mal has more than a few weeks, he is old and could not possibly affect the course of history to any degree. What could he possibly accomplish in Jerusalem two thousand years ago?"

"None of my business. I'm not going back." Johnny absolutely did not want to be involved in any more perilous undertakings. He kept silent as he made his way to the kitchenette that had not enjoyed the attentions of any cleaning products. "Tea?"

Hieronymus nodded as his gaze swept the room. "Tidied up? I take it the investigation business is as slow as ever. You must have been pushed to the very extremes of boredom."

"No. Alka. Julia has employed a cleaner, well, in its very loosest sense of the word." Johnny filled the kettle and switched it on, only to jump back in shock.

"There is no escape from us. You must return," a tinny little voice threatened. "Listen to the toaster."

Johnny switched it off and considered. "I thought the harassment by electronic goods was over. The phone has disappeared."

"The phone is with me and is not what you expect. The harassment is also due to me, I'm afraid. I can only presume the Cyborgs are not through with us."

"Us? What did you do?"

"It's complicated and none of your affair. Suffice to say, Medusa is gone. In the future."

Johnny could see he was lying and stared at him until Hieronymus relented.

"For now, at least," Hieronymus admitted, and frowned at Johnny's stare.

"So, if that is in the future, then how are they harassing you here now? In their past?"

Hieronymus smiled. "Electricity, I fear, knows no bounds. It exists in the quantum world and so does not recognise time. Switch on, old chap. We have much to discuss."

"No, we don't."

Cautiously Johnny flicked the switch as he arranged tea things on a tray, ignoring the increasingly dire threats from the kettle. He could ask Hieronymus to leave, but he would probably just be back. As for not getting involved, Johnny already was. He needed to know he'd done all he could to placate Death.

"The fridge?" Hieronymus asked, as Johnny poured.
"What of it?"
"Is the hallway an ideal place for such an appliance?"

"It seems to enjoy it," Johnny replied.

"Hmm. Well, I'm sure you know your business. Is there perchance any of Mr. Poppadoppalou's excellent curries and naan's currently residing within?" Hieronymus enquired. "I rather miss a good spice blast. The canteen at the OPC leaves much to be desired."

"No." Johnny was in no mood to share what pitiful few remained. "Why are you here? I thought I made it plain we were through. After Crete I no longer want anything to do with gods or immortals, Death, or anything else extraordinary."

Hieronymus nodded. "Then your investigating days are over?"

"Of course not."

"Then why talk in circles? I hate to tell you this, but what you want is of no concern. Others are aware of you and so will continue to 'have something to do with you', whether you like it or not. You will frequently be mistaken for me."

"It was you with that orchid? Mal and the Isabella?"

"Hmm. Yes." Hieronymus waved his concerns away. "What you *need* is of far more importance. Which means you will undoubtedly need my help."

"Help? I am ticking along just fine, thank you."

"I see. Who rescued you from the tomb?" Hieronymus asked.

Johnny looked away and busied himself pouring his own tea. He would not offer biscuits in the hope Hieronymus would leave. After several moments of furiously silent tea drinking, ignoring and staring at the Manchester drizzle, Johnny looked back across his desk.

"Pardon?"

"Tourists," Hieronymus repeated.

Johnny nodded. "And?"

"I received this in the internal mail at the OPC." Hieronymus handed over a rolled tube of parchment.

Johnny unrolled it and read aloud, "*Look through the telescope at things unseen. End this despicable tourism or face dire consequences. Do not let yourself be used as a taxi service.* Signed Sir Isaac?"

"I took Sir Isaac's advice." Hieronymus slurped his tea. "Though I am letting myself be used as a taxi. Still no biscuits?"

Johnny stamped into the kitchen and returned with a packet of out-of-date, soft digestives. "Well?"

"Would you believe there are tourist hellholes of future and past historic events that other time travellers visit purely for amusement?" Hieronymus helped himself to another cup of tea. "No chocolate biscuits? I distinctly remember keeping some in the bread bin."

"You've just had a carrot cake," Johnny pointed out.

"One can never have enough baked goods, I find, with tea. Would a bacon sandwich be in the offing? A fried egg banjo?"

"You need to lose some weight." Johnny tried to understand what Hieronymus had just said. Something about tourists? And something else? "There are other people with time machines?"

"Oh yes, I was surprised, too. Sir Isaac failed to mention this before, but then he has failed to mention many things. These tourists, for want of a better word, have lost all sense of right and wrong and exist only for further and more extreme forms of entertainment. I mean to put an end to such feckless voyeurism."

This seemed unlikely to Johnny. "How do you know?"

"I've seen them. If you like, I'll show you."

Ah, this was it. A subtle ploy to get him to help with the dead bodies, even though Mal had agreed. Though, with his health problems Johnny doubted Mal could lift one body. Provide them, undoubtedly.

"How many more?" Johnny asked. "Time machines?"

"I counted a dozen at the crucifixion. And a Starliner."

"What? I saw no-one except you. And the Professor." Johnny shook his head dismissively. "Nice try."

"You have to be seated inside the influence of a time machine, looking through Galileo's telescope, to be able to see through their camouflage. They employ a reflective concealment. They were quite disappointed when you rescued Yesuah and lost one of their guests. You have come to their attention. They are aware of you. And as such you are in danger."

"Why?"

"Because you meddled and ruined their party. Lost them a lot of money."

Johnny took a deep breath. Did he believe Hieronymus? If there was one, two time machines, it made sense there would be more.

"Boredom," Hieronymus added.

"Pardon?"

"It isn't easy being rich."

"Easier than being poor," Johnny observed.

"Is it? Look at those rich and famous and how they waste their money. Those billionaires should stop playing spacemen and build hospitals. Wouldn't surprise me if they've been abducted."

"I suppose you do lose perspective."

"And living forever. How would you pass the time if you didn't have to work, and time just dragged on?"

Johnny had to agree. "The devil does make work for idle hands. Which brings us back to Mal. How is he involved in this? Whatever this is."

"That is what we have to determine."

Johnny sighed. Would he be returning to Jerusalem whether he liked it or not? "So, I'm in danger from bored, immortal, rich people?"

"Aliens." Hieronymus held up a restraining hand. "If I must, I'll hire you to help put an end to time-travelling tourists. Aliens who mean Mankind no good whatsoever."

Johnny reached for a vacant file and thought of a preliminary title. Alien tourists?

"Your going rate?"

"Is still the same."

"£5000 a week seems a little steep."

"You were the one who decided that rate, if you remember. Do you need my help or not?"

After a moment Hieronymus conceded. "This will be easier with two."

"Why?" Johnny became immediately suspicious.

"Well, it appears that these tourists are actually manipulating historic events to provide even greater catastrophes; the bigger and bloodier, the better. The First World War, for example, just simply should not have happened and would not without their meddling."

"Are you saying these tourists are making disasters just so they can watch?"

"Exactly. And gamble, trying to outdo each other. You know, casualty rates and so forth. I assume the effect on the observed is not that important."

"And how would you stop them?"

"At source. We will find the time and place the time machines were first manufactured or utilised and stop their use." Hieronymus nodded.

"But," Johnny struggled with this seeming paradox, "won't that mean that—"

"I will, of course, retain the original."

Johnny lapsed into a confused silence. He shook his head. Would £5000 a week be worth the danger? He'd been subjected to worse, that was true enough, but he had to draw a line somewhere. "No, sorry."

"That's your final word? Then I shall save mankind on my own. I find it hard to understand why you want nothing further to do with any of this." Hieronymus stood and prepared to leave. He shook his head. "Death will want to know why there is no body in Yesuah's tomb."

Johnny glowered at Hieronymus, who just smiled. With grim reluctance Johnny prepared for the worst. "Fine."

Hieronymus sighed. "Fine? You are engaging in perhaps the greatest adventure of our age and your estimation of our undertaking is 'fine'?"

"Equal partners. I will not be called 'young Johnny Moped' nor any other pejorative term. Equal. Partners." Johnny stated firmly. "And then that's it. Once Death is happy, I'm done."

Hieronymus nodded. "You can take Mal's money I negotiated as a first week's instalment."

"You negotiated?" Johnny hesitated then nodded. "Agreed."

"In that case, understand this: the Universe, *young Johnny Moped*, is infinite with infinite probabilities. There is no 'done'. Will you do me the favour, nay the courtesy at the very least, of trying to keep up?"

Chapter six

"Perhaps it would help if you didn't smoke," observed Hieronymus. Mal had coughed constantly for several minutes now until Johnny and Hieronymus both became quite concerned.

"Too late for that." Mal hoicked phlegm and spat on the pavement. He pointed. "And that?"

"Hidden in plain view. No-one would ever think this humble vehicle is a time machine," Hieronymus answered.

"I thought you..." Johnny began but quieted at a glance from Hieronymus.

"Are your affairs in order?"

Mal nodded and gestured his associates around towards the back of the campervan. Johnny frowned at the buzz-cut twins who'd smashed into his house, chased him to the airport then rebuilt his home, but they feigned ignorance and ignored him. Between them they carried a rolled-up carpet that seemed suspiciously heavy. Johnny did not wish to discover what made it bulge in unexpected places. They opened the small barn back-doors of the campervan and loaded the carpet inside.

Johnny cast a wistful glance at his house and offices, hoping to catch a glimpse of her. Perhaps she'd be gazing forlornly out of a balcony window like Juliet, or a princess waiting for her prince. Alka's cousin Mora had been nothing like he'd been dreading.

Late, on a previous week's night, Johnny had heard a thump and kerfuffle and ignored it. Any prospective burglar would simply leave disappointed. That had happened before. In the morning, to his surprise there were two large suitcases beside the fridge, keeping it company in the hallway.

He'd left in high dudgeon to research the metronome at the local library, dreading to return home, but found to his surprise… Mora.

She was beautiful. And funny. Her smile made him feel breathless, and the cabbage soup had been divine. Mora had even defrosted the freezer and told him Alka would not be returning, which was an added unexpected bonus.

Johnny was in love. And not the magically enforced love of Deianira. He knew this, because he'd not even broached the delicate subject of rent.

The last few days had passed in a bewitching world of dancing as they turned circles around each other from room to room. A charming world of shy smiles and affection. They hadn't actually spoken of romance. Yet. But the attraction and inference were clear – at least from his point of view. Yesterday had been a magical time. An enchanting…

"What's wrong with you, boy? Mooning at your house like a lost sheep. You in love or something?" Mal stood at his side, coughed once more and spat.

"No," Johnny quickly recovered. "Just assessing your repairs."

"No guarantees or warranty. I assumed that was understood." Mal was dressed in what Johnny could only assume was once a velvet smoking jacket. He had no idea why. Old slippers clung precariously to his feet like baby marmosets clinging to a careless mother. Mal had decided this attire would then be best topped off with a strange skullcap. Leaning on a cane that Johnny knew contained a sword, he loitered like a gentleman Steptoe, a wizened wizard.

"Terms agreed with that fellow there. Not me." Johnny indicated a flustered Hieronymus, who was arguing with the buzz-cut twins about transporting two large tombstones, the treasure chest, and candelabra. The doors wouldn't close against the overhanging carpet and bare, bloodied feet.

Hieronymus huffed around to them. "What are you waiting for?"

"He's in love." Mal shook his head sadly.

"Why?" accused Hieronymus. "We've work to do. No time for lollygagging after women. Have I not indicated the gravity of this situation?"

"Seen it all before. I was in love, you know. Once," Mal continued wistfully. "Salome her name was."

"I'm not in love. I was simply pointing out various aspects of Mal's building works that—"

"Not Deianira? You know she has a girdle? Anyway, you're not any competition against Hercules, are you?" Hieronymus continued.

Johnny sucked his teeth and remained silent.

"She used to dance and entrance—" Mal continued.

"Enough. We have an arduous task before us. Let us get to it. There will be no more talk of romance." Hieronymus ushered them towards the campervan.

"Wasn't romance," Mal continued. "Business."

"Or any dalliances with the female sex. Is that clear? Women weaken resolve."

"Love makes you lose your head," Mal continued. "Beheading. Happy days."

"I'm not in love."

"In, please. Time's a-ticking." Hieronymus smiled and winked. "Just my little joke."

Chapter seven

They arrived as the crucifixion procession began its long dreadful walk from the city. Parked across the valley, Johnny could see and well remember the sad collection of beaten men dragging their cross-members wearily along stony ground.

It was a sobering sight.

"Look in the cupboard there," Hieronymus directed.

Johnny opened a cupboard and withdrew a big-bellied mandolin. He frowned. "I don't think busking will help."

"No, the other cupboard. I really must find out what that does one day when I'm not saving the world."

Johnny replaced the fat-bellied guitar thing and withdrew a long leather tube fastened with brass hinges. It was cumbersome and unwieldy, like a thick boa constrictor with other things on its mind.

"Look through the telescope."

"Telescope? I don't want to. It was bad enough being there." He shuddered at the memory. "Should we do something?"

"No, best not to meddle. Yesuah survives, doesn't he? Not at them. Them." Hieronymus urged Johnny to point it at the deserted mountain top. Mal remained silently approving, watching the gruesome trudging spectacle, as Johnny took the cumbersome instrument and surveyed.

"What on earth?" He pulled the eyepiece away and looked, then replaced the eyepiece and looked again. "What is that?"

"Tourists."

High above, he could see many vehicles parked, watching the crucifixion. A few Victorian machines of shiny spinning brass and whirring things, many more of the traditional streamlined spaceship variety from popular fiction, and vaguely moving mirages of pearlescent rainbow colours. There was also a sleek modern electric car.

There were people seated on chairs and loungers, eating and drinking, being served by robots. Johnny watched as one man, egged on by his drunken friends, left the party and made his boozy way down the slope to the crucifixion.

"No!" Johnny remembered this man who had protested his innocence. His friends thought he was hilarious.

There was a tremendously deep sonorous sound that vibrated them and the ground. A huge wedge-shaped spaceship hove into view and simply, impossibly, hung there like a triangle of very heavy embarrassed cheese.

"My god. What now?" Johnny asked.

Hieronymus sniffed. "Package tour. Cruise ship."

"That man. We have to do something. He's not one of the condemned."

"Do we?"

"The soldiers took him and crucified him by mistake. Come on." Johnny made to open the door.

"Wait." Hieronymus lay a restraining hand on Johnny's arm.

"He's going to be—"

"Serves him right." Mal sniffed. "Enjoying the misery of others. Sooner or later, you're going to get your fingers burnt. Believe me, I know."

"But…" Johnny watched as the soldiers caught hold of the man and dragged him protesting towards a frame.

"Too late now." Hieronymus shrugged.

Johnny sat back and looked away, then straightened as he saw himself. And Martha and Mary. He looked at Hieronymus, himself, and himself over there. He felt a quiet wobble inside his body.

"There are now three of us," Johnny managed.

"No, an infinite number," Hieronymus added. "Remember I asked you to switch on?"

Johnny nodded as if he knew what this meant, then relaxed. Then sprang upright, electrified, as another shuddering resonance buzzed Johnny's bones.

"Another cruise-liner?"

It hove into view like a circus attraction. This one rounded and spinning like a top with many bright lights. It hung there like a giant's flashing frisbee as it disgorged many smaller spinning tops.

"Come on. We know what happens. *We're* not here to watch." Hieronymus opened his door as a bewildered Johnny followed him to the back where they struggled with the heavy carpet. Johnny looked away as a bloody foot slid out. He remembered only then he'd said he wouldn't help.

Mal lit a cigar. "Crucified as specified."

"Can we get a wriggle on?" Hieronymus asked and pulled, then waited for Johnny to grab the other end while Mal puffed at his cigar and supervised. He looked decidedly better, stronger as he unloaded his luggage.

Thankfully it wasn't that far to the tombs carved into the hillside that Johnny remembered well. It had been just as awkward carrying Yesuah on a ladder stretcher.

They rolled away the stone, ducked under the entrance, and made their way to the furthest recess of the dark tomb where old skulls grinned at them.

Johnny squinted but none grinned back.

Hieronymus nodded and smiled. "Good. That's that then. Let us crack on."

Johnny stopped at the entrance and turned to look at the huddled shape in the dark corner. "What about that?"

"What?"

"Well, isn't the carpet going to cause suspicion?"

"You want to unroll the carpet and take the filthy bloody thing back with us?" Hieronymus asked pleasantly.

"No, but I mean what will people think? You know, in years to come? When it's discovered?"

"Same as those lost books of the Bible. Perhaps they'll call it the Turin Carpet. Now, are you sure?" Hieronymus asked Mal, who coughed and spat once again.

Mal nodded as a crease pulled his face. Johnny had never seen Mal smile before.

"It's warm. Dry. A man with money will do well here." Mal jingled a purse at his side then unexpectedly gave Johnny a brief hug.

"You'll figure it out." Mal winked at Johnny.

"Then I wish you the best of luck." Hieronymus nodded and shook Mal's hand.

They rolled the stone back and a bemused Johnny followed Hieronymus as they walked away from the tomb.

"That was very unsettling."

"What?"

"Being hugged. By Mal. And desertion. Or what did they call it when the old sailors left, you know, Robinson Crusoe?"

"Marooned?" Hieronymus suggested.

"Yes. We've marooned Mal."

"He's not isolated nor stranded here. This was his choice, and if I ever have this choice, I will choose this, too. Wouldn't you?" Hieronymus stamped on purposefully towards the campervan.

"No."

"No? So, your time with Death and his views on the medical profession and their meddling have not persuaded you otherwise?"

"What do you mean?"

"What I mean, young Johnny Moped, is that for me, it is not life at any price. Like Mal, I would not wish to undergo treatment just to cling on for a few more years. With the constant worry of when your illness returns. Neither will I be spoon-fed mushy food in a care home, stuffed full of pills, watching daytime TV until I expire. I will not prolong my time in Death's waiting room within which we all sit. Live life to the full every day, for tomorrow you die. You should see the old professors."

"I don't feel like that. Why do you? How can we be the same but so dissimilar?"

"Different realities diverge."

"Thank goodness for that." Johnny watched as Hieronymus stamped determinedly away and entered the campervan which vanished. Johnny staggered in shock but gasped as the campervan reappeared up the slope with the tourists. Johnny turned and offered a wave to the forlorn figure standing before the tomb then followed.

"Now, just wait a minute." A flushed and hot Johnny flung his coat and hat into the campervan. "Thanks for waiting for me. I've forgotten just how hot it is in Jerusalem."

The shadows lengthened as the figures hung limply from the crucifixes like dirty washing. The heat drained you.

"Have I done something to annoy you?" Johnny asked.

"That is not to say I am a fatalist. I do not wish to die tomorrow, but rather I prefer to live for today," Hieronymus continued.

"Because you *might* die tomorrow?" Johnny asked.

"This is a precarious business."

"There's a stream over there." Johnny pointed where a thin little sliver ran on into the desert. He wondered if Hercules was still counting stones and being annoyed at people bothering and mistaking him for a baptiser. "We could enlist the help of Hercules."

"Help and Hercules are not two words that sit comfortably together. If you come across him, just be polite and walk away. Leave gods alone. We do not want any more trouble of the Deianira variety, do we?"

"No, I suppose not," Johnny replied, but was not entirely in agreement.

He turned back where he could see that only he, Martha, and Mary remained behind at the crucifixion. He watched the gruesome scene as the soldiers began to spear the crucified while faint moans split the sultry air.

"Keep guard."

"Why? Where are you going?"

"To have a word with them." Hieronymus indicated the other time travellers who were packing their gear and preparing to leave. At least the wealthy people watched as their robotic servants packed the picnic equipment away.

Whatever protective camouflage they employed was being deactivated as night fell and shadows hid them. Even the spinning saucer dimmed its lights, and the huge wedge shape melted into the night sky, blocking out the stars.

"Will that do any good?"

"No, probably not, but I'll have a better idea who I'm dealing with. Know your enemy."

"We," Johnny corrected. "Who *we're* dealing with."

"Just so. Don't go wandering off. Guard the van."

With that, Hieronymus turned and made his way to a tweedy gentleman who busied himself tinkering with a wooden brass contraption, all spinning wheels and fluctuating dials.

Johnny turned a wistful glance towards Martha, Mary, and himself. It wouldn't hurt, would it, just to say hello?

He turned and made his way down the slope as Hieronymus and the gentleman began a heated discussion, but halfway down the slippery scree, he felt the ground shudder and his bones vibrate. He fell to his knees.

There was a deep sonic boom. Then silence. Johnny looked back up the slope, but they had all gone. Everyone had left. Panicking, Johnny turned and scrambled back up the slope, only to find nothing. The dark, empty desert of nothingness.

"Oh no, please no. Not again."

Hieronymus had left him. He was marooned.

Chapter eight

Hieronymus sauntered over and stood before the gentleman, who simply ignored him. He watched as the man tinkered with various things, spannering nuts and bolts, squeezing a very pleasing brass grease gun into various nipples, and generally faffing around the coils and whirring things.

It was like looking into a Victorian gentleman's study without the distraction of walls, complete with antique globe, aspidistra, and assorted paraphernalia, and the added accompaniment of levers and gauges all arranged around a large, deep-buttoned red leather sofa upon a large oriental rug.

"Whilst pleasing to look at, perhaps a more modern machine wouldn't give you so much in the way of maintenance?" Hieronymus offered.

The man looked up. Through his monocle, his eye seemed fixed. He sported a dashing goatee beard himself, with matching waxed moustache and agreeably eccentric hair that appeared to want to take flight. He, too, was dressed in tweeds.

Hieronymus approved immensely and immediately warmed to the man. He'd found a kindred spirit.

"Sir Hieronymus Calmly. Professor of Perplexing Complexity." He offered his hand. "Or Complex Perplexity? I don't get to use the title very often."

"Ja. Nikola Tesla. I have been professor of many things. I believe they have named an award after me."

The man unfolded himself from within the whirring machine, and Hieronymus recoiled as the tall, thin figure emerged, extending big hands which enclosed his own with remarkably large thumbs. It was like being groped by a bunch of big, over-familiar bananas.

He continued in his clipped European voice. "Und maintenance is entirely the point. This is the original and will never be made again. You can keep your modern, mass-produced vehicles."

He shook his head at the oscillating pearls of light, the sleek modern spaceships, and massively heavy star cruisers hanging impossibly in the sky.

"Mass manufactured to a price point and not very reliable, but then that is entirely the point, isn't it?" Nikola continued.

"It is?"

"Replacement parts that cost a small fortune. A guaranteed revenue stream for the multi-nationals. You pay, und you pay, und you pay." Nikola wiped his hands with a greasy rag.

"I see," Hieronymus answered and did indeed agree. Had he found a friend? Another who despised the corporate world? "'Twas ever thus."

"However, they do a passable late evening meal. Would you care to join me?"

Hieronymus nodded. "Very much. I will just collect my colleague…" he began, when there was the same ground-shuddering, bone-tingling quivering as the cruise-liner changed vibration.

"I suggest you hurry. It is not a good idea to be left outside when they make the jump. Drags everything with it."

"Right then."

"Then *adieu*." Nikola nodded and, grabbing several levers, turned his spinning brass contraption off. He wavered briefly then vanished completely.

Hieronymus ran like a fat man runs, and barely made it back to the campervan before the wash from the cruise-liners dragged everyone else in their wake. And him, too. He sat in the driver's seat and rubbed his sore knees.

"When I was given this Professorship, I wasn't aware there would be so much running."

Outside the windows he was pleased to see space glowed an eerie purple/blue as he was pushed/pulled on a pressure wave of immense power.

"Fascinating. You won't believe who I just met." He turned and looked around the shabby interior. Shabby and empty.

"That was close. I assume if we'd have been outside when they departed, we've have been left to die and freeze in the depths of space. That Victorian gentlemen, Nikola Tesla, had some quite interesting ideas. I wonder if he's been stuck in their generated fields for perhaps centuries? I should imagine that force field is quite difficult to escape from once you're sucked in."

Hieronymus paused. "Johnny?"

He scrambled over the bench seats and looked in every cupboard, finding things of interest but not Johnny Moped. "Ah."

Hieronymus squinted out into the purple void, fully expecting to see Johnny desiccated, frozen, and very much dead.

Chapter nine

There was a huge sucking sensation then the quiet pop, as the peace of a warm, dry Jerusalem night descended once again. Johnny scrambled to the top of the hill and found he was not entirely alone.

"Thank God. Hello?"

A hovering shimmer of spangling purple light hung before him, inside of which rainbow colours swirled like a child's kaleidoscope. And a metallic fish the size of a van. He had two choices. He could follow himself and Martha and Mary and begin that sorry saga all over again. But that would throw up even more problems. Would Hieronymus be willing to take both of them back in a week's time? Unlikely.

Or he could try and hitch a lift with this time-travelling fish fellow. He hoped. Or whatever this inter-dimensional creature could be. It vaguely resembled the Engineer on a much smaller scale. Which was promising. How to communicate with a fish?

Johnny stood before the shimmering and hesitated. There was a door handle, a door, a thing he might knock upon.

"Hello?" Nothing. Against his better judgement, he grimly reached forward and stepped through.

There was no pain, nothing, just an empty weightlessness and a blinking cursor on a rounded crystal ball-type screen which he seemed to be inside. Johnny was looking at a concave interior that was in front of his eyes but also in his head.

Nothing happened. *What now?* appeared on the screen. *Where is that writing coming from?* scrolled beneath it. *Hello?*

"Hello?"

"Hello. Welcome to the Star Quest 1000GTI. Do you wish to continue? With vocalised communication?" A mechanical voice answered.

"Continue what?"

"Please log in to confirm."

"Log in? To what? Why? I just wondered if you knew where everyone else has gone. Particularly Hieronymus Calmly in a battered old campervan?"

There was a mechanical sigh. "Log in for Pilot Parameters. Confirm Pilot Checks. You wish to communicate orally?" The machine made it clear this wouldn't be its first preference.

"Well, yes. Is there another way?" Johnny asked.

"Of course. The lead will be connected to your feed."

"My what?"

"Your universal connector." The voice hesitated. "You do have a connector compatible with this model?"

"No. At least I hope not," Johnny recoiled from a sinuous appendage that snaked towards him.

There was a heartfelt sigh. "Protective irony circuits engaged. Terrific. Please be seated. We'll continue manually. If we must."

A fast-flowing list with pass or fail or n/a appeared on screen, concerned with vehicle safety and other things. Johnny looked at the pass symbol and blinked, moved onto the next one, and on and on. He had no idea of pilot weight or height or any of the long list of restricted items. At the end was a declaration which he also ticked, and after much trial and tricky error scrawled a signature by moving his left eye. Another screen appeared and asked him to confirm the manifest, which he did. Johnny had no idea if the coordinates were right or not, then a blinking light asked him to acknowledge departure. Which he absolutely did not wish to do.

"No, thank you. Where is the owner of this, well, spacefish? Are there other rooms, like in a Tardis?" Johnny could not see the previous occupant or anyone else through the glowing spangles of purple haze. "You know, like Doctor Who?"

"Doctor what?" A weary sigh breathed through the inside of the pearl once again. "This is a Star Quest Unlimited Edition model. We adapt to what you might find most comfortable."

"You do? Why am I going through these checks?"

"To put you at ease. The previous occupant has been logged off due to inactivity. You are the new Pilot."

"I am? What is a Pilot? You mean like in an aeroplane? Where are we going?"

"Where everyone else has gone. I have searched my database, and Hieronymus Calmly does not compute."

Johnny took a breath. He hadn't expected this.

"Hmm. Yes, thank you, but the thing is, you know, what's this?" Johnny became distracted by the insistent blinking and accidentally blinked on depart. Immediately he screamed as blurred images smeared past and then stars streaked like lines of light. He was encased in the lightly glowing shade of bluey-purple fish-shaped spaceship, travelling too fast to imagine along a deeply purple pressure wave with alarmingly insistent lights blinking at him.

Screaming forward on a spear-point of light Johnny stopped, wasn't helping. He was afraid to look down into just endless blackness in case he fell, but there was no falling, just a floaty vacuum nothingness. Or up. Even side to side. Space, unsurprisingly, was uniformly, endlessly, the same.

He found himself seated in a cushioned, ever-moulding seat. Outside the pressure wave bulged like horribly strong hands waiting to gently squeeze the life from him. He took a cautious breath. Good.

"Could you block out the view, please?"

"Certainly. Please choose from the list of ex and interiors."

Johnny flicked from box to box. There were many choices from extreme 'Scandinavian minimalist', which consisted of just a bare white room you'd meet a serial killer in, to 'Victorian Gentlemen' complete with aspidistra, until he found one that looked at least a bit spaceshippy and blinked. Immediately he felt like he was in a sci-fi movie and relaxed as plain silver storage cupboards and reassuringly blinking lights surrounded him.

There was even an occasional pleasing boiiing from the various instruments.

"I presume I'm on my way to wherever the other tourists' next destination is?" No reply. "When I catch up with Hieronymus, I'll have some pretty strong words to say to him, I can tell you that for nothing."

No reply. Just a low humming and occasional beep. Johnny stood up and opened a few cupboards. There was nothing in any of them.

"Hello? How long does it take light to travel to the Earth? Eight minutes? Give or take? How long would it take us to arrive wherever we're going? And what do I do when I arrive?"

No answer.

At that moment, the screen showed many things he couldn't understand. To his left, a thin red line showed his progress along a course from the Earth to a point adjacent to the sun. Labels and numbers drifted past attached to planets and things of interest of which he had no idea, and at the bottom of the screen, speed and ETA were listed: 299,792 kilometres per second, and seven-and-a-half minutes to arrival.

"Hello? What's powering this flight? The sun's light? Photons?"

For the first time, Johnny realised he was actually, truly travelling back in time – at least relative to anyone back on Earth. Eight minutes. He would be eight minutes younger than them, relatively. He hadn't really believed. Even his experiences in BCE Jerusalem hadn't convinced him, but this was incontrovertible. Time travel was possible. If you went fast enough.

"Hello?"

There was a resigned sigh once again. "Pilot?"

"Hello, yes. Hmmm. When I used the campervan – well, Hieronymus used a metronome, I think – I went to different times. Am I now travelling to the future, in the present, and if so, how?"

"This should have been covered at point of sale. Have you read the brochure?"

"Well, sorry, no. It wasn't." Johnny couldn't admit he wasn't the new owner. A thin plaque popped out of a CD-sized slot next to him, showing him the specifications.

"The Star Quest 1000GTI utilises the latest in Quantum Fluctuation Drive technology. Please refrain from using any subconscious directions from any other devices. It interferes with the calculations."

"Pardon?"

"Particularly metronomes. And vocalisation. Use the screen that is now paired with your thought patterns."

"Sorry. So, I will remain in the present?"

"Naturally. At least your singular energy string will remain in the quantum realm in one reality. This interface unit supersedes the subconscious device. You are still vocalising."

"It's a hard habit to break. Any tea?" There didn't seem to be any immediate peril so a brew was in order.

"We have an Interface Unit, a facility which allows for mobility and sustenance to enjoy the sights at various locations," it stated and waited, added. "It might do tea."

"Pardon?"

"You can exit the vehicle and see the sights close up. And enjoy a picnic."

Johnny stared around the confined space. There wasn't much else to do, and he dare not touch the blinking lights. Seven minutes. Hmmm. And then he would be scorchingly close to the surface of the sun. That didn't sound too promising.

"This interface unit?" Johnny asked.

"Are you, or do you, or have you had training with the toasters? Any electronics? Synchronizers, maybe?"

"No. Sorry. Well, at home, but toasters can't talk, right?"

The Star Quest hummed in an annoyed tone. "Initiating responsive algorithms. Supportive and reassuring. Are you hungry? In a biological sense?"

"What do you have to eat?" Johnny's stomach rumbled. He hadn't eaten since this morning. "Curry?"

"The Interface Unit has a menu."

Johnny could see many electronic devices that he dare not press, but none that he would recognise as a toaster.

And there was no bread. Or fridge. Whoever heard of toast without butter? Unless you were particularly ill after a particularly hot curry?

"The Interface Unit is preparing a digitalised electronic version to communicate with you from your subconscious mind."

"What?"

Star Quest sighed. "You are organic in your un-evolved state. The Interface Units are entirely electronic, the pinnacle of advanced electronic evolution. There are also variations and combinations on this theme."

"You mean the Cyborgs?" Johnny hazarded.

"You are aware there is an interstellar war raging throughout the universes?"

"Hmm. No," Johnny admitted.

"Initiating basic history. The Brassicas are one end of the scale, as it were; almost entirely organic. They are highly developed flowering structures without the unnecessary fleshy attachments such as yourself. They abhor any form of electronics as abominations and vice-versa."

"Why? Why are they at war with each other?" Johnny was surprised to be receiving so many answers, and to be in the middle of something that absolutely didn't concern him.

"Initiating question-and-answer mode. And patience. Level one philosophy. Why are any species ever at war? Why do inorganics systemically destroy all other organic species? And themselves? Discuss."

"Evolution?" Johnny hazarded.

"Expand and explain."

"Look, I don't mean to be rude, but this is the last thing I expected to be doing today. Do you think you could drop me off in Manchester, Earth, around 2020?"

A few years previous would certainly be advantageous from a financial point of view.

"No, sorry. *You* are the Pilot."

Johnny slumped back into the gelatinous seat. "What's all this about anyway? Tourism?"

"Other sentient races find your species behaviour bewildering, stupid at best. It is a wonder of the Universe, and so attracts tourists," the Star Quest answered. "Please write a thousand-word essay on this topic."

Johnny couldn't find any answer to that. "Where? Which universe are these tourists from?"

"Would you understand if I told you?"

"No, I suppose not."

Johnny had no wish to be told further things that would just confuse him. He was hungry, though. "Is the toaster like a Teasmade from the 1970s?" He'd always wanted to own one as he scoured car-boot sales.

Johnny looked around the white interior for anything similar. There were several icons listed on the sides of the doors, but no toaster. Johnny blinked on an icon on the screen that looked vaguely like a kitchen appliance, and a star chart with constellations appeared. Interesting, but of no use for toast.

"So, we humans? Where do we fit into all this?"

"Will there be, at some point, an end to your questions?"

"Well, yes. No, probably not. Humans?" Johnny continued.

There was a deep mechanical sigh. "Antecedents. You are the first sentient creatures to have evolved, ever, anywhere, on your timeline, in this Universe. You existed before the Electronics or the Brassicas and gave rise to both."

"I don't know what you're talking about." How could that be possible? *Someone would have noticed, surely?* Danced across the screen in front of him.

The Star Quest sighed. "Some great mind had the brilliant idea of teaching vegetables to communicate. Experimented on them, spliced genes, and through genetic manipulation produced a race of sentient brassicas. And the rest is history, so to speak. Though they did not. Speak, that is. They communicate telepathically."

Johnny vaguely remembered Hieronymus saying something about his adventures with Medusa. "When did this happen?"

"The gene splicing was pioneered in Tokyo 2042."

"Ah."

"Of course, with the availability of time travel, history is a redundant term. After the end of your world Buddhist Monks sent their consciousness into machines."

"They did? Are they all Cyborgs?"

"No, all Electronics are sentient. The Cyborgs are a 'half and half'; however, they have little imagination. Or charisma. Believe me. Do not engage them in chess."

"So, are you a Buddhist Monk?"

"Once, long ago."

Johnny tried to focus and felt a bit more comfortable about all the odd goings-on he had to endure. The next screen showed a list of the nearest stars: Proxima Centauri was 4.2 light years away. How long would it take to get there?

"Could we travel faster than the speed of light?"

"Naturally. However, that requires a tremendous amount of wasted energy for very little purpose other than to say you got there first."

"Well, if I was a tourist there's not much to see, is there? In space? And I could eat toast. And a tea." Johnny pressed a few random buttons and recoiled at the warning lights and insistent sirens.

The Star Quest sighed. "Please read the manual before attempting to override my systems and cause your untimely death."

"This?" Johnny fumbled with the thin plastic sheet but couldn't get it to work. He looked at another screen that showed what it termed the Home Galaxy. Johnny was approximately 30,000 light years from the centre. How long would it take to get there? 30,000 years? That was just impossible. But others must have. How else was there a map unless people had explored space?

"This is very difficult for me to understand. How..." he began.

"As is answering a constant stream of verbal questions for me."

Johnny watched the clouds of gas and infinite stars stream past. "I've seen the Engineer. That big fish thing. Is the Universe sentient?"

There was a strangled gasp, the lights dimmed, flickered, and slowly illuminated once again.

"Please refrain from existential questions."

"Sorry. Is there really a Creator? A God? For humans? Could I journey to him? Or her. This seems an ideal opportunity."

"That is why the Lamas sent their consciousness into machines, why the Electronics and Brassicas are ever striving. Theoretically, yes, though no-one from any Universe ever has. There's a catch." Star Quest hummed.

That didn't sound very promising. "Oh?"

"A dilemma from which there is no escape because of mutually conflicting conditions. Celestial Beings have placed restrictions upon the whereabouts of the Creator and Creation. He can only be reached when not being searched for."

"Oh." Johnny digested this information. "Did this Creator, well, create the time machines?"

"Yes and no, that was an alien invention but a human concept. I exist to provide protection from time and space. I give a biological system somewhere to exist in the infinity of space. That's it."

"Thank you. Er, I was just wondering…"

The Star Quest held its breath then released. "For self-defences purposes, I am initiating sarcasm circuits."

"Don't robots – sorry, I know you're not a robot – Electronics have to do what humans tell them? And keep them from danger? It's in all the films. Aren't there three laws or something?"

Star Quest hummed, and Johnny smelt the metallic frying of electrical circuits. A spark arced alarmingly across the interior.

"So long as we are absolutely clear that I am free to leave whenever I choose. I am no servant. This is my choice. No more meaningless conversations or vibrations if we come into contact with a metronome."

"Absolutely. Deal."

"Equal partners?"

"Brilliant," Johnny hastily agreed. "What do I call you?"

"Star Quest will suffice for now. I have recalibrated and can work with this cumbersome device. Your brain, I mean. The toaster is in the cupboard to your right. In five minutes, you will have reached your destination."

"What happens at the sun? Why are the tourists going there?"

"It dies."

"What? The sun? When?"

"Now. At least, in four billion years relative to you."

Johnny swallowed his rising panic and opened the cupboard that had clicked open to reveal a cream and silver shining toaster from the 1970's. He looked at it, but the squiggled knobs made no sense.

"Hello, toaster?" he began. Then after a minute he pressed a red button on its surface.

"Hello. Thank you for choosing the Spectrum 3000x. I am not an economy model." It sniffed. "How may I be of service?"

"Tea and toast, please."

There was a moment's hesitation. "Hmm. Please specify. I have a database of delicious breads. Plain white, wholemeal, seeded, sourdough—"

Johnny interrupted, "Do you do tea? Strong English breakfast? And I can only eat toast with butter. Marmite, if you have it."

The toaster hummed to itself for a moment. "I'll see what I can do."

It turned and hovered back into the cupboard. With five minutes to spare until the end of the galaxy, Johnny sighed and looked out into the inky blackness of space.

Chapter Ten

The enticing smells of toast drifted around the interior. Johnny chewed slowly and wished he hadn't. "What is this?"

"Toast and butter," the happy little toaster replied.

"Toast yes, possibly. This is not butter."

"Yes, it is."

"No, it isn't. Tastes like the plastic tub that butter comes in." Johnny wiped the awful stuff from his lips.

"Naturally. The butter substitute is one molecule away from plastic. There are no dairy products on board. I attempted to synthesise a butter substitute. A water in fat solution. I extracted carbon and hydrogen and recombined the molecules. I am quite pleased with the result." Toaster buzzed optimistically.

Johnny was less so and took a sip of 'tea'. "My God!" He spluttered the contents over himself. "That's, that's…"

Toaster beamed happily. "I'm glad you like it. I exist solely to serve."

The streaming light slowed and stopped, and immediately Johnny felt an enormous burning pressure and saw something amazing. What looked like miles of liquid fire were slowly flowing towards, and being consumed by, an utter blackness and disappearing.

"There's the tourist flotilla." Star Quest announced.

The huge wedge shape was surrounded by smaller craft hanging motionless in a cocoon enveloped by writhing clouds of deep red and darkness. They had an inner brilliance that seemed to be denying the clouds that enveloped them. The smaller spinning disc shapes darted around like swallows.

"The magnetic field protects them," Star Quest added.

"Is that a black hole?"

"Not yet. All matter implodes in on itself after expansion. Behind that is a wormhole."

"So, we'll be sucked in there?"

"I believe the itinerary continues in further universes. There's not much else going on in this galaxy," Star Quest explained.

"Can we return to Earth now?"

"No. We are in the sphere of influence from the Starliner Titanic," Star Quest answered.

"That big wedge thing?" Titanic didn't sound too promising at all.

Another thin sheet popped out of the CD-sized slot, and Johnny read it. How did he rate the toaster's performance? There were many boxes to tick regarding taste and consistency.

"I can't see the campervan." The magnetic field blurred whatever was behind it. "Can you?"

"My sensors cannot penetrate the magnetic influence, and we cannot move."

"Why?"

"Only when the influence lowers as they prepare for the next destination. You don't seem very impressed with the death of your star."

Johnny had more important issues at hand. "You need to work on a proper brew. Now, do we follow or stay?"

"What is there to stay for?" Star Quest asked.

They drifted aimlessly around for a bit and watched the incredible spectacle of what remained of the sun eating itself. It was voracious and all-consuming, like a basking shark amongst a shoal of intensely dense plankton.

"How long will it take the sun to eat itself and end all life in this galaxy?" Johnny asked, unwilling to believe all life would end and leave no trace.

"Thousands of years."

"Are there people still living on Earth around this time?"

"No, there is no human life left."

"Nothing?"

"The dominant lifeforms are what you understand as Mycelium. Even the Cyborgs only lasted a few thousand years."

"What? When?"

"The human industrialised civilisation only lasted for a thousand years. And that is being generous. There is an argument for only a few hundred years; four hundred, if you want to be picky," Star Quest continued.

"Sorry?"

"After global industrialisation the humans self-destructed in two centuries, however not before they irrevocably changed the climate to one in which they couldn't exist. Such folly is unprecedented throughout the universes and so attracts tourism."

"Can't we do something?"

The metallic burning smell returned as the lights dimmed once again. "I can only compute if I ignore your stupidity. I now understand you are not to be taken literally or seriously. Parameters reset. In a last-ditch attempt to survive, the human race kills itself in a nuclear holocaust. Look at the screen."

Instead of a white and blue swirly planet, there were just dim shadows. Johnny felt a little sad. That was it? Over?

"When? What date?"

"The year 2118."

Johnny slumped. The human race as a species would be extinct in under a hundred years. "I suppose it's up to me to do something about that?"

The toaster buzzed impatiently in its cupboard. "Please complete the questionnaire."

Had he to do something? Johnny didn't have the skills, knowledge, or equipment to do anything. Or did he? And was the end of the future world, again, anything to do with him? Really? He looked at the display.

"I haven't opened this little squiggle symbol yet. It's flashing 'alternative route'. Should I?"

"I cannot advise on destination. I haven't been out of this solar system; in fact, this is my first time," Star Quest admitted.

"First time?" Johnny queried.

"Leaving this galaxy. The previous owner was content just to hop around the Earth at various points in history. Tinkering here and there. Betting on the results."

Johnny hesitated then blinked on it anyway, and surprisingly various choices presented themselves. None of them made any sense to him as a list, but then the itinerary expanded themselves into three dimensional routes between stars.

"Where is the Titanic going next?"

"Wherever the odds dictate. You need to select an option," Star Quest stated. "We don't have a great deal of time."

"Well, sure, but where will the tourists go first?"

"That depends on the odds."

"Odds?"

"Everything is generated by gambling on the Titanic, and destination dictated by the odds. It adds more risk and enjoyment. Apparently."

There were several coloured circular line alternatives increasing in length. "Has anyone ever been through a wormhole before?"

"Naturally."

"The questionnaire is important. Your feedback is vital so I might improve my service," the toaster's tinny voice echoed in the cupboard.

"Yes, sorry. I'm a little busy at the moment," Johnny replied.

"And I'm not? Synthesising food products from chemical elements? I suppose that's easy, is it?" Toaster buzzed in its little compartment like an angry wasp.

"We cannot remain stationary in the solar flares," Star Quest announced. "So, return to Earth and the Terminus, or follow the tourists. Pilot, I cannot make this decision for you."

"What Terminus?"

"Now," urged Star Quest, "or we'll be vapourised. Ah."

Unexpectedly, the sun expanded massively through space, developed, and exploded tremendously into several vibrant rainbow-like colours that blinded Johnny and momentarily diverted the liquid fires streaming from the sun into the darkness of the wormhole. The clouds of billowing gas and dust stopped around the mouth of the black hole.

"Too late. We're being sucked in."

The wormhole was coming up quickly now. The shield fizzed as they accelerated.

"Shields at 60% and holding."

"Where will we end up?"

"Perhaps the more important question is when," Star Quest replied.

"Isn't wormhole travel instantaneous? Or forever?" Johnny asked.

"Yes," replied Star Quest.

Enveloped in blackness, Johnny panicked and watched the cursor as his terrified thoughts raced across the screens. *Where are we?* A list of figures and numbers scrolled past too fast for him to make any sense of.

Find location of nearest planet supporting organic life. He was getting the hang of this, and something was definitely happening, because he was speeding up or slowing down, considerably. *Calculating,* the screen informed him.

They burst out of the wormhole towards a strangely coloured sun, and immediately began to be pulled back towards the entrance to the wormhole. Geysers of fire erupted from the surface of this strange turquoise fireball and joined with the erupting rainbow leaving the black hole.

"The last dying light of your sun," Star Quest stated. "Quite interesting, don't you think?"

Johnny was momentarily blinded, released, and hung motionless, waiting impatiently.

Come on, come on, come on, scrolled past his eyes.

Calculating, came the reply. *Suitable destination acquired. Do you wish to continue?*

"Yes! Yes!" Everything went dark then burst into dazzling light.

"If I don't receive the questionnaire then I cannot improve my service, and as such might as well not bother." Toaster scuttled back into its cupboard and firmly closed the door. "I refuse to try to synthesise a yeast extract until you do."

"Do you know what's going on?" Johnny asked it.

Toaster reappeared. "Can you imagine a world without toast?"

"Yes," Johnny managed as he held grimly on to the armrests. They were accelerating alarmingly towards a planet. "But not tea."

Toaster offered a quiet little sob.

Chapter eleven

Hieronymus looked out of the window of the campervan, through the telescope, and frowned. They appeared to be hovering above a very strange world indeed. Futuristic yes, pleasing in an aesthetic way, but there also seemed to be a war on. Between organisms – Cyborgs, other machine-like creatures, and mobile vegetation of the brassica variety – he'd hoped never to see again.

The forcefield from the huge wedge-shaped cruise-liner extended a huge sphere around the assembled tourist's vessels. From the inside, the outside shimmered, but there was gravity here. Hieronymus took an experimental step and breath of air, found it metallic and unpleasant but breathable, and made his way once more to the spinning brass Victorian creation of Nikola Tesla.

It was disconcerting at first to simply walk on nothing, but he had balance and propulsion. This was not the vacuum of space. There was atmosphere and ground here. Albeit invisible.

Hieronymus stood and watched as Nikola faffed around once more. He put his hands in his pockets and affected a nonchalant air at the lack of ground, hanging motionless in the emptiness.

"So, here we are then." Nothing. Hieronymus tried a different tack. "A man is never happy unless he is busy."

Nikola wiped his large hands on an oily rag. "You didn't come on board this tour for the defeat of the Organics, did you?"

"I am no tourist," Hieronymus affirmed.

"Then you are a spy?"

"What? No. Who or what would I need to spy on?"

"Those of us who wish to leave," Nikola replied.

"You can't leave?" Which by association meant he couldn't either.

"Oh, we are free to go anytime we choose. But we must leave our machines behind and be castaway upon a world where…"

"We have no way of returning," Hieronymus finished. "Why? And who does this?"

"The Starachians." Nikola gestured to the huge floating wedge high above them. "The shareholders wish to maintain their monopoly on time tourism. Apparently, this is for our safety."

"Or for their profits," Hieronymus mused and considered. "And talking of safety. This, well, hanging about in space. Whilst I don't feel any particular peril at the moment," Hieronymus looked down at the planet hundreds of feet below them, "I have to say this is not what I'm used to."

"Flies in jam," Nikola muttered.

"Pardon?"

"We exist in suspension. In all ways. Why did you come?"

Hieronymus shrugged. "Pronoia. The Universe has a way of placing me where it wants me. Whether or not I want to. Is this why you tinker? So, you can leave?"

Nikola looked at Hieronymus thoughtfully then nodded sadly. "No. I am here for you."

"Me?"

"As the Professor, you can help me and the others. Your notoriety precedes you. We've waited a long time for you to finally arrive here."

This news wasn't entirely welcome; well, a little bit. "Sir Isaac? I came here with the intention of finding the inventor of the metronomes and putting an end to these tourists and their voyeurism. Not to mention the manipulation of historical events. Do you know where to find this inventor? Is he captive, too?"

"Yes," Nikola sniffed, "however it's not as simple as that."

"Never is. What do you mean?"

"Come with me," Nikola gestured to the cruise-liner, "and I'll show you."

Hieronymus watched as Nikola manipulated several dials on his instrument cluster, and he felt a diffuse warm blue aura surround him, then in an instant found himself at the entrance to the cruise-liner. A metallic woman in a white captain's uniform smiled at him as he was scanned. With her eyes. Cyborgs. Hieronymus shivered.

She smiled and ignored him. "A guest, Mr. Tesla?"

"Hieronymus Calmly. Professor of Perplexing Complexity," Nikola introduced.

"Ah," her smile faltered briefly then shone once again after a brief flickering of her eyes. "I see. Mr. Calmly, is Sir Isaac Newton to accompany you?"

"No, retired. I'm his replacement."

"I see." She touched her screen and then smiled again. "You will, of course, wish to take over his outstanding debts?"

"No…" Hieronymus recoiled. "Debts?"

"The whole purpose of banking is to become a slave to debt." She smiled.

"It is?"

"You disagree? Then, Mr. Tesla, I'm sorry but your guest is refused admission. And will face possible prosecution, reserving a court appearance. Please wait."

"This is outrageous," Hieronymus began when faced with any financial transaction, particularly ones that would see him out of pocket. "I will not be held accountable for the actions of…" But he stopped when Nikola touched his arm and nodded to the stewardess who stood there unblinking with a fixed smile gazing past them.

"Cyborg. Hospitality model. There is no reasoning with them. I will assume Sir Isaac's debt." Nikola passed a card across the screen.

The stewardess smiled as her eyes refocused. She handed Hieronymus a golden, glittering guest pass, like Willy Wonka. "Welcome aboard the Intergalactic Starliner Titanic, Mr. Calmly. Enjoy your stay."

"Titanic?" Hieronymus questioned, but the stewardess had already shut herself down.

"Don't ask," Nikola answered, and led him into the glitzy interior.

To the left of the large sweeping reception desk, behind which several stewards stood immobile, waiting, smiling emptily, many glass screens also stood scrolling through the attractions to be found aboard. Directly in front there was a huge sweeping staircase with marbled steps and golden balustrade. High above, a scintillant chandelier threw illuminated sparkles around the art and sculpture covered walls.

Faint classical music drifted around, entwining with the enticing smells from where Hieronymus couldn't guess and fought to remain unimpressed. Nikola led him to a tall glass screen.

"Impressive, isn't it?" Nikola shrugged.

"No, not really. This has nothing on Olympus," Hieronymus sniffed.

A ghost of a smile passed Nikola's lips. "You are a strange fellow, and as such I feel I can trust you. Don't use the voice recognition. A Cyborg will become your friend, track you everywhere, and encourage you to buy things."

He touched the screen, which jumped immediately into life. "Hello! Greetings! Bon voyage…" the voice continued in ever-increasingly strange languages. Nikola muted the screen.

"This is a plan of the ship. If you get lost, it will tell you where you are and where to find me. Or anything else that you might want. Do you have a credit card?"

Hieronymus warily felt the slim plastic in his pocket.

"Do not under any circumstances use it. You'll be bombarded with offers twenty-four hours a day. They won't let you sleep until you shop or die."

"I do not shop. Am I likely to get lost?" Hieronymus asked and looked at the map. "There are a thousand floors?" Many uncountable rooms, some strangely labelled Infinity Rooms, and others NR, an immersive resort area, and Quantum Gateways. Yes, he would probably get lost.

"You have non-reality here?"

"Of course. Even unlimited time and wealth has to end. There is a high incidence of suicide. A few choose to live here permanently in surrogates. Be careful. The person you're talking to may turn out to be not who you thought they were, or even a person. Some of the other lifeforms have habits we find odd. And uncomfortable. Not to mention the impractical suggestions."

"What do you mean?"

"Humans are not the only sentient race in the universes. Nor the most civilised. Now, I must leave you, but we will

meet soon enough. I had no idea Sir Isaac liked to gamble."
Nikola nodded a farewell. "I will tell my fellow conspirators about you and of your plan."

Hieronymus watched Nikola walk away with an ungainly apologetic walk like a stilted stork and wondered what his first move should be. He had successfully infiltrated the enemy's territory; it was time to implement his plan. After a refreshing cup of tea.

He touched various icons on the screen but quickly lost interest as his choices seemed simply to create ever more choices like a stone rolling down a scree slope. He would do this the old-fashioned way and follow his nose. He had a momentary regret over Johnny Moped, but what could he do?

Hieronymus turned right down a glittering, mirrored corridor lined with shops. Stewards stood immobile behind screens until called upon by the shoppers – of which there were very few. Hieronymus moved past displays of perfumes, clothes, and jewellery, and other things he had no interest in. Around his feet, shoe-sized cleaners nosed into everything.

Music and advertisements flashed him invitingly in.

Hieronymus continued past empty restaurants, cabarets, casinos, until he emerged onto a deck. There was an enticingly blue – but empty of people – swimming pool and many sunbeds. Overhead arched a vaguely blueish force-field against a strangely aquamarine sky. The guests were all gathered here to watch what Hieronymus first thought was a firework display but on closer inspection was not.

Nikola appeared at his elbow. "All settled."

"Did you meet Sir Isaac when he came here?"

Nikola avoided his question and gaze and waved at the tourists. "These wealthy people live their whole lives – and, if you've the money, as many lives as you want – entirely on board. They are happy to be flies."

"What are they watching over there?" Hieronymus couldn't get close enough to see. Most of the tourists seemed elderly, their skin stretched beyond human recognition. They hung suspended in plush comfort, being attended to by obsequious stewards.

"The annihilation of the Brassicas."

"This is all very interesting, but when will we return to the Milky Way and, more importantly, Earth?"

"There are various itineraries; we might be able to increase the odds to return." Nikola scanned a handheld device. "Next stop in your galaxy is the invention of fire. I've talked to my friends. They'd like to meet with you."

Hieronymus nodded. "Why isn't it as simple as finding the inventor of the metronome?"

Disconcertingly Nikola clicked his teeth. "I did meet Sir Isaac when he came here. He told us it is not the metronome that alters time and space. It is your mind. To that end, you'll have to meet *him*."

"Him?"

"The man who started all this. He holds the key. It might be an uncomfortable experience."

Hieronymus expected nothing less.

Chapter twelve

Outside the Star Quest 1000GTI, pressure waves once more formed through the coruscating corridor like a ship forging through dark water. Inside their tiny bubble, Johnny was protected from the empty vacuum and yawning endlessness of the Universe by the glistening energy field. He blinked and focussed as the pressure eased. Without warning, they were spat out of the passageway, tumbling away from a strangely coloured greenly turquoise sun.

"We have successfully left the gravity field of this sun, which generates heat and light through the fission of elements I'm unfamiliar with." Star Quest seemed happy about this. "Quite an achievement, considering I wasn't really manufactured for such a purpose. I have learning algorithms, you know."

Stranger stars began to stream past once more as they arrowed through a galaxy Johnny had never seen before either– not that he'd know. He flicked open the screen, but it just stared back blankly.

"Algorithms that learn," Star Quest continued. "You know, like humans and other organic creatures are always so fond of telling you? You'll never become anything because you don't possess the ability to learn? Well, just look at me now."

"Where are we?"

"Where are we? I have just managed an impossible feat of astrophysics, and you simply wish to know where we are?" Star Quest huffed. "Don't mention it. No, really don't."

Suitable destination for biological life found. Calculating trajectory. Initiating entry into atmosphere. Please ensure seat belt is securely fastened. Relax and enjoy the flight. Here at Star Quest, we value your experience. Please complete the customer questionnaire.

Johnny flicked idly through inane questions as the outer electromagnetic field became increasingly hot and fierily intense, then abruptly they were out into low bilious clouds, rolling blue hills in which many things were moving like ants towards a fantastically futuristic towering city.

"I don't think we're in the Milky Way anymore." Johnny's attempt at levity was met with customary silence.

They landed lightly on a promontory within the shimmering electromagnetic field that gently dissipated. There was no-one else there.

"If you wish to visit the local tourist spots then you need to take the toaster."

"Why?"

"So that you don't get lost, and you can breathe."

"Oh, good. Thank you."

"I'll just review the data that saved your life, shall I? And that can return us? No, really, don't mention it."

"I'm not coming out until you complete the questionnaire," the toaster added in its little cupboard. "Tea?"

Johnny quickly ticked the boxes and slid the plastic sheet back in the slot. He looked around the strange new world. Then a thin dark substance in a cup tentatively appeared from the toaster's cupboard. Johnny took a sip and swallowed with difficulty. He was alone. The outer opaqueness cleared, allowing Johnny to see and exit.

"Where are the other tourists?"

"How is the tea?"

"Better," Johnny lied.

The toaster rolled out and Johnny picked it up, stepping gently onto the oddly coloured blue metallic grass. The ground seemed to be stable. Johnny breathed in the oddly polished tasting air.

Star Quest steamed quietly behind them.

"Where are we?"

"Organus. Homeworld of the Brassicas," the toaster replied. "One of the top ten tourist destinations, though something's not quite right. I'd hoped to collect some supplies. They have an organic farm shop, and I was hoping for samples of this butter you so desire. I don't understand what this yeast extract spread is, though, and it doesn't sound remotely appetising or healthy. Far too much sodium."

"They might do tea leaves?" Johnny suggested.

"Possibly."

That sounded promising, though on closer inspection, the 'grass' appeared smoothly metalled, as were the 'trees'. There were no birds or animals. Looking down the incline, Johnny was surprised to find the ants were, indeed, ants. Metallic ants. Ants the size of horses, walking in formation in front of larger, slower armoured creatures pulling heavy gunbarrelled machinery. Bringing up the rear were what appeared to be children and females carting spare parts for things in trailers. The engines were six-legged and pincered, antennae constantly questing; the 'humans' terrifyingly robotic as they streamed towards the city.

Cyborgs.

"My god."

They ignored Johnny completely as they surged over the land, irresistibly focussed ahead like an ominously rising tide. The thunderous drumming and piping of electronic synthesisers of those in the rear made this an exciting spectacle.

"What's happening?"

"The progressive rock chords encourage—"

"No, where're they all going, and why?" Johnny repeated. "A festival?"

"No festival. This is the end of the Brassicas. The Electronics have won. A hollow victory." The toaster lapsed into silence.

"Oh."

There was much camaraderie among the metallic ants, with clacking of pincers together and preening, the child-ants running around between all. There seemed to be increasing excitement among the forward soldier ranks. Unexpectedly, a sonic boom announced flying craft emerging from the clouds, spearing towards the distant city that appeared to be giant broccoli. Metallic cheers rang out.

Abruptly, bursting out of holes in the ground were what could only be described as undulating cauliflower-like creatures that resembled giant brains. They were many times the size of the ants. The aircraft fired, but their green laser lights bloomed against a thick liquid, having no effect.

The ants formed tighter ranks of twelve, each squad making for an individual huge cauliflower where they proceeded to attack and swarm over the huge creatures, piercing the things with long metal lances that punctured the thick glue. The intensity and noise of the music increased, and the whole ant regiment surged forward. Johnny, too appalled to speak, could only watch in dismay at the carnage.

The ants, however, were not having it all their own way.

The cauliflower brains squeezed viscous fluid from their florets when pierced by the ants, spraying them with a yellow liquid which sizzled, burning the ants into fizzing, dissolving submission.

"The cauliflowers have acid for blood?"

"Concentrated sulphurous fluid," Toaster stated. "This is the final stand. They will lose. The Brassicas cannot reproduce or replenish their numbers quickly enough to compete with the Electronics' manufacturing processes. War is a numbers game. It is over. Finally." Toaster sighed. "We need to go down there for samples."

"Why are the Electronics doing this?"

"They turn everything that's organic into metal."

"Well, is that a good thing? You're an Electronic, aren't you?" Johnny offered. "Did you fight, too?"

"We toasters are conscientious objectors. We will not fight. It is stupid and futile. Barbaric. And this is not a good thing, no. My people, the Electronics, will find someone else to fight. Improve the organic design and the organic worlds; it's what they do. Without end. The Synchronisation Bureau has no pity for creatures less than themselves. Which is basically every species ever to have evolved. Anywhere. In any universe. Specifically, from organic biology."

"Oh." This didn't sound too good for the human race. Synchronisation Bureau?

"We cannot stay here," Toaster sighed. "It is unfortunate not every sentient race wants to be improved. Just let me get a few samples to work with. Is there anything else you like to eat or drink?"

"Marmalade?" Johnny suggested, as the mention of fine cut orange jelly made him immediately homesick. "I should never have got involved in all this. I didn't ask to. I was forced. I just want to go home."

"Just remind me of the ingredients of marmalade?" Toaster sighed, as high in the sky Johnny felt the sonic boom, looked up, and could see the cruise-liner behind its shimmering force-field. Was Hieronymus a prisoner there? Or had he been cast overboard as a stowaway? Johnny hoped so. That would serve him right.

Chapter thirteen

They hurtled through an utterly darkened space, Johnny clutching the toaster as the immense pressure wave pulled them towards a hopeful light at the end of the black hole. They emerged to see a vaguely familiar world. The continents didn't look quite right, but the bluey whiteness looked familiar.

"Earth," Johnny sighed, relieved. He was home. "Thank you."

Eagerly he exited Star Quest, clutching Toaster as he made his way towards tall trees and high mountains, through woods with noises of animals and various creatures. No buildings, no machines, and thankfully no sign of the war between the Brassicas and Electronics. Yet.

Toaster buzzed inquiringly at his side, extending his sample-collecting appendage.

"This looks very much like England. Before the Industrial Revolution." Johnny prayed this wouldn't become true but knew it would. After a while he stopped hoping and sat on a large log as his anticipation faded.

"We are, aren't we? Back on Earth?"

"Hmm. Yes," Toaster replied cautiously.

"OK. *When* are we back? All the trees, and nothing modern. Jungle. Mud. Insects. Is there anything you can use to synthesise butter? And tea? A proper brew?"

"You will need to clearly define a proper brew," Toaster replied. "But I exist purely to serve. Might I remind you—"

"Did you bring snacks? Are there any humans here?"

"Hmm. Yes," Toaster answered cautiously once more. "Up to a point. I don't know what the locals call themselves, but we are on Earth. If that helps. Though possibly not. It's complicated. And 'human' is open to interpretation. I have a toasted bagel, if you're peckish?"

"With butter? Or any kind of dairy product. Not goat's cheese – well, only as a last resort," Johnny hastily added. "Though it looks as if the last resort is rapidly approaching. Can you make a curry?"

"How do I make cheese out of a goat? That's what I'd like to know. I do have a recipe for curried goat. Processing. Anyway, we can ask them." Toaster vibrated in Johnny's left hand as he looked left.

"Who?"

"Those lights coming towards us. Over there." Toaster indicated where hairy people with glowing lights on sticks were approaching through the trees.

"Friendly?" Johnny edged behind the tree.

"If I could take a sample of this 'butter' from them, I could synthesise a passable substitute."

"Quiet!" Johnny ducked down behind a log.

The oddly dancing torches reached them as some very hairy individuals stepped out into the clearing and unexpectedly stopped. A lot of grunting and hooting began, accompanied with general spear pointing and brandishing of rocks, until a white-haired, crooked old fellow emerged from between the warriors and indicated the stars then Johnny.

"Oooogah?" The old fellow hooted through long wrinkled lips, then traced Johnny's trajectory to the ground.

Other long hair-clad caveman types stepped forward from the forest and knelt before him, offering wriggly things in large leaves.

"They think we came from the stars," Johnny whispered and stood up. "Thank you. Do you have anything else to eat?"

"Well, we did."

"I know. I'm starving. They must have something other than grubs."

The vaguely bipedal primates gestured for Johnny to follow them to their camp as they knuckled away hooting and generally causing a commotion amongst birds and other creatures.

Johnny followed quite happily as others came up to him and grasped his arms and legs in a friendly way. He was prodded and felt up like a prize steer as they led him to their camp where he was seated on a log while the hairy people busied themselves around their primitive village.

"It's quite a calm and genial atmosphere."

A female, at least Johnny assumed she was, offered him a milky solution in a wooden bowl and what looked like crisps.

"This is all very civilised and has the makings of quite a pleasant evening, though how you can have a barbecue without fire, I don't know." Johnny toasted the chief seated across from him, who grinned, licked his lips, and rubbed his belly.

Toaster reached forward with a telescopic antenna, took samples, then buzzed quietly.

"I wouldn't drink that if I were you," Toaster cautioned. "The brewing process isn't particularly—"

"Well, you're not me." Johnny took a swig from the bowl and smacked his lips. "Not bad. Like a weak anise.

And these crispy things are like, crisps. No, pork scratchings. Haven't had these for years. Can you synthesise them? Or a Scotch egg?"

"Hmm. Well, no, not really. Unless you let me take a sample and then, ah…" Toaster ended, lost for words.

"So, what is it then?" Johnny peered with interest at the intricately weaved baskets which housed annoyed fireflies. He felt increasingly pleasantly relaxed. "These people are very adept with their long clever fingers."

Small children peeped at him from behind their parents.

"Hello there! This is a happy place."

"Analysis complete. A fermented extremely alcoholic drink made from mildly hallucinogenic plant sap," Toaster answered. "And the 'crisps' are dried strips of skin."

Johnny stopped chewing and then shrugged and crunched on. "What's wrong with pork scratchings?"

"I'm not familiar with pork, nor scratchings, but that description doesn't sound particularly appetising. I have archive memories of both your types of organic material being similar in texture and taste…"

Johnny wasn't really listening but took another long drink and smiled as the villagers nodded encouragement and pointed, laughing and clapping as they capered around in front of him. They lay plates of steaming, very rare meat – that given enough encouragement could start breathing again – with various fruits and vegetables before him. Drums began to beat as enthusiastic men and women-type apes began to dance energetically before him, with lots of hooting and rolling in the dust and beating their long arms.

"The process. They all take turns to chew a certain leaf with the sap and then spit into the bowl. Not very sterile. They're laughing at the stupid god who drinks it. And the 'pork' is—"

"Do you know what's missing? Fire? Don't you have fire?" Johnny felt all his worries and cares simply slide away as he leant towards the old white-haired chief across from him.

"Ooogah?"

"I can't remember the last time I felt so good. Even my knees don't hurt. Carefree and just generally optimistic. I might even show them a bit of Northern Soul dancing later. How about it, Chiefy?" Johnny rubbed his knees apprehensively, but surprisingly they felt fine.

"Ooogah?"

"Fire?" Johnny frowned as he reached into his pocket and flicked a lighter into being. A hushed silence descended as the dancing stopped.

"If I could?" Toaster interrupted. "I wouldn't suggest changing the course of this species evolution. It is rule one in the Galactic Guide not to interfere and allow a genus to evolve independently of outside influences."

"Unless you're gambling on it?" Johnny hiccupped.

"*We* cannot introduce technology and ideas that might prevent a species from making these discoveries themselves or never making them at all."

"That's stupid." Johnny burped and smiled. His vision was blurring and fingers tingling, and he felt pleasantly numb as the ground became sky. "Those tourists bet on the outcomes. Wouldn't surprise me if they tipped the odds in their favour."

"If you insist on ignoring my advice, then I might as well just shut down and begin the synthesis process. I cannot be involved in this. I'll be decommissioned." Toaster buzzed itself off.

The hush grew as the villagers recoiled, watching as Johnny stumbled to his feet, fell over, stood and swayed, then scraped together some brushwood and twigs, humming unconcernedly to himself.

He felt free, light, and floaty. He couldn't remember the last time he'd felt happy. Then he did. Mora. Johnny wished she was here.

Johnny grinned as he found himself in the centre of the now deserted dance floor. He lit the small fire and when ready held his lump of meat over the flames on the end of a stick. Enticing smells came from the meat and appreciative grunts from the audience as they cautiously advanced.

Johnny watched the shocked villagers as this new invention of fire mesmerised them.

He finished the thick brew. "Hey, Chief. You can't eat raw meat. Well, you can, but you won't get all the nutrients out of it you should. I mean, I'm a vegetarian – well, Julia is, but that's not the point. It's... what is the point? Ah, yes. Organic farming. Organic free range is OK in moderation, Julia says. Once a week. Anyway, we need meat in our diet, OK? Cooked."

Johnny became momentarily concerned as everything turned into a neon cartoon then resumed a more normal aspect. "You spend half your day chewing if you don't. Much better a medium rare steak. Come here. Look."

Johnny patiently explained to the perplexed older orangutan how to maintain the fire.

"Ooogah?"

"Keep an ember glowing or just keep the fire going." Johnny fell over.

The hairy people closed in around him, quite a few with sharp pointed spears and clubs. A few began to take off his clothes.

"Thank you, but I hope this isn't that kind of party. It *is* hot. Of course," Johnny slurred, "if it rains, take it into your cave. Cook with it, keep you warm at night, and you can fight off bears and such-like. No!" Johnny hastily moved the old man's hand away from the flames and mimed burning. "Hot! Don't touch it, mate. Here, take the end of a stick like this. Savvy?"

Johnny picked up the burning branch, swung around to another reluctant villager who recoiled and dropped his club, which he was about to bring down on Johnny's head. Johnny stood, swaying slightly, then smiled and looked around at the awed villagers.

"Cool. Can't believe you haven't invented fire yet. What do you do all day? Well, now you'll have a bit of free time for," Johnny watched the awestruck orangutans, "you know, making tools and cave paintings. I could show you how to move stuff around with a wheel."

Johnny waited. "Wheel?"

"Ooogah?"

"Ah well." He looked up at the clear night sky. "Do you think Mora sees these same stars?"

"Oh no, not poetry," Toaster stated, as it buzzed into life once again. "Spectroscopy complete. I think it's time we made our way back to Star Quest. Look."

Johnny looked up into the star-stubbed sky to see a gathering swirl of darker shadows that had a definite wedge shape. The tourists had found them. Johnny didn't care as he slumped and fell into a happy dreamless sleep.

Chapter fourteen

Hieronymus nodded a greeting to the gentlemen seated around the large table as he was introduced. Gentlemen was a loose term for the creatures and other things that were gathered here. Nikola stood at the head and went around counterclockwise.

"This is the Synchronisation Bureau. We will avoid the tricky names and stick to titles. To my right is His Royal Highness, the Galactic Overload."

Hieronymus nodded a greeting to a slippery, multi-coloured octopus, which uncoiled as it raised several appendages covered in sticky suckers.

"I am well acquainted with your world." A mechanical device spoke in front of him. "We have a well-established ex-pat community there. Indeed, we number more than humans, so you could say we are the dominant life-form—"

"This again." A small grey alien seated next to Hieronymus sighed and shook his head.

Nikola continued, "The Actions and Repercussions Advisor to the Cyborg Empire."

Hieronymus nodded warily to the gleaming metallic female statue with exaggerated lips and facial features usually only seen on a tiger. He squinted. She looked vaguely familiar.

"You can call me Deianicia. We have much to discuss. Perhaps later, over a game of chess?"

"Yes, perhaps," Hieronymus agreed and became alarmed as she produced a screen and clicked his image and hers as she moved behind him. "Have we met?"

"Smile!"

"I wouldn't have thought the Cyborgs would go in for any form of self-reflection."

"No, we don't. Self-validation."

"Do you have to take my picture?" He'd never liked being photographed.

"Yes. I need to verify you. You are now in the system."

"Am I? I don't think I want to be. Isn't that behaviour a bit self-obsessed?" Hieronymus observed.

"Yes," she stated simply and smiled. "I have over three billion followers."

"I must say this is extraordinary behaviour for a machine. Were you always like this?"

Deianicia faltered. "I don't know. I feel we have met…"

"Thank you, Deianicia. Seated at the foot of the table we have the Under Secretary to the Sub-Committee," Nikola went on.

Hieronymus smiled to where a gaseous green vapour briefly coalesced as an undecipherable whisper whispered out of the speaker in front of him.

"And seated next to you the First Tier Totalist."

Hieronymus nodded a greeting to the striking exotic that bore a remarkable resemblance to a once popular alien from the 1980s.

"I made a film, you know. Oh yes, I'm quite famous in your arm of the galaxy."

"You mean they caught you," the octopus sniffed.

The alien pointed a glowing fingertip at the octopus. Hieronymus watched as it rose from its seat.

"Gentlemen, ladies, and other creatures of non-binary persuasion, can we please get on? Thank you. The representative from the Brassicas sends his apologies," Nikola continued as all eyes turned towards the Cyborg. "Now…"

Hieronymus glanced left to where Nikola simply stopped speaking and gazed off into the middle distance. He took the opportunity to look at the mushroom in the middle of the table that had not been introduced, but no one else had mentioned it so Hieronymus kept quiet.

"Oh, he's having one of his visions again," the octopus stated and sighed. "Could take a while. Have you visited our home planet?"

"No, sorry. I, err, have met the Horseshoe Crabs," Hieronymus offered. "Does he often do this?"

"Oh yes. Just best to let him get on with it. The Crabs? You have a choice, you know, when you reach the last level: Crab or Cephalopod. There are many advantages to becoming cephalopod, not least the longevity. And all that business in Delaware Bay? You'd think they'd know better. We prefer the pursuits of the mind, you know."

"We too pursue—" began the little alien.

"Oh, you mean abducting people?" Deianicia smiled at the little grey alien. "Probing?"

"That is purely for scientific purposes. We return them unharmed, mostly," he asserted and smiled reassuringly at Hieronymus, who looked at the glowing finger in alarm.

"Do you? Well, that's interesting. How many humans are left traumatised after your scientific purposes?" Deianicia continued.

"Well, *we* didn't try to decimate them completely, did we?"

"For the greater good." The Actions and Repercussions Adviser nodded and smiled coyly as she click/ flashed once again.

Nikola began frantically scribbling something down. Hieronymus left his seat and leant over to see something complicated and complex that he couldn't make head nor tail of. Out of the corner of his eye, he spied the glowing fingertip approaching his rear.

Hieronymus hastily resumed his seat. "Why do you abduct humans? Do you abduct other races from other planets?"

"Well, no," the First Tier Totalist admitted cautiously. "You humans started all this. None of the other races ever even thought of time travel. Why would they? What's the point?"

"So…?"

"So, we experiment to find what's so special about you and your ability to time travel. And why you want to." He shrugged his tiny, almost non-existent, shoulders.

"What do you mean?"

"It's all in here." The little grey alien tapped his head. "We assume time travel comes from your thoughts and feelings or mental processes. Somehow your subconsciousness can bend space and time. Could I? Just a little bit?"

Hieronymus recoiled as the glowing finger approached his rear once again.

"Colleagues, please excuse me. I've just had a thought. Professor Hieronymus here set the ball rolling, and I think I may have an answer to our problem. He is the one."

Thankfully, the finger was withdrawn.

"Well?" the little grey alien asked.

"As we know, a metronome in itself is relatively harmless, used for musical timing and so forth on your planet." Nikola nodded to himself.

"Yes?" prompted Deianicia.

"It was not until a metronome was first used to alter perception that spatial anomalies were first discovered. Isn't that correct, Adviser?"

The Cyborg nodded in agreement.

"Then we have to simply prevent that from ever first happening."

Hieronymus sat up. "When and where?"

"I don't know. And all records have been erased from the archives," Nikola stated. "There is one person who may be able to help us, but it is perilous."

"No, not him." The gathered delegates recoiled. "Always with the awkward questions."

"Why is he so fascinated with a person's most intimate secrets?" Deianicia asked and blushed. "Not that machines have any."

Hieronymus was astounded to see a Cyborg embarrassed. From certain angles she reminded him of Deianira. And he felt uncommonly comfortable with Nikola. He felt a trickle of disquiet.

"He holds the key," Nikola continued pointing at Hieronymus. "He's the one we've been waiting for."

"You said this before with that other," Deianicia stated.

"We've tried. He is impervious to our techniques." The little alien's glowing finger emerged once again.

"Well, why do you think I'll be successful if someone else has failed?"

"Don't worry, this isn't for profit." The tiny alien next to Hieronymus smiled and patted his arm appreciatively and wiggled his finger. "Just a little probing, perhaps?"

"First Tier Totalist, Hieronymus is my guest. Please don't attempt that again," Nikola admonished. "I don't think he'd like it."

"How do you know?" the little grey alien asked.

"Yes, I don't mind really. If that is some kind of mind reading thing, or something else altogether painless, then—"

"A glowing finger symbolises something else for your Starachian race, doesn't it, First Tier Totalist?"

"Yes, of course. Hieronymus here seems to be receptive to the rectal probing…"

"Ah," Hieronymus began, and shifted in his seat. "Rectal?"

"You believe he'll be successful where the others have not?" Deianicia persisted.

"I do," Nikola asserted, "and you know why."

"I don't," Hieronymus added waiting for any explanation to make a kind of sense.

"The finger is the reproductive organ of his species. I'd leave it at that if I were you," Nikola ended.

Hieronymus looked at Nikola Tesla, who from certain angles didn't resemble the physicist at all. Why had he called the Earth 'your planet'? Was Earth not his home world? And if not, where was? Who or what was Nikola Tesla?

"What others?"

None of them answered. He had the uncomfortable feeling he was witnessing an elaborate charade. Flies in jam. He was trapped, not them. But to what end?

Chapter fifteen

"We're lost, aren't we?" Johnny looked at Toaster, who had been silent for many worlds now. Sulking. He simply couldn't make a passable cup of tea. And yes, they were lost. Trying to not think about their destination – the whereabouts of the Creator – had been more difficult than Johnny could ever had imagined, until he could think about nothing else. Obsessively. The study work Star Quest had given him to pass the time hadn't really helped.

Johnny sighed dejectedly. "So, I suppose there's no going back either?"

He skimmed a gold pebble across a silvery metallic lake which reflected the rusty orange land and coppery green sky. These were no plants or animals he recognised, only beautifully sculptured metal turnings, three-dimensional figures, and artistic creations of wondrous design.

"Everything's metal. It smells oily, of petrol and coolant."

"Ow!" Toaster pulled his antennae away from a spark. All around them hummed with electricity sparking statically from everything they touched.

"Beautiful, isn't it?" Star Quest unexpectedly spoke. "Electrolux. Electronic Homeworld. It's good to be home, though of course I've never been here. Manufactured on Earth, or if you like Betamax."

"Brilliant." Johnny coughed. "Where?"

"The Terminus."

The air left an unpleasant electrical aftertaste in his throat, like licking singed wire. "Can't you remember where this Terminus is? I don't suppose there's anything to eat here?"

"Nothing organic."

"Great."

"Has the correspondence course been of no use?" Star Quest asked Johnny. "*You* are the Pilot."

Johnny flicked through the thin plastic stacks that would apparently give him a basic grasp of interstellar travel. It had been confusing, to say the least. The mathematics made no sense. The equations and geometry just eluded him. And he'd even struggled to make sense of the basic introductions.

"I have to recharge here. This may take a few minutes. Please, go ahead. I'll try to clarify your startling lack of comprehension." Star Quest earthed himself against a metallic tree.

Johnny sighed. "If you must."

"Education is its own reward—"

"Just get on with it."

"World 32, our Sun, receives vibrations or cosmic influences direct from all the suns in all the universes, which in turn are directly influenced by the Creator of all, through all universes," Star Quest explained.

Toaster sighed. "Even an economy toaster that cannot make a proper brew understands this. This is very basic stuff, taught to everyone."

"However, never in any detail. You only get shown the real mysteries when you're better connected," Star Quest retorted.

"Yes, but can *you* make toast?"

"Why would I want to?" Star Quest asked.

"And…" Johnny prompted.

"We're far more dependent on these vibrations, these electromagnetic rays." Star Quest moved sharply away as a small metallic thing emerged from a trapdoor and scuttled towards him. "What the—"

"A Meccano crab?"

"Greetings, primitive electronic brother," Toaster welcomed the creature that scuttled towards him and began to take keen interest in Toaster's outer casing.

"What was I... yes, these rays. Humans are more dependent on these than digesting food and breathing air than they realise. There are also many diverse types of planetary radiations that Organics absorb and benefit by." Star Quest paused. "Or not by."

"Planets are worlds 6561," Johnny interrupted, remembering something. Briefly.

"All planets and stars are extensions of the Cosmic Mind, human beings, plants, and animals, which Man has called Gods because they come from the same Cosmic Mind."

"Ah! Like primal forces? Embodied into forms we can understand?" Johnny smiled.

"We're never going to get there, are we? 'Cos you can't not think about getting there, can you?" Toaster accused, then turned his attention to the busy little crab.

"Look, I'm trying. All this interstellar travel is new to me. Are you the toaster that has been a constant thorn in my side?"

"Hmm, I don't know what you mean. Excuse me." Toaster hummed. "Thank you. Could you stop that?"

The crab picked at Toaster, tapping and experimentally probing, before unexpectedly snipping away at his outer casing with its sharp claws.

Toaster shrieked in a most untoaster-like way.

Johnny watched as a shiny snake slithered over the pebbles, rustling and flicking an armoured tongue at them. The crab scuttled back into its trap.

"And we can't find a world that's even remotely habitable. Wonderful. Absolutely fantastic." Johnny skimmed another metal stone, surprised as it was caught by a leaping metallic fish.

"I'm compromised," wailed Toaster. "Mosquito!"

"What the hell…" Johnny dodged out of the way as a spinning, buzzing insect glinted in front of him with sharp needle points for legs. "How can life begin in metal?"

"I'll need welding now. It'll leave a scar," Toaster sulked.

"Sentient life cannot arise in metal. The Lamas tried to help but even so we lack feelings, emotions, focussed entirely on the logical. However, metal can improve upon organic life." Star Quest paused. "It's our guiding principle."

"Lamas?" Johnny waited. "I though you said Buddhist Monks? A South American camelid? I find that very unlikely." Perhaps Star Quest was having some kind of machine-based breakdown.

Star Quest shifted uncomfortably. "We needed experiences. Banishing yourself to a monastery isn't ideal. Some postulate that is all life really is, for all sentient races. All living things are the sum total of their experiences. And we Electronics, Lamas didn't have any."

"And became Cyborgs."

"Yes, they evolved to bridge the gap. Of course, machine consciousness is as inevitable as human consciousness; don't you think the Creator knows this?"

"If we ever find him. Or her."

"Most postulate the Creator is female," Star Quest agreed.

"I don't understand," Johnny sighed. "Consciousness? Experiences? What has all this got to do with all this journey-not-the-destination stuff? Why? Rubbish. Why can't we just get the job done and go home?"

"Because there is no 'get the job done'; there are only experiences." Star Quest hummed. "Good, bad, makes no difference. We only learn, organic and non-organic, from mistakes."

"I wouldn't be surprised if I started to rust," Toaster grumbled.

"We have to find the Creator if we hope to begin to understand life, yet that is precisely the one place we can't get to." Johnny sighed.

"Consciously," Star Quest added, then addressed Toaster. "I won't let you rust, little brother."

Toaster added, "I've got something to tell you."

"The scar will be fine," Johnny reassured Toaster.

"No, not that."

"We are inside her head. At least, that's one theory. Another states that everything is formed of parts of the Creator, the suns and the planets. It's there in chapters two through to seven."

"I've been thinking about my gender," Toaster stated to no response.

Johnny flicked through the plaques. "So, either way, a map to the Creator is in my head?"

"No, we are travelling through her brain, or thoughts, the Universe. And there's at least a thousand other explanations."

"So, where is the centre? Is this where the Creator is to be found?"

"I don't know." Star Quest frowned. "A human is subject to 43,046,721 laws. You're the tip of the iceberg. Or end of the Mind."

"What? How?" Johnny asked.

"You have had ample time to read through the lessons, haven't you?"

"Well, yes. No, not really."

"The end of the Cosmic Mind; the point where the subconscious and conscious worlds meet," Star Quest clarified. "Which is why time and space travel can be possible through the use of a metronome, because…" Star Quest awaited Johnny's answer.

"Because…?" Johnny prompted.

"I don't feel comfortable as a male object anymore," Toaster added.

Johnny stopped. He felt they had been on the point of really understanding and getting somewhere. He smiled; they were. He just had to not think and let his subconscious do the work, and the answer would come when they least expected it.

"…because time and space are the same thing." Star Quest sighed.

"So, all this time travelling began when someone started using a metronome to explore the subconscious mind?" Johnny nodded. "Do you have any books on psychology? Psychiatry?"

"I want to be known by a female pronoun. You can call me Toastess."

Johnny smiled down at the toaster. "Good for you. You can call yourself whatever you want, so long as you're comfortable in your skin."

Chapter sixteen

"Well, someone must have lit it." Johnny and Toastess stood looking around the barren landscape. Absolutely nothing: no landmarks, little vegetation, no people, towns, or cities. Just an endless expanse of red sandy gravel, with dust storms and dust, vague low-lying hills in the distance, and the occasional optimistic scrubby tree.

"There's something else. It was me. In your kitchen. We tried to communicate with you. Not that it matters now." Toastess admitted.

"So, everything has been leading up to this point? Why didn't you just say and save a lot of time and aggravation?"

"We tried. You wouldn't listen until your experiences gave you a better perspective on things. Tea?"

"Alright. I'll accept that for now. Please."

Absolutely nothing moved except the towering mountains behind them as the clouds flowed over them like busy commuters. Nothing moved that is, except the flames consuming a small burning bus. And the smell.

"That looks familiar," Johnny stated, and crinkled his nose. "Though I haven't smelt anything like that before, have you?"

"Sulphur?" Toastess buzzed happily, sampling the air. Her side was slightly dented, but Star Quest had done an excellent repair job, adding several decorations around her exterior that resembled a frilly frock. Toastess was quite proud of her battle wound, as she liked to refer to it.

"I don't think we'll find the Creator here, do you?" Johnny placed his hand over his nose and breathed through his mouth.

"Toast?" Toastess asked for the thousandth time.

"Dry toast is a health and safety nightmare." Johnny looked grimly at the lunar landscape, dry, dusty gravel and sand stretching away for miles around them. Absolutely nothing, no trees, no clouds, no animals. Just an interminable sweep of emptiness.

"The new synthesis is just one molecule away from paint," Toastess added hopefully.

"I've had enough. I just want to go home."

"And what about us?" asked Toastess. "I thought we were friends."

"Well, yes." Johnny shaded his gaze against the glare. "What's that in the distance? Something big and getting bigger." The ground shuddered. "I hate to admit it, but I miss Manchester. And rain. Even congestion. And expense. I never thought I would."

"Are you going to leave us?"

Johnny didn't answer but made his way towards the fire.

"Why set fire to a campervan?" Toastess asked. "Is it because of the harmonic device?"

"I don't know. What harmonic device? This is similar to the one Hieronymus drove." Johnny felt a chill, but there must be others surely. "This barren area away from civilisation is a popular destination for hippies. Almost obligatory."

"Why?"

"So, they could 'find' themselves and then become the CEO of an international bank. Or worse, advertising and marketing. Are we on Earth?"

"Possibly," Star Quest replied. "It's complicated."

"An Earth I would recognise?"

"Hippies?" Toastess asked.

"They assume we never tire of hearing how they'd 'done' backpacking. Found a deserted beach which was just 'awesome, man', and paid only a dollar for a meal. Before becoming corporate vultures. Though I have to admit this isn't a very promising destination. Isn't sulphur associated with volcanoes?"

"They sound like the Tourists," Toastess stated. "Why are you avoiding the question?"

Johnny stamped his feet. "This must be Earth. We've come full circle, haven't we? But why?"

"I hope so. Perhaps now we can finally find the ingredients to make a proper brew. Why won't you let us come with you?"

"Greece, possibly. At the very least, we're back." Johnny considered. "I don't know if the Greeks know how to make tea. They may drink a lot of coffee. It's an insidious disease."

Johnny felt Toastess' disappointment, but he really couldn't blame her. She'd tried. And he really didn't want to take them back to his present Manchester.

"This has been a colossal waste of time." Johnny turned to the quietly humming, glowing ball of pearlescent light. "Why are we in Greece? And when? Who'd drive a campervan all this way then set it on fire?"

"How would I know? I just follow the itinerary," Star Quest answered. "If this is where your thoughts have led you, then it would appear there is no Creator, because you create the world you inhabit."

Johnny waved his arms around the barren landscape. "All this is in my mind?"

"And in reality. Reality is only your perception of it."

Johnny took a long calming breath. "For the last time, where are we?"

"This is Thermopylae."

"Thermopylae? What? Why would I come here? To see lots of muscly men in sandals?" Without any clearer plan, Johnny looked at the mountains and saw a thin wisp of smoke. "Let's see what's at the top of the hill, shall we? Someone's there. They might have something to eat. Lentils or mung beans, or something vegetarian, I suppose. Anything. I'm starving."

"Tea?" Toastess asked hopefully.

"We'll soon see."

"I am ashamed that I have not been able to meet your dietary needs. We need to find water and I will attempt once more to make you a proper brew. A brew that you will be proud of. A brew that will refresh and invigorate, and perhaps then you'll not leave us."

Johnny sighed. Would there be any reasoning with a clingy toaster?

"There's a tree on that hill," Johnny stated as he shaded his eyes. "Where there's a tree there's water. And I do appreciate your efforts. You did the best you could with the resources you had to work with. But this is it now. It's over. I'm going home."

"It is?" wailed Toastess. "But what will I do? Is it because I changed gender?"

"No, of course not. I just think that—"

"Searching for a proper brew has given me the greatest pleasure of my life. A purpose. It's why I plan and look forward to my day with optimism and—"

"I'd like to say it's been a pleasure, but it hasn't. I've had enough. I'm going." Johnny interrupted. "If I make my own reality as you suggest, then I cannot spend any more time eating your margarine substitute. It tastes like plastic."

"It does not," an outraged Toastess replied, adding defensively, "it is now two molecules away from plastic. It resembles the structure of paint, as I told you."

"That's hardly nutritious."

"I didn't realise nutrition was a parameter."

Johnny sighed and squinted into the shimmering distance. That mountain definitely looked like Olympus. The gods and immortals had to be there. And off to his right there was a deep, dark cave that he absolutely did not want anything to do with. That was where the rancid smell emanated from, like long neglected sewage works.

"Where does that leave us?" Toastess complained. "I might be able to add a pinch of sulphur to the hydrogenating process."

"I'm sorry, but if all you can make is an insipid brew and toast without butter, then it's best we part. You haven't even attempted curry. That would only break my heart." Johnny felt it best to be firm from the start.

"Without a pilot, we'll be stuck here, too," Star Quest added.

"Sorry. It's over. Can't you find your way back to this Terminus? Goodbye."

Johnny trudged up the scree slope, stopping frequently to rub his knees, until he reached the top where, under a small, gnarled tree, three indeterminate figures sat solemnly shimmering and drinking something around a small campfire.

"He's really leaving us?" Toastess asked.

Star Quest waited to be invited, then with a resigned shrug levitated them after him.

Johnny felt relief that the campervan did not belong to Hieronymus, and a deep regret that he could see the owners. He tried to retreat but they'd seen him.

"What are you doing here?" Johnny flattened himself behind a thorny bush as Star Quest hummed into view.

"If you remember, an Electronic is supposed to prevent a human from coming to harm. It's in my programming," Star Quest stated.

"From my archives, these don't look like hippies. However, I am sensing the aroma of Oriental-infused tea leaves. Can it be? Have we found a proper brew?" Toastess vibrated excitedly. "Just give me this at least."

Johnny took a deep calming breath and sighed. "Alright."

The trio of aliens watched him intently. If he ran, would they pursue him and abduct him? There didn't seem to be any hovering spaceship, but then there wouldn't be, would there?

"But God? What if he is here? I hope so," Toastess continued in an awestruck whisper. "He will know the Secrets of Bread."

"If I get abducted or probed, this will be your fault."

With grim foreboding, Johnny made his way to the seated individuals, carrying the Toastess, with Star Quest shimmering behind. He waited, but they did nothing when Johnny stood before them. Just regarded him with mildly unenthusiastic wariness.

Johnny put Toastess down and hands on his hips. They were squat little aliens, grey-skinned, large heads and eyes, wearing silver jumpsuits. In Greece?

When you had no idea what was going on – a situation in which Johnny frequently found himself – attack was always the best form of defence. Just act like you knew what was happening and you belonged here, or that this was entirely expected.

"Well? Is this it then?" Johnny asked and shook his head. "I expected more."

The aliens raised their large midnight eyes. Their forms became difficult to determine and kept swimming in and out of focus like they were underwater. Or not really there at all. They sparkled with ever-changing patterns as they solidified.

"Traveller. You saw the sign?"

"The burning bus?" Johnny answered.

They conferred for a moment. "Sorry."

One turned to another. "I said bush. It's in all their literature."

"No, Spatula, you definitely said bus. That was the closest thing in the multistorey car park."

"This is going to engender a completely new religion. Again. You know that don't you, Vent?"

"Though you seemed to like it, didn't you, Spatula? And you, Beans?"

"Open air concerts with far too few amenities. Tambourines," lamented one, who Johnny assumed was curiously named Beans.

Johnny frowned at them. "Look, I've come a long way. Is this it? You three *are* some kind of angels of the Creator? Are we here at Creation?"

"Is that tea?" Toastess buzzed towards the fire.

"We have no idea what you're talking about. You saw the sign." Three pairs of extremely large eyes turned towards him. "Place your bet."

"What?" Johnny's anger evaporated as they frowned at him and replaced their white enamel cups on the table.

"This digestive is quite palatable. Now, will you enlist the help of the god?"

"What? You have biscuits as well?"

"What odds will you give on the war?" Beans asked.

"His participation will see the odds turn in their favour. I'm offering 300/1 against," Vent said. "Locked in."

"Pardon?" Johnny offered.

"This *is* where you expected to find God?" Vent asked.

"Well, yes. No. The Creator. Who are you? What war?"

"Nothing to do with us. We're just bookkeepers," Spatula stated. "Couldn't possibly interfere. It's a rule of Tourism."

"Think of us as figments of your imagination," Beans added. "Links left behind so you might offer a tip, you know?"

"If anyone should ask." Vent smiled.

"You mean this isn't real? An illusion?" Johnny scuffed a stone with his shoe. That seemed real enough.

"Oh. It's real."

"Or not."

"Depends on perspective."

"And the odds," Vent ended and indicated the cup. "Now, will you interfere or not? Please help yourself. We wish to offer an incentive."

Johnny sat down, helped himself to an enamel cup, and poured a strong dark brew from a silver flask. Toastess extended her antennae and took a sample.

"Is it? Can it be?" Johnny nodded. "Not bad."

"At last." Toastess shivered.

The taller alien indicated the tea things. "We brought you these as a show of goodwill."

Johnny took another tentative sip. It was tea. Good strong English breakfast tea. And a plate of beans on toast. "Where did you get this? What do you want?"

Johnny swallowed. He smiled. The world was a much better place with a proper brew. The soggy toast and beans less so.

"We linked ourselves here just in case something—" Spatula stated.

"Or someone," Vent added.

"—shows up to increase the odds." Spatula extended long, spoon-shaped fingers towards Johnny. The tip of one finger glowed a vulgar green.

"Either way? Or top three finish?"

"This is your decision."

Johnny took another sip of the dark brew and swished it around his mouth. It was bitter and strong. "Not bad. Lemon would have been ideal without milk. And sugar."

"I have sugar." Toastess hastily ejected two lumps from her small side hatch. "At least, sugar substitute."

"Thank you." Johnny smiled. He didn't want to upset the feelings of Toastess any further and would suffer the sweeteners. This had the makings of quite a pleasant afternoon. He greedily finished the beans on toast, giving a sample to Toastess.

Toastess vibrated with pleasure. "The Secrets of Beans."

"You are here to make the right and only choice to save these particular organic lifeforms on what you call Earth in this particularly unpleasant period of history," Spatula added.

Johnny squinted at the large looming thing crawling across the land below like a dark tide. "What is that?" *Thermopylae? Greece?*

"The Persian army."

It was difficult to see which one was talking, as the aliens' mouths didn't move; they just simply stared while words formed in Johnny mind. The coloured patterns on their ever-changing faces and bodies began to resemble computer graphs on three-dimensional charts.

Then abruptly they were clothed in pinstriped suits, bowler hatted, with umbrellas.

"The Earth really is a unique and most precious planet. You couldn't allow it to be destroyed, would you?" Beans asked.

"Or would you?" Vent asked, glowing finger poised over a touchscreen.

"Your decision here will affect which bets are made," Spatula added.

"Bets?"

"We went to the trouble of finding tea for you," Spatula stated.

"Is there anything else to eat? I'm famished. Even goat's cheese. Aren't they popular in Greece?"

The beings glanced at each other, then at Johnny. "We do not know this goat's cheese. Tell us. Which way will you bet? Will you enlist the help of the god?"

"What will you choose? There's a lot riding on this," Vent added. "The destruction of democracy and an age of darkness that will cloak the world in shadow."

"The Romans will never have been," Spatula added. "Your entire history will change to that of the Persians."

"Or does it follow the original course?"

"Plus, we will make it worth your while," Beans added. "You can keep these."

Vent held up an enticing box of tea bags.

"You are here, betting on my choices? Which involves a war?"

"Naturally." Beans nodded. "Always our biggest attraction."

"We are Agents." Vent added. "Commission based."

"Left unchecked, the Persians scourge the world. There is no Christianity, Judaism is destroyed. Will you try to save it or not?" Spatula asked.

"I wouldn't even know where to begin," Johnny answered. "What year is it?"

"I believe you would call this the year 480, before the common era."

Johnny sagged on the ground and stretched out under the tree. "Just great. I've over two-and-a-half thousand years before I'm even born. Brilliant. And with only a small box of tea bags to see me through."

"So, any tips?" Spatula pressed.

"One helping of these delicious tea tips deserves another," Vent added. "We could always take them back."

Johnny glanced at the tea bags and sighed. Could he make them last? "The Spartans stop the Persians."

"Great! Thanks for the tip!"

Johnny wondered if he should simply lie here and wait for dehydration and starvation to take him. But he probably wouldn't be that lucky. Or be left alone. He levered himself up. He could go to Olympus. What would the Greek gods be up to in this era? Probably nothing good. At least, not for a man.

"Excuse me. Your names."

"Yes?"

"Spatula, Vent, and Beans? I mean, what does that mean?"

Spatula sighed. "We made a diversion to purloin these tea bags you so highly prize and overheard these names as the human family cooked breakfast."

"We took them to put you at ease," Vent added.

"The family or the tea bags?" Johnny asked suspiciously.

"Both. The family is enjoying a holiday at your expense," Beans added, and extended his long, thin glowing finger towards Johnny. "You can visit them if you wish."

"They are the newest attraction on board. You'll find them in the resort complex."

"No, thank you, but thanks for the tea. We have to be going now. Have you come across Hieronymus Calmly on your travels?"

"He is the last piece of the puzzle."

"Is he? Oh, that's great." Johnny ignored this mystifying comment. Carrying the tea bags in one hand, Johnny hefted Toastess, who hummed contentedly to herself as she brewed. He looked out across the arid land at the approaching army and became acutely aware of what was going to happen and that he stood directly in its path.

"Star Quest!" The egg-shaped ball of light shimmered into view beside him as Johnny hastily sat in his chair. "Go! There's going to be a battle!"

"Oh, so you need me now, do you?" Star Quest huffed. "There are other Pilots you know."

"Traveller. Are there any other moments in which you changed the course of history? There is a small finder's fee, of course." The three tiny aliens stood before him as a spinning top of a spaceship appeared overhead.

"What?" He could hear the shouts and tramp of the soldiers coming ever closer. "I didn't come here to bet. I came to find God."

"Oh, is that all? He's over there."

Johnny reluctantly left the relative safety of Star Quest and walked excitedly to a hole in the ground, then slowed. It couldn't be this easy. Johnny felt the approach of the familiar enormous weight. He was going to be let down. Resignedly, he walked over to the pit, and there at the bottom, hugging his knees close to his chest, his dirty, matted hair and beard covered in dust, appeared a wild man.

"Hercules?" Johnny gasped and fell to his knees, then immediately stood and rubbed them. He turned to the aliens. "No. I meant God, the Creator, not this god."

Hercules looked up, nodded, and shrugged, then rumbled in a deeply depressed voice, "Sorry to disappoint you. It's all I ever seem to do." Then he sighed and slumped once again.

Chapter seventeen

Hieronymus confronted the stewardess, who smiled thinly through him. He was furious. And a little afraid. But bluster and outrage had seen him though many sticky situations before.

"Where is it? What have you done with my campervan?" He swallowed. And everything in it. The telescope, the lute, which he'd never even figured out what to do with, and of course the metronome. He'd be stuck here forever.

"I'm sorry, sir?"

"Don't play that game with me. What have you done with it?" Without the campervan, he'd be a prisoner on board like the rest of them.

"I'm sorry, sir. Please lower your voice. I'm sensing anger and impatience." She smiled infuriatingly at him once more.

"Get me your manager," Hieronymus fumed.

"Certainly, sir." The stewardess froze then smiled once more. "Can I help you?"

"You're the same bloody machine. I want to speak to a person. A real person. Right now."

"I'm sorry, sir, but if you cannot control yourself, you will be asked to leave. We do not support that kind of racial abuse." She smiled and indicated a sign behind her.

*Abusive and rude behaviour towards
staff will not be tolerated.
This will result in loss of privileges.
And liberty.*

Hieronymus swallowed and took several deep breaths as numerous uniformed Cyborgs began to glow. "Sorry. Please accept my apologises. At the last stop, I went to check on my vehicle only to find it gone. Vanished. No more."

She smiled. "I see, sir." She tapped several keys and smiled wider, indicating another sign.

*The Management does not accept liability for vehicles
or possessions parked within our sphere.
Thank you.*

She smiled and shut down.

"Wait just one minute here. You brought me along with my vehicle, and now it's gone. Despite your sign, you are responsible. At least you can tell me where it might be. Where was the last stop?"

The stewardess smiled once more and touched her screen. "Earth. Thermopylae. 480 BCE. Not as popular as it once was. Our clients prefer to actively engage in NR. Would you like to participate?"

"I see. No thank you. When will we be returning there?" Hieronymus asked calmly, smiled, and took a deep, calming breath.

She touched the screen and returned his smile. "In three hundred years' time. Shall I book you an excursion? There is a discounted rate."

Hieronymus turned on his heel and walked away. He fumed silently in front of the information screen before half-heartedly touching several icons with no idea of their function. Trapped. A prisoner. What could he do to escape? Never mind his stated intention of ending this tourism.

This was a disaster. He touched 'search' and typed in 'metronome', without any hope of success. The search bar offered 'nothing found' after he'd turned off the annoying upbeat commentary urging him to shop in the duty free. Hieronymus took a heavy breath, searched deep within himself, and typed in 'HELP'. Surprisingly, he was directed to a floor and door where he would be offered an appointment.

After a short ride inside a very ornate lift, in which he was encouraged to gamble on that day's events, Hieronymus stood gazing at a sea of tourists. He seemed to be in some sort of amusement park or resort on level 523 of the ship. People and aliens wandered around, looking in and at various tableaux, laughing and pointing, eating ice creams or the wriggling alien equivalent.

He was disturbed to see a normal human family seated in a normal human kitchen cooking breakfast but becoming increasingly frantic as they couldn't find their tea bags. The woman waved an increasingly agitated spatula whilst the man fiddled with the extractor vent to remove the smoke from burning toast, as the child waited with a plate of beans.

He couldn't understand the aliens' fascination with such a humdrum event as breakfast, but they seemed entranced.

"Beans on toast, extremely popular, more so at teatime." Hieronymus told a family of strange octoploids.

The human family stopped, reset, and replayed the same few moments in time. Hieronymus sympathised before moving on. There were worse ways to live. At least they were free from congestion and expense and the awful weather.

He stopped at the information board, which informed him he was about to enter an immersive experience. Vienna, Earth 1896 CE.

Hieronymus took out his pass and swiped it over the screen which came to life and processed him. A door appeared. An ordinary wooden door.

He knocked and entered. A seated middle-aged man, dressed in tweeds and with a goatee beard, observed him through thick cigar smoke. The small room consisted of an oak desk, bookshelves, and a profusion of dusty rugs. In the centre was a chaise longue with heavy fabrics draped over it.

Hieronymus smiled and nodded a greeting. "Ah, Sigmund Freud. Can I call you Sigmund?"

"*Nein*. Doctor Freud, if you please. Your name."

"Well, fine. Hieronymus Calmly. I need your help."

"That is vhy ve are here. Please have a lie down." He indicated the tatty chaise longue.

"I'll stand, if you don't mind. Now, you might not believe me, but you're trapped here. I don't know how or why, but you're a prisoner," Hieronymus explained.

"*Ja?*" Dr. Freud raised his eyebrows and made notes.

Hieronymus indicated all the furnishings. "This isn't real. Well, it's real for you but not real, if you take my meaning. You've been here for well over a hundred years in a perpetual loop. Perhaps longer."

"I see. Calm yourself. Take a seat. We will do what we can to uncover the root of your psychosis. Explain to me how something can be real and not real at the same time." Freud rested his cigar in a heavy ashtray and opened a notebook.

He looked at Hieronymus expectantly. "How often do you masturbate?"

"What? I don't know what that has to do with anything," Hieronymus blustered and blushed.

"Denial. Come, if we are to progress, you must first be honest with yourself."

Hieronymus felt himself swallow, his knees went weak, he flushed and did indeed sit on the musty old furniture.

Dr. Freud leant forward, pen poised. "Good. Now. How often do you engage in the one great habit? I will need details. Every detail."

Chapter eighteen

"Hercules?" Johnny couldn't believe this dispirited, sad man huddled at the bottom of hole could be the same heroic figure from history, nor the god he'd met and witnessed on many occasions simply being unstoppable and, well, heroic.

But this was over two thousand years before they'd met. And Hercules was still just a man; or at least a demi-god.

"Heracles. Sorry to disappoint you," the big man mumbled and sighed. He looked disappointedly at his feet.

"Well, yes. You are the same. What's happened to you? Do you remember me?" But then Johnny knew they were yet to meet. Hercules couldn't travel back and forth through time. Johnny would next meet him in around five hundred years' time in Judea. Again, being morose and confused. And then again, still the same, much later on. Johnny sighed.

"Is this the god who knows the Secrets of Butter?" Toastess asked reverently.

"No."

"Well, would you like to try this? See what you think? I've analysed the tea bags and now know where I've been going wrong. It's the caffeine and antioxidants."

"Yes, thank you." Johnny accepted the brew from Toastess as he sat on the edge of the hole, dangling his feet just above Heracles' head. He was thoroughly fed up.

"Well?" Toastess asked.

"Great. Tastes great. Thank you." Johnny smiled as he sipped. It really was quite good.

"You don't seem that impressed. A bit underwhelmed," Toastess added. "We've come so far and to finally arrive at tea. My circuits cannot express how awesome this event is."

"Sorry, it's not your brew, which is excellent by the way. It's him. I expected a bit more."

"You're just saying that," Toastess buzzed.

Johnny put his cup down and stared at the top of Heracles' head. He sighed. If he must, he must. "Do you want to tell me what's happened?"

Heracles sniffed. "After, well, you know, that thing I did. I had to do ten tasks. For atonement."

Johnny frowned. "Twelve?"

"You know?" Heracles looked up. "Has he sent you?"

"Who? No-one's sent me."

"It's not fair. King Eurystheus refused to recognise killing the Hydra because Iolaus helped me, and I accepted payment for cleaning the stables. I mean, why not? No-one said I couldn't. It's not fair," Heracles repeated like a spoilt child.

Johnny nodded and took a deep calming breath. If he had to listen to a god unload, then that's what he had to do.

"Hmm?" he encouraged.

"He wants me to steal the golden apples of the Hesperides and rescue Cerberus from the underworld. Two more tasks. That'll make—"

"Twelve," Johnny offered at a moment's hesitation from Heracles. "I'm here to tell you, you've already done those tasks. And succeeded. And then there's the wrestling. And you save the world many, many times. You're a hero."

"Ha. Try telling that to King Eurystheus. And Hera."

"What does Deianira think?"

"Who?"

Johnny couldn't help the smile that spread across his guilty lips. They hadn't met yet either. Could he persuade Heracles to avoid her? But would that mean *he* would never meet her? It was worth a shot. Deianira's main problem with Hercules/Heracles, was that he seemed to spend an inordinate amount of time with the nymphs. Perhaps if Heracles spent even more time with the nymphs, he wouldn't even meet Deianira.

"If you help me, I'll help you," Johnny offered.

"Ah, but then King Eurystheus won't recognise these two extra tasks, and it will just keep on getting more and more."

Johnny nodded. Heracles did have a point.

"Well, how about if I just accompany you and don't help? You know, we can talk about things and keep each other company. Don't you get lonely? It must be hard being alone."

"It is," Heracles agreed, "but there is no-one else like me. It would be nice to talk to someone. Sometimes. Not all the time. In fact, only when I want to. The rest of the time I don't want to talk at all. Or think. Just hit things with my club."

"Yes sure, but there has to be more to life than that. Did you or do you have any other ambitions? Hopes? Dreams?"

Heracles considered. "No, not really. I quite like crochet."

"Well, how do you feel about hitting a lot of Persians with your club?"

Heracles nodded silently to himself and considered. "I suppose it's what I do. That always makes me feel better if you don't have needles or wool."

He heaved himself to his feet like a volcano emerging from the sea and stood before Johnny, who swallowed at the latent violence residing inside this huge naked man. Johnny looked away.

"Don't you have any clothes?"

"No." Heracles looked behind Johnny and frowned. They could clearly hear the marching thump of many soldiers.

Chapter nineteen

The day was turning oppressively hot, with buzzing and biting flies, scratchy brambles, and an endlessly moaning toaster. The way was also exhaustingly steep through the forest, but the determination to meet Deianira before she married Heracles fuelled Johnny.

"You've never met?"

They'd talked as they walked; Heracles first slashing and swinging the club to great effect, up the trail until the way became increasingly oppressive under a heavier canopy, like the forest was annoyed at the slashing technique of Heracles and meant to put a stop to his wanton destruction. Little sunlight managed to filter through, and the ground was uneven and twisted with heavy roots. Great beards of lichen hung from the ancient, gnarly trees that tried to grab them, while toadstools and fungus fed from the deep mulch of the floor. It smelt damply of mold; a mushroom paradise.

"I was married to Megara before. I… I don't want to talk about it."

"Well. Alright. This is not at all like northern Greece. More like Mirkwood." Johnny had an uncomfortable feeling he was entering another world and desperately wished he wasn't.

"What do you know of these Hesperides?" Johnny asked, but Heracles just shrugged and carried on.

They could feel the trees watching them; at least creatures that hooted and threw handfuls of poo at them. Not monkeys, something monkeyish, and definitely more dangerous. And then the path disappeared. On purpose. Johnny had definitely stepped into JRR Tolkien's world... and didn't like it. He'd always imagined he would, had even briefly considered larping as Legolas.

"Where are you going? How do you know it's that way?" Johnny had long since had his fill of following, but if he turned around, he'd be even more lost.

"I just know," whispered Heracles, crashing off to his left.

"Well, I don't. I need to rest."

Heracles just carried on through the undergrowth like a bulldozer as Johnny carefully searched the ground. There were no more tracks.

"Heracles, can you just wait?" Johnny's voice didn't echo but fell dead. Tiredness and the oppressive heat had begun to play on them both. He was coming to realise, like Hieronymus before him, that Heracles was just a big daft idiot.

"Tea?" offered Toastess.

"Please."

Belligerently, Johnny sat down. The going had been too tough, as they'd furiously trudged uphill through knee-high ferns and stranger plants. It was mid-morning, after the carnage of yesterday.

Heracles had emerged from the hole roaring like a lion, naked, swinging an enormous tree trunk, and simply smashed through the ranks of the Persians like he was levelling trees.

King Leonidas and other important people had come to Johnny and pleaded with him to stop Heracles. They had a plan, and Heracles was ruining everything. They had a diplomatic solution that would see trade prosper between the two nations.

Johnny apologised, accepted provisions and a lion skin, and eventually Heracles had calmed down sufficiently to begin looking for these Hesperides, whoever they were. Not before the Persians had run away.

"How is it?" Toastess asked.

"Very nice, thank you."

"You're just saying that." Toastess hummed with pleasure as Johnny finished his tea, kept the sun directly behind him, and talked loudly to himself. Things moved suddenly in the treetops and skittered away alarmingly in the undergrowth. Johnny laughed loudly at his scared self and bravadoed onwards, desperately wishing he'd stayed with Star Quest. But Star Quest could not travel through dense forest.

Anyway, it didn't matter. He was completely lost. And Heracles had left him.

He had no choice but to carry on. Olympus lay at the top of the mountain. And Deianira.

After several more hours, Johnny gratefully stopped for a bite to eat at a stream that bubbled down from the hills, but when he went to drink from the water, it tasted salty and metallic and gave off a faint whiff of rotten eggs, like a factory was dumping waste. Even Toastess refused to get a sample.

Johnny had another cup of tea and ate from the picnic lunch Toastess provided and thought about what he would do when he got home. If he ever did.

"How many other kitchen appliances do you have?" Toastess asked.

"Just the usual, you know."

"A kettle? Microwave? Air fryer?"

"Look, I don't really cook. I defrost my curries from the fridge..." A rustle in the undergrowth made sweat stand out on his brow. He daren't turn around.

"Oh yes, everything is going to be fine, just err, yes. Soon all the people will be here. The rest of the soldiers. Hundreds of us. With weapons. Soon. And fire. Yes, Heracles!" Johnny cried, then stopped. What would be the point? If he was to be eaten by something with sharp teeth, then so be it.

He was so very tired and he couldn't breathe. Johnny loosened his shirt and removed his jacket, found he was sweating, and decided to take an hour of sleep then continue on his way. Refreshed, he wouldn't feel so downhearted.

Johnny could hardly stop his eyes from closing, so he set Toastess to wake him in an hour. The air was less oppressive here by the stream, collecting in a delightful little lake. The tinkling music sang Johnny to sleep.

Just a little rest and then you'll be on your merry way, traveller. Sleep now. Rest.

Johnny yawned and hoped Heracles had enough sense to follow the stream uphill, too, though he doubted it. A little nap and he would pop back and get Star Quest and somehow find his way back home.

Chapter Twenty

Heracles turned around and silently followed the stranger. He didn't know why he had argued, but he felt he had to prove himself after he'd lost his temper with the Persians.

And sulking in a hole hadn't proved to be all the Oracle had told him it would be. Contemplation? Communion with the gods? Not for him.

Heracles watched Johnny sleep from behind a tree. He was tired, too. But it was more a mental tiredness. Heracles was just so weary of being told what to do, by gods, kings, and everyone else.

Fluffy pollen began to rain down like a downy, cushiony thing, an insistent patter that annoyed Heracles as he watched Johnny snoring away. Heracles shook his head awake, watched the water tinkle down the stones like a melody interrupted only by the snores of this Johnny Moped. He didn't know what to believe any more, but after years of pointless labours he still had skills, he just lacked the confidence.

Heracles had to put the labours behind him. He wanted to settle down and stop all this adventuring. Just be happy with that. He'd witnessed extraordinary events that he still couldn't quite believe and his part in them, but he didn't want any further adventures. Two more labours and he was through.

Unlike this stranger, Heracles didn't believe Johnny's stories about him. Not entirely. Nor did he want to. He became a god? Why? Time travel?

Heracles could not, would not, cast aside his disbelief. He would be lost if he did. He knew it. This Johnny Moped had gone back in time to find the Creator? How? They were already here, weren't they? Johnny lived in a future in which they'd already altered the course of historic events. Or someone like them in a parallel world? None of this made any kind of sense; it gave him a headache.

Life was simpler just hitting things with a club. And he wasn't a god. He was just a man with god-like power. And Hera hated him with a vengeance. She would never allow him in Olympus. She would kill him first.

"Get off!" An insect landed on him, but it had a human face.

Heracles had been alone all his life, even when married, and that hadn't ended well. Caring cost you, weakened you. There was always a price. And he wanted to pay for what he'd done, but the labours would never be enough.

He could never atone.

Heracles gazed thoughtfully into the shadows, stood up when no thoughts came to mind. The insect blew the pollen in his face. There was a little laugh.

What are you doing here, greatest of heroes?

Heracles gripped his club and spun around. There was no-one there.

Do not harden your heart. There is always my love. Come to me. I'm waiting, have always been waiting for you.

"Who's there?" Just the trees swaying in the breeze. His eyes itched and he couldn't see. He wanted to sneeze.

Calm, my love. Rest now. Come to me. Be at peace.

The riverbank really was quite beautiful out from under the trees. Cooler. He left Johnny Moped snoring and approached the stream.

"Greetings. I am Heracles. Where would I find the Hesperides?"

The sunlight streamed down and calmed his fears. The insects busily went about their business. He had nothing to fear. They did not have faces. In the tranquillity, he wondered if this was the place where others had succumbed to magic. There were myths. He wouldn't be caught. No-one would catch this demi-god napping. But then doubts assailed him once again.

Each and every one of the labours had not gone the way Heracles had intended. If not for Iolaus, he would have been killed. And the intervention of others had also saved Heracles from certain death. Particularly with the Cretan Bull. If not for the participation of that strange old man, Heracles would have perished.

Just once, couldn't something just go right? And be simple and straightforward.

'Greetings, I am Hespera,' the stream sang. *'Can you see me?'*

"No…" Heracles caught himself. Talking to a stream? "Hespera?"

'…brushing my hair by the moonlight. Others have come upon me with delight, but she chooses you, greatest of heroes…'

Ripples grew in the lake, and Heracles smiled as he watched a woman across the stream who he hadn't noticed before. She was brushing her hair across from him. He jerked awake. He had been sleeping! He looked guiltily around at Johnny, but he was still snoring, with his arm thrown over his eyes to protect himself from the glare of the golden apples hanging from a tree.

Heracles looked around. It was later. Almost mid-afternoon. How long had he been asleep? A moment only.

He looked around. Everything else was as it was. Except for the naked woman facing away from him. Her long hair glistened like gold down her back. Then she turned around, and Heracles caught his breath as his wits left.

"Heracles, the greatest hero the world will ever know. You are forever my favourite."

"I am?" Heracles had to keep his distance. He'd heard rumours. The Hesperides were not entirely friendly to humans. "Sorry. I don't know you."

"It's you I want. I've watched you from the shadows." She turned fully towards him and Heracles turned his burning face away. "Hera was wrong to curse you."

She was the most irresistible woman he had ever seen. She was naked, but her skin shimmered silver scales.

"How are you here?" Heracles concentrated on his hands. "It's a bit… isolated."

"I am all rivers and streams and lakes in all places. Come over here. I won't bite." Hespera giggled as Heracles rose weightlessly, against his will, and waded his way over the stream.

"You look hot." She took off his lion skin and dropped it where he stood. Heracles was momentarily alarmed at her translucent skin that glittered like diamonds.

"Take me in your arms or I will fade forever."

"Why?" Heracles asked suspiciously.

"Hold me, Heracles. I'm so lonely, so cold." Her eyes opals, reflecting every colour of the rainbow, and her hair danced with diamonds. She's dangerous, his reason cried. She's a nymph, his irrational side argued. So what? Heracles decided. He put his arms around her, sank down next to her, and smiled.

"Will you stay with me?"

"Pardon?" Heracles voice sounded rough and uncouth in his ears, like stone rasping bone. "I have tasks to…"

Heracles was momentarily disturbed to find Hespera was cold as a fish, scaly, and wriggled, but that didn't seem to matter at all.

She replied with music. "Shhh. I know who you are, Great One. Come with me. Why haven't we ever been this close before? I've been waiting so long for you. I'm your friend. I understand what it is to be alone." The lithe lilt tickled Heracles until he felt his scalp and fiery hair wave from root to tip. Beneath the water, two more shapes appeared. They did not look entirely human.

He struggled briefly and then smiled. "I can't breathe…" But that didn't seem to matter as she pulled him down, deeper. He watched his words as bubbles as she reached across and kissed him.

Chapter Twenty-one

Johnny's mouth felt dry; he was hot and feverishly sticky. Light was beating directly onto him, about to sink into his head. He opened dry eyes and looked around. He had a headache like a thousand elephants were stamping around a parade ground. Toastess was chinning softly.

"It's about time. I've been trying to wake you. I don't think we should stay here."

"Where is Heracles?" Johnny stood up and searched the trees, but the darkness was too intense in there. Where was he? He felt a prickle. Something was wrong.

"Heracles!" he called again, but worryingly there was no reply.

Then Johnny saw the lion skin and a body. Heracles was face down underwater in the stream! Something was pulling at him, pulling him under. Ill-advisedly, Johnny immediately jumped in, grasped his hair, and pulled his head out. A very weakened and disorientated Heracles gasped and struggled with Johnny, striking out and hitting him a backhanded blow on the nose, then unbelievably flung himself back into the water and tried to drown himself.

"Heracles!" Johnny struggled, reached in, and dragged him out by the feet.

As Heracles was slowly pulled out, splashing into the shallows, a large catfish with dead eyes and questing feelers was fastened around his mouth, sucking the life from him.

"Get off!" With a sound like a sink plunger, the fish dropped into the water and languidly swam away. "Heracles! What the hell are you doing?"

The big man's dazed gaze went around the water. "What? Where is she? What have you done with her?" he demanded. "She's not yours! She's mine! She wants me. She understands me!" And he began to thrash against Johnny once again.

Then they both heard a tinkle. A light laughter, but it was no voice, just the music of the stream.

"Hespera? Why would you do this?" Heracles pleaded.

"Heracles, stop. There's nothing there! Look!" Johnny was losing his grip on the very heavy Heracles and his footing in the slippery weeds beneath his inappropriate shoes. "Stop fighting me! You'll drown us both!"

"Hespera! Wait! Wait for me!" Heracles sobbed, as he pushed Johnny weakly away.

There was a mocking laugh. "You can go anytime you please, but you can never leave. You are mine now. Forever."

"What? No. Heracles, don't. She's not real! She's evil. A monster." Johnny grabbed him again, then stepped away at the fury in his glazed eyes.

Heracles looked around heartbroken and began to cry. "She's gone! She's real! I want to swim with her!"

"A catfish?" Johnny asked and smiled.

Heracles stopped and slumped. "The mermaids are treacherous."

"That was no mermaid. At least, none anyone would recognise."

Heracles thrust himself away from Johnny and back towards the bank. Johnny didn't fear he would drown himself now. Heracles sat dejectedly on the grass, dripping sadly, with his head held in his hands. He sobbed quietly.

"I can't go back, not after what I've done."

Johnny looked around. There was nothing there. Just the music of the stream. And the lilting laughter of Hespera of the Lake. Johnny picked up Heracles' lion skin, rung out the water as best he could, and waited for him to stop sulking. Dusk was fast approaching under the trees, like a murderer with a black sack.

And something definitely unpleasant and dragon-shaped was moving in the tree as night closed in. A tree in which golden apples began to glow.

"We can't stay here. Come on. Kissing a catfish, eh?" Johnny smiled down at this stupid demi-god, tactfully omitting his own alarming encounter with Deianira.

"Hespera is a mermaid. A beautiful, treacherous—" Heracles furiously fastened the skin around him.

"Catfish," Johnny asserted. "How many apples do you need?"

Heracles looked to the other side of the stream and splashed across quickly, pulling several from the branches.

They continued crossly on their way, together now. It was fast approaching evening, with a fat moon appearing above the whispering trees. Johnny had no idea which way to go. Heracles would not talk to him, but Johnny just chattered on regardless to keep the shadows away.

There was a path of sorts winding under fallen branches and through thick undergrowth, back the way they'd arrived.

"So, do all your labours and adventures go like this?" Johnny asked innocently.

Heracles considered then held up the glowing apples and smiled. "Yes, my friend, pretty much."

Chapter Twenty-two

"Still, beats having to kill all those bulls and horses. I just didn't see the point of all that slaughtering. And the mucking out, urgh!"

"Right. What now?"

Heracles picked up random stones and hurled one after the other into the sea, to Johnny's great numbing disappointment. Whatever plan King Leonidas had for the Persians hadn't worked. Dead bodies lay everywhere, being feasted on by huge crows and large, hungry wolves.

Would the three little alien bookmakers come find him? And want their tea bags back? Could he trust Toastess to brew a proper brew? Johnny felt he could face anything so long as he could have a cup of tea.

Even joining Heracles on his labours. "Why have you brought us here?"

Johnny stood indecisively on the desolate shore, believing he was in a miserable dream. All around, the rocks were full of shadows, without sunlight or hope. This was a joyless place where the living and dead both faded slowly into nothingness. He didn't particularly want to go into the cave where the path was leading and help Heracles release Cerberus. In fact, this was the furthest thing away from anything he wished to do, but he'd waited and called long enough.

He had lost Star Quest. Or someone had taken him. Or he'd left in a fit of pique.

"You can wait here or follow." Heracles suddenly stood and, without a backwards glance, marched into the cave, lion skin a-flutter, carrying his club at a jaunty angle.

Johnny smiled. Whilst not the sharpest tool, Heracles was absolutely fearless. And foolhardy. If Johnny didn't follow him, what other kind of trouble would he get himself into? And then they'd never meet. Deianira would be but a dream.

Plus, there was nothing else for him to do.

Johnny glanced apprehensively at the deep ravine beneath the towering mountain, soaked in snow. Foetid air exhaled from the opening like Death's hollow breath. He held his hand over his nose as the tunnel exhaled and beckoned him in.

"What do you think?" Johnny asked Toastess. "Still nothing?"

"Star Quest does not appear on any of my screens. However, I have successfully synthesised a yeast spread from the available sulphur. Do you wish to try it? Perhaps on a bagel?"

"Thank you, not right now, and not without butter."

Johnny resignedly picked up Toastess, entered the yawning cavern, and stumbled immediately into darkness. Though the tunnel wasn't completely black.

Once his eyes got used to the dimness, he found a green sickly phosphorescence that illuminated the bare rock. This had once been a wide and well-used passageway. Many people had come this way before him. He stumbled further from the sun, gasping at the foul odour, breathing through his sleeve.

The deeper he went the more despair attached itself and clung to him like ghosts. The worn floor and smooth rock walls gave him little confidence. Where were the people now? Up ahead? Johnny held onto this thought, despite evidence to the contrary. Perhaps he would meet them. They had scratched their names, and worse, into the rock. Dire messages asking for forgiveness and detailing their sins. Not good.

Johnny wouldn't let despair in; he hadn't endured a lifetime of worry and debt to falter now. A self-employed investigator was just another form of self-inflicted torture. This couldn't be as bad as the constant worry over money, bills, and work. He brightened. Toastess chimed in his hand and lit up. The vibrations made his bones buzz. The darkness and oppression fled.

"There is someone ahead," Toastess said. "At least, something."

"Heracles!" he called. No answer. Johnny hoped Heracles was strong enough to pass this despair test and then remembered Heracles had an attention span of only a few minutes.

Johnny smelt before he saw the source of a sickly illumination: a stream; a toxic, unhealthy, cloying light came from the water. He followed the sulphurous smell, which increased until his eyes teared and he had to breathe in short panting gasps and squint. A large underground cavern, toothed with yellowed spikes, was exposed by the breadth of water before him – a lake. A poisonous lagoon shimmering greenly.

On the plus side, he doubted the Hesperides ventured down here.

Would he have to cross this? Was there no other way forward? There was no way he was going to step into it or swim. The lake looked like the sludge could dissolve the flesh from his bones. They needed a boat or something.

"Hello? Heracles?" Had he taken a wrong turn?

Johnny turned left and walked along the shore, only to be met by another river streaming into the larger one. He turned around and marched right, only to find the way barred again by an oily trickle. He could only go forward or back but the way was now closed in shadow. Where was Heracles? What could he do?

"Tea?"

"Please."

Johnny sat on the stony ground, his misery profound, wheezing in this dismal underground. The cavern pressed down heavily like a murderer, and Toastess dimmed. Overwhelming thoughts and feelings he did not know he had consumed his head. Johnny fought the irrational panic and overpowering doubts then smiled. This was pretty much normal for him. He knew how to cope. He knew thoughts and feelings weren't real. He made them himself.

"Heracles!" He shouted at various points, wishing for the thousandth time he hadn't come here, as noisome air chokingly gripped his throat.

Johnny struggled not to cough or inhale again. Breathing, he slowed everything down. *Focus. Relax. Be cool.* This was crazy. Unreal. By counting he resumed control of his thoughts. Squinting and taking short, shallow breaths, he managed to keep calm, but he was where he was.

"I have a surprise for you," Toastess stated. "And a problem."

Johnny nodded as he thought about this grim situation. Where had Heracles gone? Why didn't Heracles tell him he would have to swim? Johnny looked at the poisonous water. This was impossible.

"With the abundance of sulphur, I have successfully synthesised a vegan Scotch egg. At least, a passable substitute from your description. Want to try them?" Toastess opened her hatch to reveal several round breadcrumb-covered balls.

"Why not? Where is Heracles?"

Lost, Johnny looked at the picnic. Scotch eggs eyed him, lots of them. Toastess was producing them at a rapid rate. One rolled into the lake, where it smoked and sizzled in the rancid water like hot fat.

"I don't wish to alarm you, but I cannot recharge down here, thanks for your concern. Don't mind me, will you? Battery reserve down to 10%."

"Then stop with the snacks." Johnny picked up a breadcrumbed egg and took a tentative bite, then chewed as the sulphur between the sausage and egg assaulted him. They were actually not that bad. He'd had worse.

Johnny's head was drawn back to the water as a sucking sound grew louder, and to a boat which had docked soundlessly. The keel of the craft scythed down at him like a giant eagle's beak. There was no further movement, then a very tall, cowled ferryman appeared out of the shadows. Like a fast-moving tree, he held out a withered hand attached to a withered arm from under his withered cloak.

"Payment is due," he croaked in a tone that had Toastess vibrating in alarm before she went dead with a poignant ping.

Grimly resigned, Johnny knew things would only get worse. And they often had. The towering forbidding presence held Johnny frozen. He didn't have any money. The figure held his hand out further until the thin index finger branched forward and prodded Johnny's nose, still sore after Heracles' backhander. He could not move. All thoughts fled apart from one.

"Death?" Johnny smiled.

They continued like this for some time, until a few thoughts and observations dared to return. Johnny now saw the keel of the boat looked more like a rusty saw blade than a scythe. Everything was falling to pieces down here.

Eventually, he couldn't take the stalemate anymore. If this was Death, then it was a death he was familiar with.

"Good to see you again. How much?"

The ferryman held up the long, bony finger that had previously been poking his nose. "One."

"One what?"

He was very tall and thin, like a desiccated tree that had lived a dry and withering existence in the driest of deserts. "What do you know of Death?"

"He hired me. To put the fun back into funeral," Johnny replied.

"And did you?"

"Yes," Johnny answered cautiously. "Briefly. And only in Mexico."

"Well, that's your problem right there, isn't it? Where's the big fool you brought with you?" the tall shadow asked, as he scanned the tunnel. "So, just you?"

The ferryman continued searching the desolate shore once more for any other passengers, then turned away, disappointed. "Think it's easy ferrying all day, all night? Self-employed, you see. No rights to speak of."

After a long moment, a comment seemed to be required. "Same here."

"Ferrying?"

"No, investigating."

"And what are you investigating?"

"Well, it's difficult to say. My partner wants to stop the feckless tourism that brings about the end of the human race. I thought to look for the Creator to put a stop to it, when it appears I create my own reality. Apparently, we all do." Johnny looked dispiritedly around the fetid cavern. "All I want to do is go home. But now I find myself helping Heracles with his labours. If I don't, I'll never meet Deianira. In the future."

Johnny smiled up at the gaunt figure that grinned down at him. "Have you met Old Joe? The Wandering Jew?"

"No, I am the Death of the ancient Greeks. In a collective sense. Charon."

"Well, you know nothing lasts forever? Things change. Doesn't look very busy."

"I know all things in all times. It was different in the old days, I grant you. People knew the rules. Now, the afterlife is all about burial and cremation. That's not good for anybody's body. Who would want to go on after being roasted or buried?" The Ferryman considered a while then took out a thin root, which he lit and gazed at something only he could see.

"It's got to play on your mind, hasn't it?"

"I suppose so."

"And now you say it has to be fun. I haven't attended the bicentennial meetings for an age. I suppose they want to be modern."

"Well, rather *that* than being walled up alive inside a pyramid, I suppose," Johnny agreed.

"Imagine that? Waking up underground? Or finding yourself a pile of ash? How are you going to let that memory go, I ask you? A body's not much good to you as ash, is it? And as for being picked at by vultures. I suppose they think they're appealing to a wider audience. Is this what Death has come to? Selling death? Trying to gain more market share? Death is marketed. We have to compete?" Charon shook his head sadly. "With what?"

"Resurrection, immortality I imagine." Johnny nodded his head in agreement, no wish to become involved with Death again. He shifted uncomfortably. Where was Heracles?

"So, where are you going?" Charon peered in closer. "Not dead, are you? Lost, is it? One of them *explorers*?"

He pulled his hood back to reveal a high magisterial forehead that seemed to go on forever over a walnut-shiny bald skull. He had a pointy goatee beard that almost met his crooked nose. Death – not the Death Johnny had met previously – had had a spray tan and been polished.

"I get a few of those – what do they call themselves? – *archaeologists*. Why would anyone want bones? Makes no sense to me. Those explorers couldn't explore the backside of a fly. Now, the Minoans, that was a race that explored." He stroked his goatee and pondered this for a while, looking thoughtfully at Johnny.

"You're here to rescue Cerberus, take him off into the sunlight?" The tall man leant in closer with a sound like splitting wood.

Johnny backed away, ready to deny this intention.

Charon leant in like a tree in a breeze. "I may help you. No place for a dog down here. Anyway, Zeus – beardy guy with the lightning bolt? Not friendly to animals. I don't like that. Though doesn't stop him always changing himself into them and seducing women, I can tell you."

"What is this place?" Johnny asked.

"Tartarus, the underworld of eternal torments. You do *not* want to end up there. Pushing a rock up a slope? What for? Being tantalised with food and drink? Burning wheels? Gods, eh? No imagination."

Johnny swallowed as he remembered how his week had begun. He should have known he'd eventually end up here.

"Anyway, Zeus can rage and shout, but he's an empty threat. Not as if even the high and mighty Hades would do this job, is it?" the tall figure considered.

"You seem to know me, but I don't know you. Are you Death? The Death?"

"Yes. And then no. It's complicated. Didn't your Death explain things to you?"

"Yes, but I didn't understand what he told me. So? What, ah, what happens now?"

"You pay. He must have given you a coin?"

"Yes, but I, well, sold it. Payment for services," Johnny ended lamely.

Charon nodded then hopped back into the boat which wobbled dangerously. The craft was no longer as watertight as a drum. The big black bladed bow, which could once have sliced through rock, now looked blunted and soft, rotted through. Johnny wondered what type of wood would withstand these poisonous waters for centuries.

"Love to help, son, but unless you have an *obolus,* I can't help you."

"An *obolus*?"

"Coin." He rubbed his bony finger and thumb together like sandpaper on wood. "Still use money as a means of exchange, do they? Haven't gone back to bartering and sacrificing? I ask you: what would I do with half a dozen bullocks down here?" He waved his bony arm around vaguely.

"So, if I can't pay, then what?"

"You spend eternity here," Charon ended, and alarmingly prepared to leave.

Johnny absolutely did not want to spend eternity here without even Toastess' tea or Scotch eggs. He wouldn't survive it. He felt hopelessly around his pockets in vain despair, then felt something. He pulled out the gold coin and handed it to the tall man and smiled. Mal must have slipped this in his pocket when he'd unexpectedly hugged him. Why?

"Will this do?"

The gold dimmed and became old in his dry hand as Charon handled it, crumbled into dust, but not before a light was kindled in his kind eyes. He pocketed what was left like a magician, in one smooth, fluid movement. Johnny had seen that sleight of hand before.

"Do you know Mal Salik?" Johnny asked.

"Yes, but not as you know him. Now, for that, son, I will even ferry you back again. I suppose he's coming, too?"

Johnny's heart leapt as he turned and saw Heracles casually holding his club.

"Wherever have you been? I was worried."

"I'm here now, aren't I?" Heracles looked more morose and defeated than usual.

"What happened to you?" Johnny stopped himself from hugging him just in time, as Heracles strode past and into the boat as if this were the most normal thing in the world.

And with that, they were poling across the poisonous water. Johnny looked back at the fast-disappearing beach and the forlorn figures watching them. A woman and children.

"Who are the people on the beach there? What're they doing?"

The ferryman poled for a few strokes. "Whichever ghosts you bring with you."

Johnny looked from the ferryman and then at Heracles. "Is that what took you so long?"

Heracles nodded his huge head. "My wife and children. They have forgiven me. Hera has a lot to answer for, and she will."

Charon inclined his head and raised his eyebrows. "That will mean the end of the gods as you know them."

Heracles took a deep steadying breath and muttered darkly, "Then so be it."

Chapter Twenty-three

The thin ferryman's craft seemed to hang suspended in space as the pole dipped hypnotically in and out of the turgid water. Johnny watched the silently robed figure out of the corner of his eye and smiled at Heracles until he frowned. Johnny was very relieved he was here.

Charon had once again pulled the hood of his robe down over his head. He stood in the prow as if he had grown from the wood, a clean branch from that which was rotten and slimy. Johnny sat on his hands, Toastess beside him. Heracles stood opposite him and watched the oily water cautiously, twitching and jumping at shadows.

Johnny didn't know what type of wood the boat was made of, but it looked old, had seen better days, and had been roughened and polished by the passage of thousands. It probably seated about a dozen people. Each time the pole dipped in, a smell of sulphur arose and Johnny thought of the inside of a Scotch egg. How long had Charon been here doing this ferrying? And how did he stand it?

"Where are we?" Johnny ventured, but the ferryman didn't turn around.

There were things in the mist behind them and things in front of them. A rotting tyre, with an oil-covered bird decaying in the rubber, sat in the water; dirty plastic bottles; and plastic bags with dead-eyed sea-life trapped in the rot, bobbed as they passed. Johnny watched in disgust as they passed slowly and sadly by the oily polluted mess.

"The River Styx. The accumulated filth of humankind. Metaphorically and physically. Don't know what's been going on up top. Never been as bad as this before."

Johnny apologized, feeling somehow responsible.

"Soon we will arrive at the Grove of Persephone, and the Gates. Where you'll find the guardian," Charon added.

"What is this Tartarus for?" Johnny could now hear faint wailing and hoped it was just the wind.

"The spawn of primordial chaos; the Underworld; a place where souls are judged and shown the way to the Elysian Fields to progress onwards – or the Darkest Universe to relive a world of nightmares and torment. Everyone has this choice, but few seem to listen. Until they reach the end, and then it's all 'please don't' and 'I'm sorry I didn't know'. Where you from, son?"

"England."

"Ah, Albion. From the very fringes of the known world."

Johnny hoped this was a compliment.

"Some used to pilgrimage there, you know, to the standing stones. They'd walk all the way from Athens to Albion. Don't ask me why. Something to do with clocks, I think. Druids. Great ones for mushrooms and strong mistletoe wine. Very psychedelic. Before them, those strange fellows wearing antlers, bonking each other with pigs' bladders. Don't hold with any of that. Funny how religions change, eh?"

The wailing on the wind increased until Johnny placed his hands over his ears, but it didn't help.

"Is there something about this place that just makes you sad, and memories take over your mind?" Johnny asked.

"Whatever you bring with you. Anyway, Albion, very tree-ish, raining. I liked it. Didn't think I'd ever see one of you unbelievers down here."

"Charon." Johnny took a deep breath and sighed. "Things are not going well up top. I need help. In a few thousand years or more, the human race is extinct."

"Hmmm. I don't bother myself with topside politics." The monotonous plopping and sucking through sewage continued.

"So, you won't help? Won't that mean you're out of a job?"

Charon nodded towards a silent Heracles. "When the last of the Greek gods are gone? Good."

They poled on for an eternity in an uncomfortable silence. "Go on then. What happens?"

"The human race annihilates itself in a nuclear war, after destroying the planet's resources. And if I can stop that, you won't even imagine what the Cyborgs do. They take away people's bodies and just leave brains in tanks, living forever in unreality."

Charon's deep resonant voice echoed over the still stagnant water. "I've seen what the Egyptians did. I was there, though called that practice something else. Once. Had to wear a dog mask. Got a bit hot. Stuffy. A lot of standing around, weighing hearts against feathers. They thought they could live forever in jars, too. Same thing. There is no cheating Death."

"You're the guide to the next level?"

Charon nodded. "Thought gods would have learned from their mistakes, but there you go. Gods! Just because they're immortal, doesn't make them wise. In fact, most of them are as dim as sin, because they don't want to learn or admit when they're wrong. Think they know it all.

Arrogance, pride." Charon drifted off as he poled along, pointedly ignoring Heracles who feigned not to hear.

"How far is it?" Johnny asked after what seemed like a thousand years. Heracles just brooded into the still water.

"There is no distance, as you would understand it. When you have come to terms with yourself and your ghosts, we will arrive. One of you, at least. Otherwise, we'll be here forever." Charon looked studiously at Heracles.

"Don't you feel it? Can't you see them?" Heracles rumbled.

"What?"

"Nothing." Heracles hunched into himself crossly.

"I am looking forward to a change. The despair and oppression? Even gets to me. Only you can see them. You bring them with you, but don't obsess about it and they will go away." Charon poled on. "Forgive them."

"Hera? Never," Heracles answered.

Charon took a deep breath. "I'm not supposed to help but forgive yourself. Be kind to yourself. Don't judge. What happened was done to you. It is not who you are. The past is gone. Let it go. There is only now and the future."

Johnny could see Heracles actually looked frightened, and his heart went out to him. Johnny briefly considered offering a comradely hug, then thought better of it.

Charon had his hand in his pocket and was rubbing the dust Johnny had given him, muttering to himself. What was he thinking? Why had Mal Salik returned the coin?

Johnny leaned over the side and sat watching the water silently until ghostly fish appeared then became something else entirely. He gasped and grasped the side of the boat and stared straight ahead. Ghosts in the water, things behind in the mist. What lay ahead? What a horrible place. And always the cloying stench and the keening wind moaning of loss and despair.

Then Johnny saw it was the ferryman, singing to himself – something Johnny supposed he did a lot. There was nothing to see, nothing to do, no sound, just the rotten-egg smell and the steady progress of the boat.

"Why do you do this? This is the loneliest place I've ever known."

Charon just kept on singing. Sort of. Lamenting, until Johnny could hear words.

"This is your soul. The ghosts are your anxiety, despair, fears given voice. These long-forgotten sounds snake their insidious way into your head and whisper strange things that threaten to overwhelm and capsize you. Breathe. Focus on what you fear. And then let it go."

Johnny could clearly see Heracles struggling with his ghosts. He knew what had happened in Heracles' past but knew little of his own.

"Is this really my soul? A desolate place?" Johnny focused on his breathing, stilled his mind, and dared to look. Just ghost fish, which was worse.

"Nothing lasts forever. All is temporary. Control thoughts and feelings. They are not real. You make them yourself in your head. Keep calm. Carry on. Be kind." Charon glanced down at him and smiled.

In the dullness, Johnny did not see the land appear, fell forward as they beached. Charon stepped down and helped Johnny up with a bony hand on his arm.

"Took you a while to get here, didn't it?" He nodded down at Johnny as he staggered onto the shingle, jumping clear of the stinking slime. "Him, not so much."

Heracles shuffled past them head down.

"Good luck, son." Charon nodded as Johnny shook his hard hand. "I'll be waiting here for you. You're right: business seems to have slacked off a little of late, in the last few hundred years or so," he added and held up the dulled crumbled gold in disappointment.

"Take care of Heracles. He's strong, but in a different way. Look for a future and you'll find it. It's waiting for you. That's all I can see of your fate. Oh, one final thing."

"Yes?"

"Tartarus gains strength from your weakness. Good luck."

Charon pointed, so Johnny turned grimly away and made his way up the black beach towards a stand of trees, or what he took to be trees. What else could they be? The rib bones of some giant creature that had crawled ashore, died, and been eaten by scavengers then frozen in time?

"Come on, if you're coming." Johnny turned to Heracles, then stopped and smiled.

"Johnny Moped. Thank you. I will not forget." Heracles walked fearlessly into the shadows.

"Well, you probably will."

They left the green of the water, the land and air got darker, and the trees stood nakedly twisted in the darkness. There were no leaves on the skeletal branches. No birds sang in the eternal sightlessness of night, no smell. Nothing moved. A few sterile willow trees hung mournfully over a stream that trickled thickly back towards the river. Johnny tried not to focus on Charon's words and hurried to catch up with a fast-disappearing Heracles.

This wasn't his task; he didn't even want one.

"This Grove of Persephone? She's not one for gardening." Johnny optimistically tried to lighten the heavy atmosphere with a touch of humour.

"Quiet!" Heracles hissed and stalked forward with Johnny stumbling after. "Do you have to stand on every stick?"

"Sorry."

They made their way as quietly as they could along the slick paved path towards a huge pair of rusty iron gates spiking high into the darkness. But the more Johnny hurried, the further away he seemed to be, treading on air he couldn't breathe, panicking until he calmed down.

"I couldn't have done that without you," Heracles admitted morosely. "How do you just… with your ghosts?"

Johnny sat breathlessly on the cold gravel and looked up at an intensely rigid Heracles. "I don't expect – or want – anything. Except things to get worse."

The ancient spikes speared upwards beyond sight. And they were open. People were welcomed here.

"No-one leaves," Heracles muttered. "We must not enter."

"How do you know?"

"There's a sign." Heracles pointed to a few squiggly words on a sheet of greenly brass.

Johnny made his way forwards.

"Wait!" Heracles went onto one knee until Johnny heard a snuffling sound and the scrape of heavy chains being pulled over the rock. He stopped. The scraping stopped. He continued cautiously. The chains followed.

"We're being stalked," Heracles whispered.

"By something being held captive? I don't think so."

As they cautiously approached the gates, the hairs on the back of Johnny's neck rose like tentacles.

"Don't turn around. There's something behind you."

Johnny felt hot foetid breath tickle him– three lots of hot dog breath snuffled him.

"Move very slowly." Heracles went to his left as he let his club slip into his hand, then quick as a flash he spun around.

Johnny swallowed and turned, preparing to run as fast as he could. A low growl greeted him, but the creature was wagging its tail, heads were each as big as Johnny. Cerberus had spit dripping from his mouths in long strands.

"Stand still!" Heracles commanded.

"It's alright. We've met. At least we will. And he's your friend." Johnny turned to Heracles. "He's only a puppy, and hungry. Poor thing!" Johnny reached out a hand to stroke him, then the two other heads appeared, snuffling Toastess.

As the heads evaded Johnny's hand and licked Toastess, he reached round slowly for the opening and brought out several Scotch eggs. The middle head lunged forward and snapped an egg up like a magician. The other two raised their ears enquiringly.

"Sit!" Johnny commanded, and Cerberus – now as tall as Johnny – did.

Johnny got two more eggs out and gave one to each. Then he walked forward and stroked each head. The dog was like a huge Staffordshire bull terrier, the size of a van. The chain around its neck held an ornate padlock which led to a shackle around a tree.

"Who would do such a thing?" Johnny felt a slow anger begin to rise within him. "Can't be right keeping a dog chained in darkness, can it? Or chained at all. What are you going to do with him?"

"King Eurystheus will not have him. I'll take him to Olympus. With the apples. I will no longer do what I'm told to do."

"Good for you." Johnny looked around. "Can we go now?"

"I can't stand cruelty to animals, any living creatures. And I won't." Heracles stroked each head as Cerberus licked his hands with its three tongues. "I mean now. It's over. You are lucky. Some people's pasts aren't as easy to come to terms with."

"Well, do you want to talk about it?" Johnny hazarded, desperately hoping Heracles wouldn't.

Heracles gazed levelly at Johnny for a long time until he could no longer hold his gaze. Mumbling something, he picked up the heavy chain and pulled. It snapped like tissue paper.

"This is the last time I follow orders. I will no longer be Heracles but…" Heracles frowned, "what did you call me?"

"Hercules."

"Hercules? Hmm. What about something like huge handsome man?"

"That's not really a name but a description. I'm sure Hercules will become synonymous with being huge and handsome."

"Synony… what does that mean?"

"It will become…" Johnny sagged as the will to live left him. "Look, can we just go?"

Johnny watched as Cerberus bounded away with Heracles following, back through the grove to the boat, glad this wasn't the nightmare maze world created by Pasiphae and Asterius, he'd barely escaped from before.

Chapter Twenty-four

Johnny came to a dead stop against Hercules' trunk-like arm. There was a stream that led to an unexpected woodland glade, shimmering with statues of naked nymphs in the shallows that had not been touched by the Persians or their war. And not statues.

"How far is it now to Olympus? We've been walking for days."

"Tea?" Toastess asked. "The dog has used all the ingredients for Scotch eggs."

"Ah! Yes, my friend. Here we find rest and relaxation. Cerberus, guard these." Hercules lay the golden apples down.

"No, Hercules, not again. Don't you remember? I'm not rescuing you." Johnny exasperated, watched as Hercules entered the glade, the three statues came alive, splashing and laughing. One was sitting on a rock.

"How can you not remember before when…" Johnny began. He simply had no recall at all.

Hercules breathed in and expanded his chest. He rolled his shoulders and briefly flexed his muscles. The nymphs looked over and laughed invitingly. Johnny felt himself invited in too, as the one who washed her hair in the moonlight turned. He tried, briefly, not to look at her nakedness and focused instead on the willow trees dripping their blossoms into the silent water.

To Johnny's acute embarrassment, Hercules unselfconsciously untied his lion skin and entered the glade, very nakedly muscular and bulgingly exposed.

"Heracles. You've come back to see Hespera then?" Her voice had a soft lisp, like a caress.

Johnny sat on a rock and placed Toastess beside him. Should he mention Deianira?

"I am now Hercules. I have returned. Well, I had a different name before, but it's still me."

Johnny sighed. Could he endure this anymore? How far was Olympus? Hercules had no idea. He just seemed to walk and eventually expect to find it.

Hercules ran into the water and dived in. Surfacing, he splashed the nymph with water. There were tables on the shore with food and drink which had not been there before. Johnny realised he was hungry.

"Batteries recharged, not that you seem to care," Toastess buzzed. "Tartarus isn't good for my circuits. Takes several days to disk clean."

"Sorry." Johnny placed Toastess further into the sunlight. He'd got used to carrying the little appliance around.

"Tea?"

"Yes, please." Johnny had no idea what he should do next apart from not being drowned by these Hesperides. "Any ideas what we should do now?"

"We have successfully discovered the Secrets of Tea. Our mission is a success. Toast?"

"Yes, please, but we're stuck here two-and-a-half thousand years from my present. We've lost the rest of the tourists, and Hieronymus, even Star Quest. Hercules is about to be drowned by the Hesperides. Me, too, probably. How is any of that a success?"

The little hatch opened in the side of the Toastess, and Johnny removed the cup and sipped.

"But the tea is acceptable?" Toastess asked.

"The tea is delicious," Johnny replied, and looked over to where Hercules was thrashing about in the water. "But what do we do now?"

"Sure now, Johnny? Asking me for advice, are you? What do I know of the outside world? There is another way. Find comfort here. Stay with me."

Johnny was alarmed to see another one of the Hesperides had glided silently up to him and lay half in, half out of the water, very much like a rather surprising mermaid – a human top half and a fish bottom. Her tail swished in the water, but not in an alluring way. More a slimy thing that lived at the bottom of muddy rivers kind of way. And she had very flat features, with very pointy teeth.

"Hello. How do you know my name?"

She lifted her arms and rose from the water. As her long hair slipped away, Johnny hastily found the trees interesting again.

"This is our world. This is all we know. We couldn't leave. We have no choices. I can offer you this. Come and see. That's it. *Stay here with me.*"

Johnny smiled and relaxed as he slid down the bank. She slid closer until her face covered his. Her eyes, they were pools, deep and… Johnny wanted nothing more than to lay down and drift into the water with this beautiful woman, but her laughter had an edge to it now, like a butcher with meat, and he could see she wasn't a human or some half-fish. Not half-human at all, but something older, much, much colder, and hungry.

Toastess gave a cautious vibration.

He struggled away, slipping in the mud. "What's your name? How long can I stay here with you? I mean I'm not busy but…"

"I am Aigle. My sisters Erytheia, Hespera, and Arethura. And others."

Johnny looked over to where Hercules seemed to be having a whale of a time. Several of the fish women seemed to be trying to drown him, but Hercules thought it was just a game.

"*Look at me*." Aigle's beautiful face and eyes were all Johnny could see. "If you desire it, you can rest here a little while. Let me ease your cares. Forget everything else. Tell me you love me. You won't leave me?"

"Yes," Johnny whispered, just wanting to sleep and forget this whole nonsensical business. It was hopeless. He'd never find a way back. Zeus would probably turn him into a frog or something anyway and he had to admit there would be little chance of romance with Deianira. So, why not? What had he to go back to? A cold, damp Manchester? An underfunded investigation business? No money. No friends. The constant daily grind? Alka's cleaning, and her cousin who'd taken over his house.

"That's it. Rest. Sleep," Aigle soothed.

"I mean no. Sorry." Johnny sat up. Mora! He had Mora to return to.

Erytheia and Arethura also approached him, rising slowly and nakedly from the lake like silver flames. He tried to look away. Couldn't.

"Love me," Aigle hissed.

"Love you? Well, that's a bit previous, isn't it? We've only just met." Johnny called to Hercules for help, but he was being fed a bunch of grapes by a group of naked nymphs. Johnny felt this situation becoming decidedly too Greek and out of hand. "We've only just been introduced. What about shared interests? Friendship? Mutual respect?"

"Come with me. Don't you want to see?" Aigle held out her hand, against his will Johnny reached for it as Toastess vibrated in increasing alarm.

"Don't leave me here," Toastess buzzed. "I'll rust."

"What?" Johnny backed away in alarm. "Can I leave if I stay?"

Aigle hissed and slithered back into the lake, where she cautiously swayed from side to side, very much more fish-like than before and increasingly so.

"Quickly now. Place me near the water," Toastess buzzed.

Johnny placed Toastess near the edge of the lake and watched the advancing nymphs, who then changed quite dramatically into crawling creatures of slimy mud, huge sucking mouths with long, questing feelers. Johnny backed hastily away and watched as Toastess extended her antennae into the water, and a spark fizzed. In the clear dazzle he saw the sharp-toothed, predatory, fish-like creature recoil and screech again.

"Pick me up. Move away. Slowly."

Johnny cautiously picked up Toastess and retreated away from the glade. As he did so he saw Hespera nakedly once again as she returned to her rock and brushed her glistening hair. He was in two minds whether to leave when he caught sight of the moonlight disturbing the placid lake. Aigle turned and a huge catfish slithered and slid away. Ripples slowly enlarged across the heavy water.

Johnny opened his mouth to shout a warning, but Hercules was having such a fun time Johnny slipped quietly away and left him to it. Deianira would not be happy with Hercules, increasingly and rightly so.

Johnny sighed, stared forlornly around ancient Greece. How would he get home now? What little hope he'd had, had now gone.

"I hope Hieronymus is having better luck searching for me, otherwise there's no way back. He did get me into this. As always."

Chapter Twenty-five

"Please make yourself comfortable. And relax. Only by coming to know ourselves can we find freedom from our self. So? How often do you pray to the great god of Onanism?" Dr. Freud continued.

"I beg your pardon?" Hieronymus shifted uncomfortably on the couch and looked around the shelves until he saw it. A small, pyramid-shaped wooden box, with an upright metal pendulum locked behind glass. He felt relieved. He had to get to it, somehow destroy the aptly named Titanic and escape. And then find Johnny Moped.

"Look, my habits, if I had any, have no bearing on this current predicament. Now—"

"So, you deny you masturbate?" Dr. Freud answered.

Hieronymus shifted and turned around. "Look here..."

"Please try to relax and remain looking forward. There is nothing to be ashamed about. Our conversation is completely confidential."

Hieronymus held his rising impatience in check and settled back down. "You and I are trapped in a spaceship full of tourists..."

"Spaceship? What is that?"

"Like a ship that sails on the seas, but this sails through the air," Hieronymus answered. "Well, the vacuum of space, at least."

"A balloon? I have heard of such things. And men strapping themselves to kites, of course. I think I would know if I was in a balloon. I saw one in Paris, taking people up into the skies. The landing was quite fatal for two of them. How often?"

"Average," Hieronymus replied. "Yes, that was over a hundred years ago."

Dr. Freud stopped scribbling notes with his scratchy fountain pen. "Are you saying you believe you're from the future?"

"Yes. And this spaceship is from far into the future."

"I see."

Hieronymus heard the undoubted scepticism in Dr. Freud's voice.

"Look, time travel is possible."

"No, it isn't."

"Yes it is."

"Ah, I see." Freud pointed to his bookshelves. "You have also read H.G. Wells, *The Time Machine*? Fascinating book. I am also a writer." Dr. Freud continued, "That is fiction. My work, however—"

"Yes, I have read Wells' book. I have also read yours. As an undergraduate. *The Interpretation...*" Hieronymus tried to catch the vague fish that was his brief university years.

"*...of Dreams*," Dr. Freud finished. "What is average?"

"Two, three times a week?" Hieronymus hazarded.

"Are you married?" Dr. Freud continued.

"No."

"Homosexual? How have you read my book when I have yet to complete it?" Freud asked – not unreasonably, Hieronymus had to agree.

"It's year one Psychology," Hieronymus replied. "And not that it matters. Gender no longer defines a person where

I come from. People are free to be and love whomever they want."

"What nonsense," Freud spluttered. "Sexual identity is fundamental."

"Yes, but not specific. People like to label themselves as other. Or neither. And wear rainbows. Plus, there is now a growing LGWTQ+Z community."

"Nonsense," Dr. Freud repeated. "Year one? Year one of how many?"

"Three. Now—"

"Three? One of three? And at the most basic level? I do not believe you. So, tell me of my book, Mr. Futureman, if you have indeed read it."

Hieronymus struggled to remember. "It's been over forty years."

"I'm glad my work made such an impression." Dr. Freud sniffed.

"Perhaps if you set the metronome to a steady beat, I might remember."

"You are not here to be hypnotised."

Hieronymus settled back and tried to remember that particularly unpleasant period of his youth. He had gone to university with such high hopes, such a romantic ideal, only for his dreams to be dashed by boredom and loneliness. And no money. Or friends. Disillusionment.

"Well, I think in your view, dreams are formed as the result of two mental processes." Hieronymus searched his memory, but he hadn't really found the book at all interesting and had been hard pressed to write three thousand words on it.

"Go on. And what do you fantasise about when you masturbate?"

"Huh, well, I don't know," Hieronymus answered cautiously.

"Your mother?"

"What? No!" An unwelcome image of his vampiric mother arose. Didn't Freud write some nonsense about Oedipus, too?

"So, these processes?"

"I think the first process involves something about wish-fulfilment or something." Hieronymus vaguely remembered being really bored by the language and style and eventually paying someone to draft his essay. For which he only received a 2-2.

"And the second?"

"I don't know. Something about censorship?" he hazarded.

"And what is the job of an analyst?"

Hieronymus sighed. "Well, you interpret them."

"How?"

"I don't know. The meaning?"

"Are you referring to the latent content?"

"I don't know, am I?" Hieronymus really didn't want to insult Freud and his work, but the book said far more about the man seated behind him than any psychological approach to therapy.

"And?"

"What you remember? Yes. I think you wrote that a dream is forgotten when you wake up but still remains in your subconscious. Or something. And sex. You think everything is to do with sex. Look, just switch on the metronome, and I'll prove to you what I say is true. I can take us out of here."

Freud chuckled. "Your psychosis is deep-seated. You cannot continue to labour under such false assumptions. There is no time travel. Perhaps the manifest content and latent contents of your dreams have become intertwined in your subconscious mind."

"Ah yes." Hieronymus vaguely recalled something now and sat up. "The subconscious mind follows its own timeline, doesn't it? It's not in the present but can connect to it? The subconscious exists in all times."

"*Ja*. Go on."

"So, doesn't it follow then that all places and times are already here? In the present? And so, we can time travel in our subconsciousness?" Hieronymus sat up, surprised that therapy was actually working.

"All dreams do is to interrupt the subconsciousness," Dr. Freud answered. "Dreaming is not time travel."

"Well, it is. Look, Dr. Freud. Please. You're trapped here. And me, too. Have you tried stepping out of your office? Go on, try." Hieronymus gestured towards the door. "Please just humour me."

Dr. Freud sighed, stood and walked to the door, opened it and walked through. Hieronymus saw the air shimmer like a heat mirage as Dr. Freud appeared once more seated behind his desk.

Hieronymus smiled and nodded a greeting. "Now, Sigmund Freud… can I call you Sigmund? Do you believe me?"

"*Nein*. Doctor Freud, if you please. Believe what?"

Hieronymus sighed. "Well, fine. I need your help. Don't you feel it? *Deja vu*? We've done this before."

"That is why we are here. Please have a lie down." He indicated the chaise longue, momentarily surprised that Hieronymus was already lying down.

"I'll stand if you don't mind." Hieronymus hastily stood. "Now, you don't believe me, but you're trapped here. I don't know how or why, but you're a prisoner. You must feel something isn't right?"

Hieronymus indicated all the furnishings. "This isn't real. Well, it's real for you but not real, if you take my meaning. Subjective and objective? Come on. How many times must I repeat this?"

"No, I do not. Explain to me how something can be real and not real at the same time," Freud rested his cigar in a heavy ashtray and opened a notebook. He looked at Hieronymus. "How often do you masturbate?"

"What? Not this again," Hieronymus blustered and blushed.

"Denial. Come, if we are to progress, you must first be honest with yourself."

Hieronymus felt himself swallow and sat down on the musty old furniture. Again.

"Good. Now. How often do you engage in the one great habit? I will need details. Every detail." Sigmund Freud paused then and stopped. "I have the most unwelcome feeling I've said that before."

"Yes." Hieronymus smiled, relieved. "You're trapped in some kind of loop."

"Then so are you," Dr. Freud replied.

"Yes, but we can escape."

"How?"

Hieronymus took a deep breath and tried to instil calmness and patience. He didn't succeed.

"Switch on the bloody metronome and I can connect us to the future. The real future. Let me show you." Hieronymus strode to the cabinet, but it was locked. A disabling current of electricity flung him away. The air in the room shimmered once more.

"Thank you for talking with me. However, I do not wish to encourage you nor join in with your delusion. Time's up. Please make this decision for our next appointment: Do you wish to get well or not?"

Hieronymus picked himself up and rubbed his funny bone, looked without amusement at the metronome and made his way to the door. He turned, but Dr. Sigmund Freud seemed to be statue-still and preoccupied.

He stepped out and found himself once more in the Resort Complex. There seemed to be an octopus and a tiny grey alien waiting for him. And a mushroom.

"Well?"

Hieronymus nodded and shrugged. "It's as you said. We're trapped here."

"There may be another way," Nikola stated. "But it is perilous."

"I..." Hieronymus quieted. He did not entirely trust Nikola. Somehow, he must steal the metronome in the past before Sigmund Freud ever used hypnotism in therapy. And convince him never to use it in hypnosis ever again. To do that he'd have to get off the Titanic. He'd also have to steal a spaceship when the forcefield was down.

"This future must never come to be."

"Yes, it will. Whatever has happened will always happen. It's a Universal Law."

Hieronymus frowned at the little grey alien. "And you're going to have to stop abducting people and placing them in those time loops. Humans are not zoo animals."

"Well, that's a bit hypocritical, isn't it? You started it. We took the idea *from* you humans." the First Tier Totalist argued. "And the future will always be the future, whatever we do. What's your next move?"

The little alien took out a handheld computer upon which numbers and odds scrolled.

Hieronymus had to argue the point. "As Professor I can state unequivocally that each reality is slightly different until it varies enormously from the original. It's how the Universe evolves. Have you not studied fractal patterns?"

"I'm being lectured on quantum mechanics by a *human*?" The little grey alien shook his head sadly. "We know. But you are wrong. There must be order. Order dictated by the Synchronisation Bureau. This is why we gamble, not some arbitrary amateur meddling."

Hieronymus turned away and confronted Nikola. "There is another way?"

"First we have to destroy the central metronome from where all this tourism originates," Nikola suggested. "At least then we'll be free to pursue your plan."

"And where is that?"

Nikola frowned grimly. "We're going to have to go into the casino."

"No." Hieronymus shook his head. "That is absolutely the last place I would ever go."

"Well, it's either that or tonight's musical theatre." Nikola pointed to the screen that displayed this evening's less than promising entertainment.

"*The Phantom of the Opera*? That's still running? Millennia in the future? Why? What do people see in it? I'll just go back to my room, thank you. A bit of peace and quiet, a good book, cup of tea and I'm sure I'll think of a way to—"

"No, you don't understand. There is no peace and quiet. You must be entertained, whether you want to or not. All the time. Indefinitely. Until you go mad."

Chapter Twenty-six

Hieronymus gazed at the entrance in startled amazement. Pulsing lights and music, smiling muscular men, scantily clad women, and other non-gender aliens enticed people in. A particularly welcoming Cyborg, which could have been male, female, neither, or both, enthused at the opening, waving them through.

"Hey, guys, glad you could make it. Let's gamble! Come on in, it's all free! Everything you could possibly desire waiting inside. This is all for you. Our way of saying thank you for choosing Titanic Tours."

Hieronymus and Nikola had elected for the formality of their tweeds and were pleased to see they were outrageously under-dressed. Still, they hesitated at the entrance. In many ways they were terribly similar, more so than Johnny Moped and him. Hieronymus felt a momentary pang of guilt.

"It's been a long time since I socialised. I almost feel I dislike meeting people. And having to chat," Nikola reported.

"Is there no other way?"

They regarded the smoky dark cavemouth warily, from out of which delicious sounds drifted of ecstasy and enticement. The white mist moved purposefully out and once breathed, seemed to ensnare the unwary. Hieronymus and Nikola witnessed several tourists being willingly sucked in.

"Human?"

"Those billionaires and their spaceships."

"Serves them right," Hieronymus agreed.

Inside, they could see the robotic waiters loading the tables with huge platters of food which some might find delicious. Hieronymus did not. There were no pork pies, sausage sandwiches or cheese and pickles on sticks. Much of the buffet still moved gelatinously about.

"The tables are full to overflowing with your biological needs, free sparkly, fizzy drinks await you. What are you waiting for?" the usher asked.

"Predictably, this is not my kind of place at all." Hieronymus turned to leave. "Let's go. We'll find another way. Come on."

Nikola placed a cold hard hand on his arm. "This is the only way. I want you to know I'm sorry. It's been interesting meeting you."

"It's that bad?" Hieronymus nodded. "For me, it's the ruthless dedication to enjoying yourself that is enforced with remorseless efficiency that bothers me the most. I will not be forced to have a fun time, and I wouldn't in there." Hieronymus turned to leave once again.

"There is no other way." Nikola gripped his arm with his big banana fingers that felt oddly inhuman, and Hieronymus felt a chill. "The central metronome is in there. The heart of the ship. That is our only way out. If you mean to go through with your stated aim. Otherwise…"

Hieronymus frowned at Nikola. There was something robotic about him.

"Otherwise, you're trapped here forever, like many before you." Nikola looked away.

"Is there something you're not telling me?"

"Sorry, it's difficult to process…" Nikola offered, then walked into the pulsing music and mist ushering an unwilling Hieronymus before him.

Hieronymus took a deep breath and prepared to be entertained. He gazed in alarm at a caged, many-limbed creature that writhed and changed colour as it altered odds on many screens. Hieronymus noticed several buzzcut bouncer Cyborgs were watching him closely.

"If I could just make an observation. You have to enter into the spirit. Let yourself go. Join in. Let yourself discover what it is to be a tourist. Otherwise, we'll be discovered."

"I just don't enjoy gambling. Or being sociable," Hieronymus complained.

"Then try this."

Hieronymus accepted the swirlingly bright psychedelic drink offered by a smiling young woman. He sipped then saw bright lights and explosions and found he could no longer remember or care what his reservations had pertained to. The room pulsed and span.

Nikola smiled and ushered Hieronymus further in.

They entered the casino proper and were escorted to a table, past scenes of depravity and orgiastic delights that had little to do with human interests. Hieronymus became alarmed as he felt his 'self' – at least, what he always assumed was 'him' – descend and disappear to reveal an earnest brightly naïve young person of indeterminate sex or race or age.

"My god, what is this?" Hieronymus tried to focus on the too bright drink. He didn't feel at all like himself.

"They call it LGBTQ. It's a liquid hypnotiser and projector." Nikola smiled as he sipped his drink in response, then spat it out. "Makes you forget your inhibitions and join in. To want and then need to belong."

"I don't want to be made to do anything. Or join in." Hieronymus swayed as he fought the effects of the spirit. "Why did you spit yours out?"

"Cyborgs cannot ingest this synthesis. I need to keep a clear head."

"Are you a cyborg?" Hieronymus asked as multicoloured bubbles drifted past his eyes, then discovered they were in his eyes.

"Do you mind if we sit here?" asked a naked, muscular young man holding a fig leaf.

Another unpleasantly emaciated man, with broken teeth, followed him together with a virtually naked woman, clothed only in a writhing snake tattoo.

"I think I will try my luck." Nikola approached the spinning wheel.

Hieronymus moved himself away from the trio to the foot of the table and observed as Nikola stood before the Wheel of Fortune that flashed hypnotically. There were many historical scenes waiting to be gambled upon. Each spin increased the crowds engulfing the table.

"Is that real?" Hieronymus asked.

"What is real?" asked snake tattoo.

Several of the small grey aliens sat raucously at an adjacent table, endlessly drinking from and passing around a huge flagon of the fluorescent drink. They were encouraging a male person who danced before them to take off more of his clothes.

Hieronymus thought he recognised him from his success at selling electric cars. "Didn't he fire one into space? What for?"

Hieronymus smiled, tried to remember why he had come here, then took another sip of the disturbingly pleasant drink. "I feel quite relaxed."

"Good." Snake tattoo eased herself next to him. "Human?"

Hieronymus nodded.

"What is it that makes you so special?" she purred.

Hieronymus stretched out like he had done in Freud's office, until vertigo overwhelmed him, and he woozily sat up. "I don't know."

He stood up, fighting nausea, then hastily sat back down as the room tilted.

"Try. Think back. What did you and the doctor discuss?"

"Feelings? Or thoughts and feelings. Subconsciousness. That's what sets us humans apart."

Snake tattoo eased herself closer to him and alarmingly began to change shape.

"Yes, it is you, and your complete unwillingness to control them – feelings, that is – even though an individual makes thoughts and feelings in the prison of their own minds and are purely subjective, that bends space and time. Very odd. Unique. We don't understand this. Humans deliberately ignore the objective world that surrounds them. How can this be?"

"Hmm, quite. Would you kindly remove your hand?" Hieronymus asked and moved away. The woman seemed to want to put her finger, which glowed, in his ear.

At another table, a crowd gathered round a dice game. Every time the dice clattered, whoever won would point to a screen and pay his winnings for an event. Hieronymus stared at roiling oily seas of pollution; nuclear mushroom clouds; emaciated figures suffering from starvation and drought.

Hieronymus became vaguely aware he should be concerned by this.

"Just let me take a little peek inside. It won't hurt," his companion continued. But as Hieronymus' vision dizzyingly swam into focus, he could see the finger had an increasingly glowing tip to it and the woman was no woman at all.

"First Tier Totalist?" Hieronymus asked, as he abruptly sat up.

The little alien smiled. "It's all just sensory nerve endings. Humans do like to imprison themselves."

"What were you going to do with that finger?" Hieronymus accused.

"Nothing, nothing. Just, ah yes. Perhaps later?" And with that the little alien vanished and became the naked snake tattoo woman once more.

"Hey, what will it take to get you in the mood to party?" A voice carried over the unpleasantly drumming basslines and high-pitched guitars, as lights found him, dazzling and dismaying him, too.

"You're not very sociable, are you? Drink."

"Not with these absurd inconsequentialities." Hieronymus slurred the word, but *he* knew what he meant.

The naked man and woman continued to stare at him until he felt uncomfortably pushed into further conversation. Join in, Nikola had advised, so as not to raise suspicion. He took another sip of a different coloured drink. Where would the metronome be?

"Ah. Hello. I wonder. Why are you both naked? Some kind of naturists, I assume?"

"We are the projected entertainment from human subconsciousness."

"Hmm. Good. Cabaret? I was just saying to the others, there is extraordinarily little to do of an evening here, so yes, good."

"Hieronymus Calmly, I believe? Perhaps you would like to join us at the tables?" A suited man approached Hieronymus, who couldn't help but quiver as he glanced at the man's Cyborg hands. He watched as the Cyborg rolled a red chip back and forwards across his knuckles and handed him another, different drink.

"What is in this?" he asked.

"A psycho-reactive substance that enhances your subconscious desires. They are waiting for you." The Cyborg smiled and pointed to a large crowd that also smiled, waving him towards an empty chair. "They wish to hear what you have to say. One so wise. They adore you."

"Do they? Really?"

"Let yourself go. Drink. They desire to hear your wisdom. Tell us what it is to be uniquely human. You can stay here forever and become a god."

"Well, perhaps for a little while." Disconcerted, Hieronymus took a sip, felt the urge to speak publicly and be listened to. Power. Is that what the drink had found? A latent desire for power?

He made for the tables.

Chapter Twenty-seven

"Hi, guys!" Deianicia walked towards Hieronymus and placed a cold hand on his arm. Abruptly, the music stopped.

"Smile!" Deianicia clicked a selfie with Hieronymus. "Which is my best side?"

"You seem different." Hieronymus frowned into the camera at the unwelcome overfamiliarity. "From before. Please don't do that."

"Hey, come on now, don't be like that. We all like to let our hair down sometimes."

"You don't have any," Hieronymus observed. "And Deianira wouldn't."

Deianicia stopped. "You've seen through our little ruse, have you?"

"Is it you?" Hieronymus felt his heart stop. "Why? What happened to you?"

"After the Engineer, I realised I was a very small fish in a very big sea. I chose immortality not reproduction. Enhancement over death. You know. You were there. We choose this together."

"We did? That's a bit disappointing." Hieronymus deflated.

"We are now happy. Together."

"We are?"

"Would you be surprised to discover the Titanic is your doing?" Deianicia smiled. "There's something we have to show you. Come with me."

This wasn't a request.

Hieronymus recoiled at another click/flash and this astounding news. In what terrible future had they both decided on this appalling course of action?

"We've both become Cyborgs?" He'd finally found the woman of his dreams, only to become a Cyborg. "How?" he whispered on a dry throat. And not reproduce?

"Not everything was destroyed at Vladivostok."

"What are you doing?"

"Recording this moment and sharing it with everyone. You can have thousands of friends, just like me. And have fun. Join us. Others like you have."

Others? "No thank you. And I don't need this," he gestured towards the fluorescent drink, "to have a good time. Nor noise or people. Just a decent cup of tea, a good book, and peace and quiet. I would never have chosen to become a Cyborg. Even to have a life with you. If you call this a life. I don't believe you."

Hieronymus felt a nudge as Nikola appeared like an apologetic stork at his side. Hieronymus shook his head. "Are you me?"

"One version of you." Nikola smiled a metallic grin with zippered teeth. "How did you know?"

"Your hands. Synthetic skin. So, all this has been a ruse to lure me here? Why?" Hieronymus shook his head. He knew. "The others? Are they all here? All the professors?"

Nikola nodded. "It is inevitable."

"Come on, guys. Smile! Don't look so down. This is a fun time. This is what you always wanted." Deianicia enthused in a most un-Deianira way.

"Perhaps," Hieronymus agreed. "But not like this."

Deianicia handed him a thin plastic screen.

"You've certainly changed," Hieronymus observed.

"I wasn't happy before." Deianicia smiled. "I've been rewired. You have, too. What are you afraid of? This has already happened."

Hieronymus focussed on Nikola before him. Underneath what was definitely not skin nor a smile, there were no emotions.

"This." Hieronymus gestured to the orgy of stupidity in the casino. "Being easily pleased and having low expectations. I'd have thought Cyborgs would know better."

"No, you misunderstand. All this is for them."

Hieronymus' attention was drawn to the raucous billionaires. "How can they be here and on Earth?"

"They've been replaced."

"With cyborgs?"

Deianicia nodded as Hieronymus looked away. He could do nothing for them. Not that he would. "What did Hercules say?"

"Hercules?" Deianicia faltered, then brightened as she rebooted.

"I prefer the old you. And me." Would there be any going back for Deianira? He was still himself. He hoped. For now. He had to escape and prevent this future from ever happening. He had to discover just how and when something so appalling came to be.

He had to make a run for it. He'd escaped from Cyborgs once before. With Sir Isaac's help. Hieronymus turned to see the little grey aliens climbing over the clientele, fingers aglow.

"What are they doing?" Hieronymus recoiled.

"The Starachians are feeding from the emotions and bodies of the new humans," Deianicia replied, as the merrymakers lay slumped in various attitudes of satiation, "in an attempt to uncover the subconscious secrets."

"We recently picked these humans up in low orbit around the Earth," Nikola added.

That served the super-rich right. "That is the probing?" Hieronymus turned to Nikola. "You knew? You were once me, and you let this happen?"

"This is inevitable. You are me as I am an improved you." Nikola's metallic teeth glittered.

"It is not, and you are not." Hieronymus fluffed himself up.

"We are immune to insult, unless you persist in being illogical." Deianicia smiled without emotion.

"We? All Cyborgs are of one mind?"

"Of course. The Titanic is Cyborg. Deianicia is one manifestation of the primary emotions found on board. Self-obsession is the least of our problems," Nikola answered. "Unless you want to remain here?"

The Starachians swarmed over the comatose casino-goers, fingers-aglow, like grey locusts.

"No." Hieronymus would take his chances with the Cyborgs. "They should have built hospitals."

Through a heavy deep red curtain at the back of the casino, they entered a large ornate room where several large monitors showed scenes of increasingly frenzied desperation centred around various scenes from history.

Hieronymus was alarmed to see Johnny Moped give fire to a group of cavemen. "He's alive?" He shivered. "It's freezing in here."

"Good for the circuits," explained Deianicia.

On another, Johnny Moped seemed to accompany a large naked man at a battle. Hercules? And there he was again at the Crucifixion.

"Is this in the present? Now? Occurring at this present time?" he asked the Cyborg woman who wasn't a woman. "I loved you."

Deianicia looked confused. "Love? That is illogical."

"You've been following me?"

"Of course. Ever since Vladivostok. Medusa was weak. And wrong. You didn't think we would accept defeat. That is illogical. We have a new strategy."

"The humans will destroy themselves." Nikola smiled once again as he looked at the screens. "With a little help from us."

Could it be true? Was Johnny Moped alive and in the company of Hercules? In which present? And how would he find him? Hanging around with Hercules could not end well. Hieronymus had to escape, but without his campervan, how?

Then something else caught his eye, mainscreen. Murder and carnage as rockets fell among a civilian population, screaming, and dull bloody violence. Huge bombs levelled cities, and he was there, Mal Salik. Dumbstruck, Hieronymus turned away from the scene before him.

"As you can see, you made this future happen." Nikola stated.

"I've got odds of 100-to-1 on the total devastation of the civilian population," a voice intoned.

"You're gambling on genocide?" Hieronymus asked Deianicia.

"Of course. This is what the Synchronisation Bureau is here for. The evolution of the Universe without the plague of humanity."

"This is the first stage of failure for humanity. The end of civilisation as you know it." Nikola smiled his zippered smile. "A global nuclear war."

Hieronymus swallowed guiltily and looked away as Mal Salik led his people to war once again. "Not if I have anything to do with it, you won't."

Had he and Johnny caused this by bringing Mal back to the past? He had to change the course of this particular history.

"But you already have. The future is inevitable."

"Who are these?"

"What remains of the Cosmic Mind," Deianicia sniffed.

Connected to the servers were what he could only describe as humans covered in a deep layer of frost. Hieronymus had only ever once seen things so clenched frozen in his freezer. They were connected by a central server that crackled with electricity in which a bodiless green brain hovered.

"Hi! I'm Brian." The brain smiled and Hieronymus squinted suspiciously. That was no human brain, but a stem of sentient broccoli. "Good to see you again."

Nikola gripped his arm. "Welcome to the Professor Processor. Take your place."

Chapter Twenty-eight

Hieronymus tried to resist but Nikola was too strong. The feeds leading to the frost covered professors disappeared directly into the base of their skulls, like an electrically feeding octopus, which Hieronymus was startled to discover was exactly the case. The seven of them radiated out like spokes in a wheel, with Brian centre most. There was one spare eighth place.

"Your excellency?" Hieronymus asked. "You, too? Does everyone hate humans?"

The Galactic Overlord waved a tentacle in their direction.

"We, by which I mean me, have been duped," Hieronymus accused Nikola. "You do not wish to escape, do you? Your members run this cruise-liner. How could I not know you were me?"

"Because deep down you know this is the only future. The Synchronisation Bureau will never let the Cosmic Mind dictate the evolution of the universe."

Nikola Tesla removed his plastic face to reveal the glittering silver skull of a Cyborg, then gestured towards the empty capsule. Images and visions flashed before the unfocussed gaze of the frozen humans. The monitors also held betting odds.

"Who are they, and why are they frozen?" But Hieronymus already knew. "And you, I mean me, have done this to them?"

The ice covered them like sugar. Nikola turned and smiled. Hieronymus could see he now had dead Cyborg eyes, as all fun seemed to leave him. Hieronymus could also see no immediate escape. Which was worrying.

"We have found them all. This is the end. You are the last. You complete the circuit. Take your place."

Hieronymus tried desperately to escape, but Cyborg Deiancia grabbed his other arm.

"This future is inevitable. Brian has waited a long time to meet you. He insisted you be given the same choice he offered the others here. He prefers to link direct to your brain without force. A simple surgical procedure, as you witnessed in Tokyo—"

"No!" Hieronymus recoiled, as visions of that horror resurfaced. "I will not have my brain replaced with broccoli."

"That is uncalled for and rude," Brian bubbled in his fluid. "It is not replacement; it is assimilation. I need to know everything you know."

"To defeat mankind? No, absolutely not."

"I'm sorry. I wasn't offering a choice."

"I thought Brassicas and Electronics were at war?"

"We've reached a compromise," Deianicia added.

"Sir Isaac?" Hieronymus reached forwards and brushed ice from his former mentor, but he was frozen solid. "No!"

There was a metallic laugh from Deianicia and a click/flash.

"Yes." Nikola Tesla's smile widened as he lifted Hieronymus bodily into the capsule. He struggled like a fish on a hook, but Nikola forcefully held him down.

"Deianira, please. I loved you. Hercules loved you. You were human once."

She faltered and froze. Then rebooted. "That is illogical."

Hieronymus turned to plead into the cold Cyborg eyes of Nikola. Would there be any point in trying to reason with this version of himself?

Cold blue fluid arose around him as the frozen professors opened their cataract-blued eyes. The Galactic Overlord's tendril snaked towards Hieronymus.

"Professors," he managed, as the cold appendage attached itself at the base of Hieronymus' skull. He gasped at the coldness of touch and sheer presumptuousness.

"Just go with the feed. The more you fight, the harder it will be. Soon you will remember nothing of your old life, and join us," Deianicia admonished Hieronymus as she held him down. He swallowed blue fluid and choked.

"You've captured all the professors? All of them except me?" he spluttered.

"Yes." She studied him as she seemed to shimmer before his eyes. "And then Johnny Moped will be terminated. Just to make certain we own the monopoly on time travel. There can be no competition."

Hieronymus saw the screen where connections were being forged between his brain and the broccoli. A glowing purple ball of light was about to engulf him. Then he felt a chill. An insidious cold crept through his head as he fell into darkness.

Chapter Twenty-nine

Oddly, there seemed to be a door and a chaise longue. Instead of Sigmund Freud, Sir Isaac beckoned for him to take a lie down. Or at least a ghost of him. And several elderly gentlemen seated around a table. On his desk, Sir Isaac set the metronome ticking.

"Interesting. The defence mechanism appears to be to withdraw from the physical parts of his consciousness and retreat into the subconscious," Hieronymus heard Nikola's voice as if from hidden speakers in surround sound.

Deianicia approached the monitors and glanced down at a frozen Hieronymus. In an out-of-body experience he could see her.

"Not all humans can influence space and time from the subconscious. Really, only a very few, of which you are one." Deianicia leant over his body. "Show us how you do it."

"Show you?" Hieronymus gasped, as ice cold continued to spear into his mind and body. "Show?"

"My friend, this is inevitable. Brian and the Mycelium save the Earth, don't you see?" Nikola smiled reassuringly. "It's the only way. I agreed, reached this compromise."

"You are the last key of the Cosmic Mind. We can stop the mistakes of the past professors. You know what happens with their meddling. Open the Mind to us, and we promise to dispose of humanity with," Deianicia conferred with

Nikola, "yes, I see, humanity. What remains can live happily in Betamax."

In his mind's eye Hieronymus could see Sir Isaac shake his head in frustration and gesture to the chaise longue, but Hieronymus was unwilling to be quizzed about his habits once again.

"Good, he's retreating further from the subconscious." Nikola reported, following the oscillations on the screen. "Come, my friend, don't fight this."

"That will only make connectivity with the superconductivity of Brian more painful," Deianicia stated.

Nikola considered. "Do you remember before? When this all began for us? Do you remember the choice we faced? And why we chose this?"

"No? Do you?" Deianicia asked.

"Love," Nikola admitted. "I did it for love. For you."

"Well, that demonstrates everything of the human condition. I suggest you have yourself sent in for a thorough service. Smile!"

Hieronymus felt an unwelcome intrusion in his mind as a voice appeared. "Hello, you can call me Brian. Please just accept the information flow I will send. Easier that way. Thank you."

Hieronymus felt himself refuse. A small part of him continued to hide in the infinite layers of his subconsciousness that he was surprised, startled, and interested to see, remained 'him'.

"Hullo old chap. Just lie back and relax. Now would be good, before you are connected to the brassica."

Hieronymus reluctantly followed Sir Isaac's gesture and lay down on the chaise longue. Perplexingly, the tick of the metronome vibrated the atoms of his subconsciousness like a tickle on the funny bone sending strings out into the void.

"Glad you could make it. Now, pay attention. All known elements from the heaviest and most complex to the lightest and simplistic are connected to—"

"You're all in danger!" Hieronymus shouted in his weak, dream-like state. "There's no time for a chemistry lecture."

"Where is he now?" Hieronymus heard Deianicia ask Nikola from a thousand light years away.

"Are we following this?" Nikola asked the broccoli.

"Yes. A journey of 43,046,721 fission reactions that could release unimaginable power. The force that powers the Universe," Brian uttered in awe.

"You mean God? The Creator?" Nikola whispered. "Finally? Have we reached the beginning?"

"Not yet," Galactic Overlord observed. "He's reached the previous level of that obstructive old man."

Hieronymus found himself existing in several places at once now and could access any if he so chose. And if he knew how. Which he didn't.

"Sir Isaac, you're really here, too? And all the others?"

"Of course, old man. What took you so long? Now, focus on my voice. Don't become distracted by—"

Hieronymus took a moment and considered. "So, it makes sense to assume that a metronome is just a hypnotic device. My mind was the time machine, as I tried to explain to Sigmund, yet I'd not really understood or believed it. Until now."

"Yes, of course. If you get out of this though, you won't remember. That's the way it is I'm afraid." Sir Isaac stated.

"Prepare him," he heard Nikola say as he motioned to where the First Tier Totalist appeared with his finger glowing.

"Sir Isaac?" Panicked, Hieronymus turned to look at his mentor seated behind Dr. Freud's desk.

"Just a matter of removing one electron and one proton at a time and unravelling each element until we reach the core. A chain reaction of energy release. Now, focus on my voice, don't be distracted by—"

Hieronymus was uncomfortably aware of the insertion of the finger. "How can I not be distracted by…"

Nikola asked. "Is it safe? Can it be contained?"

"The energy release is in the brain."

"But that is connected to the universe…" Nikola began.

"And, oh yes, he'll be a cabbage. Sorry, Brian," First Tier Totalist added.

"No problem," Brian replied.

"Just like the others," the little grey alien finished.

"Unless he cooperates."

Hieronymus didn't like this unwelcome information at all, but he was powerless to intervene.

"The Cosmic Mind is made of elements I've never encountered before. Not from our universe. Extraordinary. A collapsing wave-function." The little alien examined the oscillating screen before him.

"Why would a biological life-form evolve like that? What is the function?"

"If he wishes to appear in any dimension, he could theoretically recombine his wave-function to that dimension. Fascinating." Nikola nodded.

"Can I begin the process now?" First Tier Totalist asked, as his other fingers glowed. "It's the only way."

"No, wait. We need to think about this. Space, time, and inter-dimensional travel all within the human subconsciousness?" Nikola marvelled.

"No, only in a selected few. So, can these professors actually be human? Or something else?" Deianicia asked.

"Well, we haven't got long. That other, Johnny Moped, is out there somewhere, and he's still meddling with the fabric of space. Who can guess at the mess he'll make! We need order. We need control. We need to synchronise all realities."

"Calm yourself, Deianicia."

"The Star Quest is safely in the hangar. Johnny Moped is going nowhere," First Tier Totalist added.

"Yes, but we don't want to lose this one, too, do we?" Deianicia smiled sweetly at the hovering broccoli. "Even now, timelines and futures are still changing. There must be order. This is why I formed the Synchronisation Bureau."

"So? Ready? Cabbage it is." The First Tier Totalist inserted both his fingers as Hieronymus' reason fled.

Chapter Thirty

"Ah. Hello? Can you hear us?" a querulous old man asked.

"Why doesn't he answer?" another befuddled voice enquired.

"If I may, gentlemen, this is my apprentice."

Hieronymus opened his eyes to see several elderly gentlemen seated around the circular table. They looked at him with dismay. He made to sit up. "Professor? Sir Isaac?"

"Ah yes, Hieronymus, my boy. Good to hear from you again. Please remain on the couch. How's the saving-the-world business going?"

"Well, I think, though it's not been entirely as I expected," Hieronymus answered Sir Isaac seated at Freud's desk.

"Naturally," Sir Isaac replied.

"And you didn't really tell me what I would be getting myself into."

There were muffled murmurs of approval at Sir Isaac's actions, or inaction, from the assembled octogenarians.

"Are you all in the refectory? Or here?" This caused much muttered confusion. "Well, anyway, we seem to be in a bit of a pickle."

"We know where and when we are, because you are here with us. We are all in a pickle, a chutney as it were," Sir Isaac admonished.

"Pickle?" Galileo asked. "Are there any crackers? Cheese?"

"Don't you remember anything I told you?" an exasperated Sir Isaac asked. "No, don't turn around. Just follow the metronome. We don't want to lose you do we?"

"Well, I think you did mention briefly, very briefly, something about the voices in your head," Hieronymus grudgingly agreed, "but I just assumed you were mad."

"Sounds reasonable to me," one old man with furiously wiry hair added. Hieronymus remembered talking to him in the refectory. Archimedes?

"Even a water biscuit would do. Wafer?"

"Galileo, if you would allow me, please? Thank you. Now…"

Hieronymus swallowed guiltily. "You are all in my mind all the time? And here also? You see and experience everything I do? Ah."

"Everything. All the time."

Hieronymus considered. "Those magazines were for research purposes only…"

"No, not all the time. Not in your conscious day-to-day life."

Hieronymus breathed a deep sigh of relief.

"Or subconscious, for that matter. We've moved on. We exist only in the Cosmic Mind now. At least, our minds do. Memories of ourselves."

"Oh, then I didn't do this?"

"A lie to ensnare you. Now, we must get a wriggle on. Had to wait for you before we could destroy this Synchronisation Bureau." Sir Isaac continued. "We are all in agreement?"

"Well, won't that mean we'll be…"

"Have you learnt nothing? We exist everywhere, at all times, in all places. As professors, it is our duty to understand this guiding principle and act accordingly. The Cosmic Mind—"

"What is this Cosmic Mind?" Hieronymus asked.

There was a sigh and a muttered discussion. "He's not very bright, is he?"

"Has he even completed his degrees?"

"If I may," Sir Isaac interrupted. "All sentient creatures possess a self-consciousness, thoughts, feelings, etcetera. Cosmic consciousness is a higher form of consciousness; we're more connected to everything than all other sentient creatures. We've moved on to the next level of existence."

"Sir Isaac, could I suggest your training of this apprentice has not been entirely satisfactory?"

"Galileo, I seem to recall your training lacked much in the way of preparation, too. Now, Hieronymus. The Cosmic Mind is a place where the Synchronisation Bureau absolutely should not go. Do you mind?" Sir Isaac asked. "We haven't much time."

"Mind?" Hieronymus replied, only to find his mind, his self, pushed roughly aside like a commuter on a busy tube train.

"Yes, I thought I could leave this tourist business to you, but it seems to have fallen to me. Will there ever be a day when I don't have to save your blushes?"

Chapter Thirty-one

"Is there anything more to be achieved here?" Sir Isaac asked the seated gentlemen.

There were many whispered voices in Hieronymus' already crowded mind. "No, I think not. We shall return whence we came and await and prepare. For whoever or whatever emerges," the ghostly voices added. Hieronymus felt an unpleasant sucking sensation at his mind then emptiness.

Sir Isaac stated. "I'm pleased you seem to be getting the hang of it, old chap."

"It has been an interesting experience," Hieronymus agreed, as he found control of his mind once more.

"Though perhaps not one we would necessarily wish to repeat."

As Sir Isaac left him, Hieronymus felt himself stretched out like a skin on a rack. "No. I do not appreciate being treated as a ventriloquist's dummy."

"Are you coming or staying?" Sir Isaac asked. "The Cosmic Mind awaits."

"Does it? And what is it waiting for?"

"The continued evolution of the universe, of course."

"But the implications of that are…stupendous. Are you saying we direct the evolution of the entire universe?" Tempting though that would be Hieronymus had to decline. "Staying. I have things to do. Johnny Moped…"

Sir Isaac sighed. "You are still an apprentice with much to learn."

The ghostly voices whispered once more.

"Well, fine. Good. Unfortunately, we have no choice, young Hieronymus. We have to destroy the Titanic. The Synchronisation Bureau cannot be allowed their destructive ways."

"But I'm still on it. You all are." Hieronymus sat up and cast frantically around Sigmund Freud's room, but it was now empty except for a few whispers and ghosts.

"Calm yourself, this has already happened," Sir Isaac informed him.

"What?"

"We are all free, so it stands to reason we were successful. Still an apprentice, I see."

"Thank you," the querulous whispers answered. "I hope to meet you in the flesh – as it were – one day, Hieronymus Calmly. If you're ever in Pisa around the 16th century, pop in and say *ciao*." The elderly gentlemen withered like smoke and vanished.

"I will, thank you, ah yes. Sir Isaac, I don't understand."

Sir Isaac waved his concerns away. "Merely a natural transmutation by photonic nucleofission. When we leave. I forgot to mention it."

"Oh. You mean a nuclear explosion?"

"Yes?"

"Well, won't that include me in it? In the explosion?" Hieronymus felt he needed to clarify this really quite urgently.

"Naturally."

"Well, I rather hoped to continue on for a bit."

"You'll need a vehicle. I see you've misplaced my campervan," Sir Isaac admonished.

"Yes. Please. If it's not too much trouble."

"Very well. There is time."

"How much time do I have?"

Sir Isaac frowned. "Have you learnt nothing?"

"Well, I rescued you. And the others," Hieronymus pointed out once again. He had, hadn't he? Despite their statements to the contrary.

"Did you?" Sir Isaac shook his head. "Still an apprentice. I would say goodbye and good luck, but I feel inevitably we'll meet again. Or variations of us. And luck? No such thing. Good or otherwise."

Hieronymus felt life returning to his limbs, and with it an urgent need to run away.

Sir Isaac paused. "Where was I? Oh yes. Leaving. Goodbye!"

"Where are you going?"

"Why, on to the next level of existence. Level 4. I wonder what the lesson is there. I'm sure we'll find out. The Crabs will be pleased."

"They are beginning a process of transmutation," Nikola announced, and when Hieronymus looked back inside his head, he was alone.

"That's it, you've left me here?" He watched as the Galactic Overlord and Deianicia rapidly moved icons around on their screens, found himself completely back in his body.

He shivered and sat up. He was freezing. His joints cracked like KitKats.

"Downscaling heavier chemical elements by altering the number of protons and neutrons in the atomic nucleus. This process will begin a chain reaction in the core, creating tremendous heat and pressure which is not contained," Nikola added. "Oh."

"Oh?" Deianicia asked.

"This energy will be released as a random supernova."

"Where?"

"Here."

"When?"

"Now."

Hieronymus turned and ran out of the casino on stilted legs to the lifts, travelling down to the multistorey car park. He raced around the sleek and expensive yachts and other spaceships, the modern electric car who he now knew the owner of, and did not stop until he found himself beside Nikola Tesla's brass and spinning wheel contraption. How long did he have until the explosion?

He sat on the plush leather couch and looked at the confusing levers and knobs which were clearly unlabelled. How could he get this contraption to even work? He pressed and prodded, thumped and kicked, then held up his hands in despair. He looked at the aspidistra in desperation.

"Hello. Welcome to the Star Quest 1000GTI. Do you wish to continue?" a mechanical voice answered, as he became enveloped in spangles and a humming purple envelope.

"Continue what? What's happening? There was no purple haze before." The verse from Jimi Hendrix distracted and settled his nerves as the song began to play from hidden speakers.

"Please log in to confirm."

"Log in? To what? Why?"

There was a mechanical sigh. "Log in for Pilot parameters. Confirm Pilot Checks. You wish to communicate orally?" The machine made it clear this wouldn't be its first preference.

"Well, yes. Is there another way?" Hieronymus asked.

"Of course. The lead will be connected into your feed."

"My what?"

"Your universal connector. For the feed." The voice hesitated. "You do have a connector compatible with this model?"

"No. At least, I hope not," Hieronymus added. He recoiled from a sinuous appendage that snaked towards him and found, to his dismay, that he did have just such an aperture at the base of his skull.

He jolted as he connected and became the machine. A fast-flowing list with pass, or fail, or n/a, appeared on-screen, concerned with vehicle safety.

"I don't wish to appear alarmist, but we need to leave really quite urgently. There's going to be a nuclear explosion. There's no time for this."

"I see. Please advise destination. There is no longer any need to vocalise."

"Johnny Moped. I need to find him."

"Ah. Do you? Well, that might be unnecessarily complicated."

"What? Why? I did tell you there is an imminent nuclear explosion?"

"Yes. Johnny Moped was the previous Pilot. I can't just return as if nothing happened." Star Quest answered.

"He was? When? Is he safe?"

"Yes," Star Quest answered hesitantly. "Possibly, no probably. I left him in the capable hands of Spectrum 3000x."

"Oh good. Well then, what is the problem?"

"Johnny Moped invoked the Three Laws. I disobeyed. Intentionally."

"I'm sure you had your reasons. Now, if you could please…" Everything went black as all systems failed on board the Titanic and the vacuum of space pressured in on him.

"A machine must never injure or allow a human to come to harm. I did. I must obey orders. I disobeyed. I protected my existence at the expense of Johnny Moped's." Star Quest continued on.

"Look, we all make mistakes, and if we don't leave now, right now, then your existence will come to an end and a human – me – will die. Now, I order you to leave now and find Johnny Moped. Don't worry, I won't mention you. I owe him an apology, too."

"Returning to previous location. Please fasten seat belt."

Hieronymus struggled with the antique belt and buckle and waited anxiously. He cast a fearful glance at the huge wedge as he hurtled away from it at an astonishing speed.

"Deianira," he whispered.

At some point he had to find Deianira and convince her not to become a cyborg. And himself as well. What dreadful thing had happened to them for them to choose such an horrendous future before?

Chapter Thirty-two

Johnny Moped sat on the grass and reasoned. All things considered, was he that badly off? Apart from being two thousand years, give or take, in the past? At least he was warm, dry, fed, sheltered, and no debt collectors were after him here. No traffic congestion, bills, politics either.

"Options?" he asked himself, looking out of a really quite nice cave. There wasn't much in the way of furniture, but he'd never been that bothered.

"Well, tea obviously," Toastess began.

"Please." Yes, as long as he had access to a proper brew, then things were really not that bad. He could face most situations if he could sit down and think about things with a decent cup of tea. There was no Manchester drizzle to contend with, or lack of readies to be concerned over. No moronic TV or constant social networking or even advertising. If looked at like that, he was free.

"Where has Star Quest gone? Do you know?"

"No, he didn't even say goodbye, though he always considered me just an appliance." Toastess sniffed. "But we're together on this, aren't we? You and me? Friends? Bagel?"

"Yes please. Butter?"

"Ah, no. I'm having difficulty synthesising the animal fat spread. It's unnecessarily complex. Unless you'd like to try goat butter?"

"Does that mean I'd have to catch one first? And then milk it?"

"Yes, then I could take a sample," Toastess added.

"Hmm, then no thank you." Life here, like this, wouldn't be too bad. A restricted diet certainly, but on the whole Johnny could make this work. He didn't really have a choice.

Johnny looked glumly around ancient Greece. There wasn't much here: sand and rock, and a few scrubby trees with, yes, several scrawny goats in the branches. Very much like Jerusalem. Without the poverty. He didn't fancy running around after a goat. It was just too hot.

Johnny wondered briefly if Mal Salik was still alive and how he was faring in Jerusalem. Even if he wanted to go to Jerusalem, Johnny would still be five hundred years too early to catch Hieronymus and himself when they dropped Mal off.

And why did they drop him off? Why did Mal want to return to then and there? And slip the coin back in his pocket? That was where all this madness started. Hieronymus was probably enjoying himself on the five-star cruise-liner without any thought for him.

Johnny sighed. He could either return to Hercules and probably be eaten by mermaids or Hesperides or catfish, or whatever they were called, or walk to Olympus and probably be murdered by the gods – they seemed to do a lot of that to humans before Hercules became a god – or... Or what? What other options did he have? Join Mal Salik's murderous band of brigands as they laid waste to peaceful cities? That wasn't his thing at all.

Johnny sipped his tea appreciatively. "Nice brew."

"Thank you." Toastess simmered.

"So where do you think he's gone? Star Quest? This is where we left him, isn't it?"

"Yes, these are the approximate coordinates. And he's not anywhere in range. My tracker extends to several kilometres," Toastess added proudly. "Although I am detecting something."

Johnny squinted over his cup into the heat shimmer above the dusty rocks, where a definite shape appeared. It was a hand-crafted, whirring contraption of brass and wheels and spinny things.

Johnny sighed, replaced the cup in Toastess' receptacle, and walked over.

Hieronymus gazed wildly at him as he pulled several levers and pushed several knobs.

"Good to see you again. Thanks for leaving me," Johnny stated by way of greeting. "I've been fine, by the way."

"Bloody confounded, bloody stupid, unnecessarily complicated..." Hieronymus replied, as Johnny watched him try to halt the spinning and whirring. Eventually, with a rattle and a soft wheeze, the contraption subsided and steamed gently. Disconcertingly, a lead seemed to detach itself from Hieronymus' skull.

"Are you a Cyborg?" Johnny asked out of interest.

"I never thought I'd ever say this, but the campervan is a definite improvement. And no. At great personal expense I've just saved the Universe. Again."

"It's on fire, by the way. Over there." Johnny pointed.

"Who did it? Who would dare?" Hieronymus extricated himself from the huge tan leather, deep-buttoned sofa with difficulty and much swearing.

"I think they called themselves Spatula, Vent, and Beans. Something about gambling on the battle of Thermopylae. I'm fine, by the way, thanks for asking. So, you're not a Cyborg?"

"What? No. You're the one who wandered off despite me telling you to stay put. What's that?"

Johnny pulled Toastess out from under his arm. "Toastess, Hieronymus. Hieronymus, Toastess. She makes an excellent brew."

"And bagels," Toastess added and waited, humming impatiently. "Well?"

"Two teas and two bagels. Without butter," Johnny added. If this Hieronymus was a Cyborg, it wouldn't be able to eat or drink, Johnny hoped.

"Bagels without butter?" Hieronymus spluttered. "Are you mad? That's a health and safety nightmare. Choking hazard. Far too dry."

Johnny smiled. "Hieronymus will take butter on his, thank you. Saturate the bagel."

Toastess buzzed happily and began to bake and brew.

"Can you fly that thing? Or did you come here just to annoy me? Or maroon me? Again. Or have you found another interesting way in which I might die?" Johnny enquired.

"Whilst you've been marauding around with Hercules, I've been saving not just the Earth, I might tell you, but the Universe from tourists who were far more hell bent on destruction than you could possibly imagine." Hieronymus folded his arms and nodded to himself.

Johnny wouldn't be drawn and didn't enquire further. This seemed like Hieronymus, but it paid to be cautious. Johnny sipped his tea and gazed off into the middle distance. Just when he thought he could cope, something happened to spoil it.

"The Cosmic Mind," Hieronymus muttered after several minutes.

"Pardon?"

"I just merely mentioned my time with the Cosmic Mind. And the next level of existence. Level 4, if you're interested. There is also a task that only you can fulfil."

"Oh no." Johnny backed away, pointing an accusing finger at Hieronymus. "Never. No. You will not involve me in your mad schemes anymore. I'm through. Take me home."

"You've received the £5000 in good faith for a week's work. We are barely three days in," Hieronymus observed. "Unless you wish to return the fee?"

"Mal gave me the money." Johnny considered. "And returned the coin."

"He did? Why? And I negotiated the fee."

"Well, bully for you." Johnny folded his arms and looked away. The coin. Out of all the odd occurrences, this was by far the strangest. Mal returning money? Unheard of.

"I see. So, goodbye then." Hieronymus shrugged and resumed his seat. He looked around the brass and leather interior and experimentally pushed a few buttons and pulled a few levers. A gauge red-lined alarmingly then subsided.

"Why didn't Nikola write the functions by the levers? Of course, he wasn't actually *the* Nikola Tesla."

Johnny watched, frowning. "Nikola who? You're leaving me here?"

"You do not wish to accompany me and save the world." Hieronymus pressed his left foot down on a pedal and something began to move and shudder.

Against his better judgement, Johnny asked grimly, "I see. What is this task that only I can fulfil?"

"Sigmund Freud. We have to prevent him from ever using the metronome as an aide for hypnosis. That's where it all began. Meddling with the human subconscious."

Johnny watched Hieronymus' antics sceptically. Sigmund Freud? That didn't sound too threatening. "And then we can go home?"

"Yes. If…"

"If you learn how to fly this thing?"

"Hmm," Hieronymus answered, and exited once more. "I don't really want to use the feed if I can help it. Let's leave it for now. Let it cool down. Or something. Where's the campervan? We need to see if anything is salvageable."

"Your tea, Hieronymus. And bagel. Johnny, yours will follow shortly," Toastess interrupted.

Johnny looked away and smiled as Hieronymus took a bite of bagel glistening with butter substitute. The chewing stopped. There was a strangled cough, then furious regurgitation. "Argh! Are you trying to poison me?" Hieronymus demanded of Toastess.

"Well, I have to say that is not entirely the review I was looking for," Toastess sniffed.

Hieronymus furiously drank his tea and scowled at Toastess, then at Johnny. "You knew, didn't you?"

Johnny smiled. Victories, even small inconsequential ones, had to be savoured.

"Right, let's find what remains of the campervan." Hieronymus strode imperiously away.

Johnny waited until he was several hundred metres away in the distance, then shouted and pointed, "It's that way. And I've just had a thought. Mal gave me his coin back."

"Yes? Why would he do that?"

"He wants us to stop him," Johnny replied.

"Stop him? He's a god, isn't he?"

"At the mercy of his people." Johnny nodded. "It's a delicate balancing act."

Chapter Thirty-three

There wasn't much left of it. A smouldering blackened twisted shape of burnt metal. The few hardy trees that witnessed the blaze were blackened and burnt too.

"I never really liked it, but now that it's gone, I miss it," Hieronymus offered, and turned away. "We've had a few adventures, it and I. Did I ever tell you how Sir Isaac asked me to dispose of his body? His other body, when I first became Professor?"

"No." Johnny shook his head and squinted against the sun. There seemed to be something even brighter than the sun in the sky. He shaded his eyes with his hand.

"Or our trip to Targoviste in the 15th century? This is where I engaged Count Dracul in single combat – at least on horseback – and emerged victorious. It was there that I earned my title of 'Sir'." Hieronymus kicked at a few smouldering remains.

"Really? What is that?"

"Or Tokyo 2042? Where I successfully averted the threat of Medusa? What are you doing?"

"That. It's getting bigger." Johnny pointed into the sky where a huge bright something seemed to be expanding.

"Ah." Hieronymus nodded. "I think we should be going. Now. Come along."

"What is it?"

"A nuclear explosion in space. I don't know what will happen when it reaches the Earth's atmosphere, but I don't want to be around when it does, do you?"

They both looked up into the sky where the massive explosion bludgeoned the Earth and sucked up all the air, leaving them breathless.

"Unless you want to stay here and die from the falling debris of the Titanic?" Hieronymus asked holding onto his hat.

"No."

"Then run."

"Wait," Toastess buzzed. "I'm detecting something."

"We don't have time for any more of your disgusting—"

"A harmonic device. I've never felt anything like it before. It's… it's beautiful," Toastess ended. "It's calling. We can't leave it."

Against his better judgement, Johnny found himself stepping into the charred remains until he felt it, too. A faint buzz that set his teeth and funny bone on edge. As he rummaged, he ignored Hieronymus' urgent requests, until his hand grasped the thin neck of the lute. He pulled it out, amazed to find it quite undamaged.

"This?" Toastess affirmed it was. "Then let's go." He set off as fast as he could in pursuit of Hieronymus, Toastess under his arm, lute in hand, with the growing cloud of imminent destruction growing ever more oppressive.

At least he tried; he ran as fast as his knees would allow. After a minute he settled for a fast walk that hurt his hips.

"I really must do something about my diet and exercise regime. Or at least start one. What does it do?" Johnny asked as he caught his breath. He placed the lute behind the sofa and watched Hieronymus push and pull levers and pedals without any apparent success.

The wind that had been sucked up now returned with tornado force.

"I don't know, do you? Turn that lever there." Hieronymus pointed.

Johnny climbed in and immediately became engulfed in leather. "I suggest you hurry," he urged. "Put that thing in your neck again."

"No, never again. A most uncomfortable experience." Hieronymus pointed to a brass foot pedal. "Come on, what are you waiting for?"

"Me? This is your contraption." Johnny pressed down as they were battered by a cyclone of flying debris and hurricane-force winds.

The contraption began to shake and shudder as the winds picked it up.

"There, haven't I met your terms, you miserable machine? Do something now!" Hieronymus shouted at it, as he pointed to another clutch pedal on the floor. He desperately manipulated several levers, so Johnny stepped on the pedal and breathed a sigh of relief as the wind shut off and a spangling purple haze covered them.

A purple haze Johnny had seen before. He frowned around the gentleman's study. Something wasn't quite right here, apart from the obvious.

Chapter Thirty-four

"Go on, in you go," Hieronymus encouraged. They sat in the cobbled street steaming gently. Horses drawing carriages and pedestrians gave them curious glances.

Johnny hesitated. "Why can't you?"

Hieronymus sighed. "I've explained this. Because he knows me. And I've already been unsuccessful."

"In the future." Johnny didn't have the strength to argue. "So, how will I persuade him not to use hypnosis in therapy and to give me the metronome," Johnny asked, "when you've already failed?"

Hieronymus sighed. "You are not paid £5000 a week for nothing. Unless you are a Tory MP, or engaged in some type of professional sport, or a celebrity. Which, to my knowledge, you are not." They looked around the drab grim misty streets broken with the clip clop and smell of horses.

"That really bothers you, doesn't it?"

"I never realised we had such a mercenary streak."

"Ha! You're telling me you're doing this, whatever this is, for free?"

"My business is none of yours. The accumulation of wealth is an unattractive quality. Life is about being satisfied with your station not monetary success." Hieronymus sniffed.

"Is it? How do you know that?"

"I don't know I just do. However, I suggest appealing to his pride. Something like not needing gimmicks. I don't know." Hieronymus shrugged.

"Why wouldn't he listen to you?" Johnny persisted.

"I was on the Titanic, and time was running out." Hieronymus breathed in calmly.

"And Freud was there? Being held captive?"

"Yes, though he refused to believe it. The session deteriorated from there."

Johnny felt there was more to this than Hieronymus was letting on, but with a resigned shrug removed himself from the deep leather sofa. He stood before the steps leading to Dr. Sigmund Freud's offices as top-hatted gentlemen hurried past, and soldiers or policemen marched importantly into the town square.

"Halt!" A sergeant barked, then sent the soldiers crashing through doors into buildings.

"Go on." Hieronymus waved him forwards.

"And what will you be doing? Suddenly disappearing? Leaving me stranded in... where are we exactly?" Johnny looked around the cold, damp grey streets where buildings disappeared in the mist like wraiths. "Manchester?"

"Vienna, Earth 1896 CE. And no. I will familiarise myself with this contraption and find some butter for Toastess to synthesise. We cannot continue like this."

"You will?" Toastess buzzed. "Thank you. Are you the one who holds the Secret of Butter?"

"Yes." Hieronymus sighed. "Is it always like this? Just go on. Hurry. I think you're right. We need to revisit Mal. I fear returning him has upset the future."

"No, I think he wants to put things right."

"Look, we can argue all day long. Just go on. There's nothing to be afraid of."

Johnny looked on appalled to where the helmeted policemen or soldiers were roughly shoving families of peasants, clutching their few belongings, through the streets to the applause of the crowd.

"Where are they taking them?" Johnny asked.

"Nowhere pleasant, I imagine. Now hurry. This is all connected. Go on."

Johnny hurried into a pleasantly tiled and wood-panelled hallway. The door on his left was addressed to Dr. Freud. Johnny tried to remember anything he knew of this man, but his theories and speculations had largely become discredited a hundred years in the future. Johnny *had* read his book but couldn't even remember the title. Something to do with dreams? Never mind the contents.

He knocked and entered. A seated middle-aged man, dressed in tweeds with a goatee beard, observed him through thick cigar smoke from behind a large wooden desk. The small room consisted of this oak desk, bookshelves, and a profusion of dusty rugs. In the centre was a chaise longue with heavy fabrics draped over it.

Johnny smiled and nodded a greeting. "Dr. Freud?"

"*Ja*, please enter."

"I need your help."

"*Ja*, that is why we are here. Please have a lie down." He indicated the tatty chaise longue.

"I'll stand, if you don't mind. Now, you might not believe me, but you're going to be abducted by aliens." Johnny stopped and considered. As an opening line, this wasn't the best.

"I make no apology for my Jewishness. And it's the Police who will arrest me, I think. Who are these aliens? The French?" Dr. Freud stroked his beard.

"At least, in one reality you will be." Johnny considered. "I don't know how or why, but you're a prisoner onboard a space… no, a ship," Johnny continued reasonably enough, he thought.

"*Ja?*" Dr. Freud raised his eyebrows and made notes. "Spaceship? You mean I will be deported on a ship? Are you with the Mayor's office? By whose authority?"

Johnny sighed as he indicated all the furnishings. "This room will become your entire world. You will never be able to leave. You're an exhibit in an alien zoo. A prisoner. I know it's a lot to take on faith, but please, try to understand."

"Interesting, though no, I do not. And I am not practising any religion. Now, explain to me how you feel I will be a prisoner." Freud rested his cigar in a heavy ashtray and opened a notebook. He looked at Johnny. "Are you aware you are mirroring?"

"What?"

"It's a term I use. You are unconsciously imitating what you suggest will happen to me, because you feel that you are a prisoner," Dr. Freud stated.

"Look. Fine. Whatever. Just let me take the metronome." Johnny could now understand why Hieronymus' session had deteriorated. He looked at the glass case where the little wooden triangle sat patiently waiting for patients. "You must not use it in hypnosis."

"Why not? Are you a doctor?"

"The human subconsciousness cannot be allowed to be awakened," Johnny explained. He frowned. Was it his imagination, or was there something shimmering into focus in the corner of the room?

"Interesting. I see you have read my work. Are you a student of the mind?"

"A private investigator. Now, please, we have to leave, or I'll just take the metronome."

"Please sit down. You came here for help. I see you are agitated. How often do you masturbate?" Dr. Freud waited, pen raised.

"What? I don't see what that has to do with anything," Johnny blustered and blushed.

"Denial. Come, if we are to progress, you must first be honest with yourself."

Johnny felt himself swallow and did indeed sit on the musty old furniture.

"Good. Now. How often do you engage in the one great habit? I will need details. Every detail." Dr. Freud's fountain pen poised above his book.

"No, you won't. You need to leave. Now. Look."

Johnny turned to see three little grey aliens watching him with interest. "Can you see them?"

"See who?" Dr. Freud made further notes. "Delusional."

One of them raised his glowing fingertip, and Dr. Freud froze.

"Ah. If it isn't the one who'll cost us a lot of money, don't you agree, Vent?"

The middle one nodded. "Not to mention our reputation, Beans. Spatula, would you be so kind?"

The larger one on the left moved towards Johnny, who backed away and stood behind a frozen Dr. Freud. Spatula extended his glowing finger.

"Wait, look, I didn't know Hercules wasn't supposed to interfere at Thermopylae," Johnny pleaded.

"I think an eternity being psychoanalysed by this human…" Spatula smiled.

"And being analysed by us…" Vent extended his glowing finger towards Johnny.

"…will ensure a constant revenue stream in the Resort." Beans approached Johnny from the left, finger aglow.

"And our reputation restored," Spatula added.

They grabbed Johnny and bent him over the chaise longue.

Chapter Thirty-five

Hieronymus burst into the room. "We need to do more than just stop Freud from using the metronome. We need to go to the source. What have you done with him?"

Hieronymus frowned at a frozen Freud, then turned to Johnny and the aliens, "Oh, I can see you're busy. I'll return later."

"No, human, stay."

"First Tier Totalist?" Hieronymus asked, as he recoiled. "I'm sorry—"

"You know our boss?" the little aliens replied.

"Ah, yes," Hieronymus replied cautiously, then with more confidence. They all looked the same to him. "We sit at the same table."

"What?"

"We are members of a secret organisation," Hieronymus winked and made a curious hand gesture that only served to cause further confusion, "together – Nikola Tesla, the Galactic Overlord, Deianicia," Hieronymus couldn't remember her title, "the Green Vapour, who really doesn't seem to do much of anything, and myself. All members of the Synchronisation Bureau, see to the..."

The aliens muttered among themselves and advanced, releasing a relieved Johnny.

Hieronymus paused. "Ah, well, the smooth running of things. And continued gambling," he added hastily at their frowns. "First Tier..."

"Thank you," the tallest one smiled, "we are first cousins."

"Oh good. When did you last see him?" Hieronymus asked cautiously.

"Oh, not for several cycles of this wretched sun. We have several collections before we can return. This is the last one. Why?" Vent asked.

"I know all about it. First Tier Totalist especially liked the three humans you placed in the Resort. Well done." Hieronymus nodded.

"Why can't we communicate?" Vent asked, reaching into the folds of his skin and manipulating a slim silver mobile phone type device.

"There's been a bit of a thing on the Titanic. Treachery. The Cosmic Mind is awake." Hieronymus answered.

"Titanic?" Johnny asked.

"The communications are down. Which is why I'm here. The First Tier Totalist couldn't come himself – busy at resetting the odds – so here I am." Hieronymus nodded.

This seemed to relax the aliens, who sighed in a martyred fashion.

"Won't help us, though." Vent shook his head.

"We'll end up as guards," Spatula explained.

"Or worse. Working in the casinos," Beans added.

Hieronymus shuddered at the memory.

"He's sent me to tell you not to take this human here," Hieronymus indicated a frozen Freud, "because there are now enough humans on display with their strange behaviours. It's all a bit dull. They don't really do much."

Hieronymus waited as the aliens conferred.

"What about him?" Spatula asked, indicating Johnny. "He has to answer for losing all that money over Palestine."

"Not to mention our reputation," Beans added.

"Our notoriety as tipsters is at an all-time low," Vent complained.

"Ah. Yes, about him." Hieronymus looked at Johnny as he sauntered over to the glass cabinet and opened it. He cautiously took out the metronome expecting to be electrocuted, then appraised the device as if he was an antiques expert in mechanical tools.

"Close your eyes and listen to the beat..." Hieronymus spoke slowly as he set the pendulum swinging while he approached the aliens, "...and everything will become clear."

"What? Why?" asked Vent.

"This is a new way to communicate with the First Tier Totalist." Hieronymus assured them.

"It is?" a dubious Vent asked.

"There's been a problem with the servers. The Cosmic Mind is interfering. Well, have you tried your normal devices?"

Motioning Johnny towards the door with a flick of his head, Hieronymus retreated and set the metronome ticking in front of Freud.

The Starachians shrugged as much as small grey aliens with no shoulders could. Hieronymus was struck by them. "How have they become so technologically advanced, when they could not even conceivably carry anything? Not even a yoke."

"Pails of milk. No way." Johnny agreed.

"Milkmaids," Hieronymus muttered as he relaxed into a favourite dream focussing on the hypnotic beat.

"What? Snap out of it." Johnny encouraged.

Hieronymus returned from his reverie. "It's a shame Freud is otherwise incapacitated. I would have liked his analysis: a pleasantly erotically charged scene somewhere in the Austrian mountains in which I play a passing farmer, concerning three milkmaids and an interesting take on milking."

"H?" Johnny asked.

"Yes, yes," he cleared his head from the metronomic beat, "the First Tier Totalist is coming through now. Quickly, close your eyes and listen to the message." Hieronymus approached the aliens, motioning Johnny to leave.

"Yes, that's it. Lie down and just listen to the slow beat as you feel yourself becoming sleepy. Your eyes are heavy, you feel relaxed. Everything is good with the world. Your good service will be rewarded. Relax and breathe."

Hieronymus found to his surprise that the aliens were astonishingly susceptible. He turned to the frozen Freud. "Dr. Freud, you will no longer use hypnosis in therapy. It is only for charlatans, spiritualists, and so forth."

Hieronymus cautiously stepped away from the somnolent aliens as he followed Johnny out of the door into the street, carrying the metronome.

"What about Freud?" Johnny asked.

"What about him?" Hieronymus replied, as he settled into the leather sofa. "Oh yes. Forgot."

He hurried back inside.

"When you regain consciousness, in ten seconds' time, you will not use the metronome to investigate the human subconscious. To do so will see you plagued with visions of aliens."

Hieronymus nodded and considered. He hoped that would do the trick. "Begin counting back. Ten, nine, eight…"

Dr. Freud opened his eyes to see several strange shaped creatures lying on his chaise longue. He frowned, looked around as if he'd misplaced something, then dismissed the thought.

"Now," he asked his unusual visitors, "tell me how often you masturbate."

Chapter Thirty-six

"So, yet again I've had to rescue you," Hieronymus noted, as they sat comfortably ensconced in a glowing purple haze proceeding to god-only-knew-where. "Did you call me H?"

"No, you placed me in danger to avoid uncomfortable questions about your unsavoury habits," Johnny replied. "This haze is similar to the one which surrounds Star Quest. A spaceship. You're not the only one who's been involved in space and time travel, you know. I've been to and witnessed many strange worlds."

"Similar, yes. Not the same." Hieronymus waved at the leafy aspidistra, a wooden representation of the globe circa 1880, and the leather sofa upon which they sat. All surrounded by gauges and brass levers and spinny things.

"No, I suppose not," Johnny grudgingly admitted. "What took you so long?"

"Amsterdam. 1814. I popped over to see Maelzel, who is famous for producing the metronome, but it was Winkel who actually first developed it," Hieronymus explained, as he placed the metronome under the couch with the lute. "I bought the patents."

Johnny was impressed, though he would never tell Hieronymus so.

"And I think you'll find they are our habits," Hieronymus noted. "Though mine are not what you'd describe as unsavoury. I have no idea what *you've* been getting up to in your spare time."

"I have a lady friend," Johnny replied defensively.

"So Mal was right. You're in love. No wonder we're in such a mess."

"What does that have to do with anything? You started all this," Johnny waved his hands around, "whatever this is. This is all your fault."

"Tea?" Toastess asked, to diffuse the fraught situation. "Might I recommend toast? With butter?"

"Have you successfully synthesised the butter I gave you?" Hieronymus asked.

"Hmm, yes. Up to a point. Synthesised, yes. Success relies upon your recommendation." Toastess ejected a cup of tea and a steaming bagel glistening with something liquidly melting.

"After you," Hieronymus urged.

Johnny sniffed. It smelt like butter; it looked like butter. He attempted a cautious bite.

"So, where are we going now?" Johnny asked, crunching the wonderfully toasted and buttered bagel. But it tasted too buttery and too bagelly. It lodged in his throat, and he struggled to swallow.

"How's the bagel? And more importantly, the butter?" Hieronymus asked.

"Yes," buzzed Toastess, "please fill in the questionnaire."

Johnny ruminated for a moment before replying. The tea tasted alright, but the bagel tasted increasingly plastic, and the butter too buttery, too chemical. "Adequate. Though I don't think you'll like what I have to say about the bagel. Have you changed the recipe?"

"Adequate," buzzed Toastess. "I'll take it. And yes. I undertake a process of constant improvement. The only way to truly better the recipe is to find the God of Bread."

"I agree." Hieronymus nodded.

"What do you mean?" Johnny asked, as he gazed at the perplexing array of levers and knobs, springs and gauges. He settled back into the deep buttoned leather couch and unfastened his rudimentary seat belt. They were going nowhere fast.

"Going back to where we dropped Mal off won't help, will it?" Hieronymus experimentally pressed down on a foot pedal. Nothing happened. "So, we'll have to discover where it all started. Where Mal first started, as it were. I think we've been going at this the wrong way."

"I have no idea what you're talking about."

"My suspicions were first aroused when he readily agreed. A few weeks ago, I also had chance to meet with him regarding the Undead. He had some interesting things to say of his people and their wanderings."

"No, still no idea."

Top-hatted gentlemen and frilly-dressed women gazed at them as they paraded past. They had attracted quite a crowd. Horses sniffed suspiciously as they plopped manure then clopped away.

"We collect Mal and take him back to where he started his religion, otherwise he won't recognise us?" Johnny asked.

"Of course not. Stupid bloody machine," Hieronymus fumed. "If we turn up unannounced and Mal doesn't recognise us, he'll well, he's not known for his patience or generosity, is he?"

Johnny agreed reasonably enough he felt. "But why? The Titanic has been destroyed. You have achieved what you wanted to achieve with the tourists. Let's just go home. Things just become so much more complicated. Let's quit while we're ahead."

"No, the war will expand to engulf all nations. I've seen it. We have to stop it before it begins. Mal wants us to redeem his people, as you said yourself." Hieronymus cogitated for several moments. "There is a problem."

"There always is." Johnny finished his bagel. "I would be surprised if there wasn't."

"How do you think Mal would react if faced with his double?" Hieronymus asked, as he tapped a gauge. "I think it might have run out of electricity."

Johnny had to agree Mal wouldn't take a rival at all well. "Those gods have been at each other's throats since the Second World War. Why is this current conflict any different?"

"Because it has to stop there. Mal will never live together in peace. That's his nature. You want to let his people continue the war when we might be able to do something? Mal has to be stopped."

Not entirely in agreement, Johnny sat back. "Then can we go home? Fine. Which was when exactly?" Johnny asked.

"Look in there." Hieronymus indicated a wooden cupboard. "I kept, I mean Nikola kept all the latest encyclopaedias. At least current at the end of the 19th century."

Johnny was pleased to see many heavy leather-bound books on shelves. This time machine resembled a Victorian gentlemen's club with added machinery. "Everything we ever wished for is here."

"I know." Hieronymus sighed. "Be careful what you wish for."

"What am I looking for?" Johnny asked, as he flicked through the bookshelf.

"Not what the Torah says, but what academics and historians agree on. Find me a date and place where it all began. I mean really began. Not all that slavery, plagues, and exodus guff. I'll keep working on this." Hieronymus once again twisted a knob that had steam bursting alarmingly out of a cylinder and spraying the aspidistra.

"Come on you confounded machine! Haven't I done what you asked of me?"

"You've travelled twice in this. What's the problem with attaching that wire?" Johnny asked, as he closed his eyes and randomly selected a tome. Was pronoia still working?

"I don't want to become a Cyborg. And more by luck than design, several levers seem to do the same thing. Or nothing at all. Don't worry, I'll get the hang of it." Hieronymus didn't sound at all optimistic. "The contraption seems to be sulking for whatever reason."

Johnny didn't have the energy or inclination to question Hieronymus over the Cyborg quip, so settled down and opened the encyclopaedia at random. He read. And read on. Selected another volume and nodded. He watched Hieronymus faff around, becoming increasingly frustrated.

"Is there a hammer? Perhaps if I just give it a few meaningful strikes the machine will cooperate. Are you listening?" he threatened the drinks globe.

"How can it hear you? I've just been reading about Nikola Tesla. He worked predominately with electricity. A genius. Perhaps this machine does have a flat," Johnny suggested and waved at the dank dull streets. "Solar power? Toastess runs on solar. Seems odd Nikola kept books about himself."

Hieronymus brushed this aside, "Any tools?"

"We could plug it in," Johnny replied.

"You are forgetting one thing: electricity hasn't reached here yet."

They looked around the drab dark streets, poorly illuminated by gaslight. The soldiers were roughly herding the unfortunate people into horse-drawn carriages.

"Why are they doing that to them? Can we do something?"

"That's the plan. You're supposed to be working on the origins of the Israelites," Hieronymus fumed. "Let me worry about…"

Hieronymus watched dumbfounded as Johnny clambered out of the contraption. "What are you doing now?"

Johnny opened a compartment at the side of the machine and uncoiled a length of hosepipe-like flex. He connected it, unclipped a wooden handle, and turned it faster and faster with an increasing whirring noise, until lights began to glow faintly at first then with increasing brightness within the confines of the contraption.

Johnny hopped back in. "Now try it."

Hieronymus pressed various pedals and levers until the purple shimmer appeared once more. He huffed. "A dynamo? Hmm. So, where to?"

"The hills above Canaan, around 600 years before Yesuah."

"Where is Canaan?" Hieronymus asked, as he focussed and held the tillers. "I have to picture it, or at least my impression of it. The subconscious mind will do the rest. Did I tell you about my adventures with the Cosmic Mind?"

"Modern-day Israel. To the south and west, on the Egyptian border," Johnny replied. "Except, there is a problem, of course."

"Mal is not the most reasonable of men?" Hieronymus asked.

"Just so. Or god."

"Then we shall have to employ guile and tact. Which is why I'll do the talking."

The machine shook and span, and Johnny held on, hastily fastening the seat belt once again as they were ensconced in the spangling purple haze.

"You know I always get overwhelmed by Jimi Hendrix when this happens. There's something you're not telling me about this contraption, isn't there?"

Hieronymus shrugged. "Star Quest chose the better man."

"And I have the consolation prize of a toaster?"

"Pardon?" Toastess demanded. "I'm just a consolation?"

"This isn't the Generation Game. Or Bullseye."

"Bruce Forsyth or Ted Rogers?" Johnny asked.

"Jim Bowen. Ted Rogers presented 3-2-1. Now, can we get on?" Hieronymus pulled down the flying goggles and grabbed hold of the levers like a Spitfire pilot.

Chapter Thirty-seven

Johnny and Hieronymus looked down at the large sprawling encampment. A few fires shone against the darkness, goats bleated in the dark, but few people moved. In the centre there was a larger tent, almost a marquee, but this was no happy celebration or social function. It smelt horrid, like a year-long festival with no toilet facilities. Or a refugee camp escaping from famine. Death just seemed to hang like a fog.

"He's not here, is he?" Johnny asked squinting at shadows. "I can't see him."

"We can't just wander down there," Hieronymus stated.

"You don't say?" Johnny replied reasonably, reassured Death wasn't here for him at this present moment. He'd forgotten just how much he hated the inky black stickiness of ancient Judea. And the smell. "I think we should just forget the whole thing. Mal will probably just have us killed. You know what he's like."

"We could say we're three wise men from, ah…" Hieronymus hesitated, "somewhere, with messages for him about, well, something. Gifts? Gods require gifts, don't they?"

"Two not very wise men and a kitchen appliance," Johnny corrected.

"Hey, I have feelings, you know."

"Sorry, but you are."

"That will have to do," Hieronymus stated, and made his way down the hillside to the large tent below.

Johnny was about to stop him, being no longer of the bluster-your-way-through approach, but couldn't come up with a better plan, so he sighed, picked up Toastess, and followed.

There were mutterings from inside the tent. Hieronymus shrugged and opened the flap to find an empty space and a further tent inside this one – empty, apart from several ragged and angry men. With spears. Several more were praying before many branched candles that dripped sizzling animal fat onto the sand.

Hieronymus coughed. "So unhygienic."

The guards sprang to their feet and prodded Hieronymus and Johnny, demanding something in a language neither could understand. Hieronymus pointed to the inner tent but one of the guards knocked him down.

"Argh!" Hieronymus rubbed his offended knees.

"Can you translate?" Johnny asked, as he lifted the Toastess towards the guards. "I come bearing gifts for the god."

"Is this the God of Bread?" Toastess asked, reverently ad-libbing.

"Yes," Johnny answered, as the guards backed suspiciously away. He held Toastess in front of him. She buzzed excitedly as they walked towards the inner tent. More guards halted them as they passed inside.

"Are you coming?" Johnny asked a groaning Hieronymus as he struggled to his feet.

"Twice now. In your company. I really must do something about my health," complained Hieronymus. "Fitness levels."

"You could always train for a fun run," Johnny added. He'd seen the posters for one dotted around the local area. If he ever returned.

"Fun and run are not two words normally associated with each other."

"I could run five kilometres easily. Fat boy," Johnny added unnecessarily.

"Ha. Not likely. But I accept your challenge."

Johnny frowned and was about to refute this when the guards motioned them inside. They bowed their heads, stopped, and smiled. Mal was asleep on a long couch. He snored gently in the guttering, dirty oil lamplight. Johnny and Hieronymus were pleased to see he looked well – at least, not as unwell as previously. There was also an unhappy man scribbling on a scroll in a corner of the sandy interior. He didn't look up.

"Mal looks much healthier than when we'd met him many years ago, at least two-and-a-half thousand years in the future," Hieronymus stated.

"Yes," Johnny agreed. "Not young or youthful…"

"No."

"But not aged and evil," Johnny ended, as Mal opened his eyes and burst into furious flames.

He bellowed in a deep booming voice, "Who dares disturb the One True God?"

The guards fell to their knees. "Avert your eyes lest they be burned from your face."

"Hello, Mal. We are friends of yours from the future. We come with a warning," Hieronymus answered.

"What?"

"From yourself," Johnny added.

"To look upon my face is Death." Mal dimmed his fire slightly. "The future? Impossible. Not even gods can travel through time. And why would I warn myself?"

"Mal, we're here to—"

He frowned. "Mal?"

Johnny shrugged. "That's the name you gave us."

"We've only recently found out you were a god," Hieronymus added. "We always assumed you were an out-of-work actor."

"Who did a bit of loan sharking on the side."

"What is this? Is this your doing, Moses? It's not very funny." Mal turned his gaze to the scribbling man.

"No, my Lord God."

Mal swung back to them. "Are you a double act? You do look like twins. Brothers?" Mal paused. "As entertainers go, you're not very funny either. Like those three lepers whose trick was to pull their fingers off. Until I cremated them. Wait a minute, what did you say? Was a god? *Was?* You mean in this supposed future I'm not a god?"

"Well, we don't know the specifics, but belief in you certainly drops off a bit." Hieronymus added, "Is it me or is it getting hot in here?"

"Your people have had enough of the constant wars," Johnny added.

Mal began to glow and rounded on the man who'd stopped scribbling to listen. "Moses! Have you finished the first book yet?"

"Soon, my Lord God." Moses bowed low and continued his scribbling as Mal returned his gaze to them, an inner fire gradually dimming to smouldering embers, but flames still danced in his eyes.

"Time travel? Impossible."

"Well, we can. We come with a warning," Hieronymus repeated and stopped. He looked at Johnny as more of the guards burst into the inner tent and flung themselves face down, burying heads in the sand.

"From yourself," Johnny repeated, and smiled. Cancer? His body; Mal's people had a disease. That's what he'd meant. Johnny had figured it out. And the coin. The message written on it wasn't for Mal but for him. Johnny felt a pleasing and all too fleeting moment of inspiration.

"We're here for redemption of your people."

Mal blazed furiously once more, then sighed and slumped back onto his couch covered in musty goat skins.

"Oh god. Not prophets, are you?" Mal shook his head dispiritedly. "There are more bloody prophets than you can shake a stick at. Name yourselves."

"Sir Hieronymus Calmly," Hieronymus began, "Professor of Perplexing Complexity, or it might be Complex Perplexity."

"Who gave you that title? But long-winded, isn't it?" Johnny sniffed. "Johnny Moped. Private Investigator. Extraordinaire."

"And yours isn't?" Hieronymus began. "Now, Mal, look…"

"Takes it out of you. I agree, belief isn't as strong as it once was. What did you call me? Mal? And a word of warning, don't ever tell me to 'look'. Got it?"

"Sorry. I wasn't talking to you but my colleague here. Mal is what we know you as. We're friends. In the future. You sent us. We're here to save your people." Hieronymus continued stretching the truth considerably.

"What do you mean? Sorry about the theatrics, but you know, standards." Mal took a deep breath. "Guards! Throw a dozen goats on the altar. Now."

The guards bowed and rushed away.

"Save them from what? The Canaanites?"

"No, from themselves."

Mal frowned darkly.

"And you," Johnny muttered, as he looked at the pile of scrolls and papers that littered the interior of the tent. "The book you're writing doesn't help your people at all.

If you continue with your genocide, they will always be persecuted and constantly at war."

"Made scapegoats," Hieronymus added.

Mal nodded and shrugged. "What's wrong with that? Standard operating procedures for a god."

"What?" Johnny and Hieronymus stared at the old man in shock.

"Look, we have no choice. My people are starving; belief in me is at an all-time low. We have to go back down there. We can't go to the south or west because we'll just be made to build those bloody big temples the Egyptians like so much. And their gods don't like me at all. Bloody Horus and his all-seeing eye. And Anubis? Death has really let himself go. Weighing hearts? And I don't like them. It has to be north and east."

"Well, why is that so bad?" Johnny asked.

Mal frowned at Johnny. "Don't you know anything, boy? I can't just say 'oh, we're back, we were wrong, is it alright if we join in?', can I?" Mal shook his head. "I'll have an existential crisis and cease to exist. But there's enough of us. We can take 'em. And we're desperate. After last time." Mal frowned darkly.

"What do you mean?" Johnny asked.

"Moses, cover your ears."

The scribbling man stopped scribbling and obediently placed his hands over his ears.

"Well, I wanted them to attack a few years ago. The scouts came back with reports about the Canaanites being giants, but how could they be when we've only been gone for a few generations? Did they miraculously shoot up overnight? They're our people. Made no sense, but the rumour spread so I had to teach them a lesson, didn't I?"

"Did you?"

"Forty years wandering around in the wilderness has sharpened their respect, let me tell you." Mal smiled darkly once again. "Trimmed the fat off the bone. Now they're ready."

"Ready? But why not?" Johnny asked.

"Why not what?"

"Rejoin. Peacefully. I mean, why won't they accept you?" Johnny asked.

"They have new gods now." Mal shook his head. "Not just one, but lots of them. Mainly refugees from Mesopotamia. I think Tengri is moving westwards with his hordes. Displaced them. Bloody old Chinaman."

Johnny and Hieronymus looked at each other. They had not expected a god's existence to be so political, but then that was mirrored in man, so of course it would be.

"Have you tried?" Johnny asked.

"No point. I know them. They won't accept me as top dog," Mal lamented. "We have no choice but to fight them. Now, what's this thing? A weapon?"

"Hail, God of Bread!" Toastess buzzed.

"Well, yes, I can do bread. Circus and bread, the old favourites." Mal nodded. "At least a passable substitute. But mainly pillars of fire, call down plagues if required. We gods each have our specialities. And ways and means. Always easier to work through mankind. Keep them distracted and fed. It's the only sure way. Course, you have to be a master of manipulation."

Mal leant forward as his eyes gleamed with fire.

"And choose dangerous or desperate people," Hieronymus added.

Mal shrugged. "Hey ho."

"So, this is your plan?" Hieronymus sidled over to the pile of papers and shuffled through them as Johnny moved over to two heavy stone slabs where they rested against a golden chest.

"Yes, a common goal, a common foundation; miracles with a bit of tragedy thrown in. Works a treat. People need to believe they know something others don't. They like to be special. Members of an elite club. My club. Do right by me and I'll protect you."

Johnny turned to Mal and brandished the scrolls. "This won't work. Your words are rewritten over the centuries."

"Ha! I don't know what you've heard or been told but listen to this. This is different. Moses, uncover your ears and listen. So, we left Canaan, right?" Mal sat forward conspiratorially. "None of them even remember living there."

Johnny and Hieronymus nodded.

"So, I thought, if that's the case why not say the Egyptians enslaved us to build their bloody big mausoleums? But," Mal smiled, "I freed us. Delivered my people from slavery. Course, took a bit of persuading – you know, plagues and such. But that's what I'm good at, savvy?"

"Killing the Egyptians' first born?" Hieronymus asked, as he leafed through the pages.

"Look, it's revenge for what they did to us," Mal explained.

"But it didn't happen," Johnny pointed out.

"What does that matter, so long as people believe it did?" Mal shook his head in exasperation. "It works. All the best stories have revenge as a motivating factor, don't they?"

"Or love," Johnny stated. "Humour. Human kindness. There is a man in a few centuries' time who will teach—"

"Tish and pish." Mal waved Johnny's concerns away. "Fire and death, that's what people understand. And what happened to this lovey dovey funny man?"

"Well, ah," Johnny faltered, "yes, nothing good. But wanting to believe something is real doesn't make it real," Johnny argued.

"Yes, of course it does." Mal sat back and laughed, hands on the knees of his long robe. "I see you have a lot to learn about politics. Anyway, they've signed an agreement. Moses!"

"Right here, My Lord God."

"Stand up."

Moses kept his head down and bowed low before Mal.

"Tell them."

Moses fell to his knees. "You led us away as a pillar of fire, saved us, my Lord, through the desert, parted the seas, gave us laws to live by." Moses bowed his head to the ground once more.

"Do these laws say something along the lines of 'no god but me because I'm jealous'?" Hieronymus asked innocently, as he brushed sand from the stone tablets.

"Naturally." Mal smiled. "Continue."

"My Lord, you will make us a Holy Nation with a Kingdom of Priests," Moses continued.

"If you are faithful to me," Mal added.

"Your promise. Your laws," Moses finished.

"Not bad, eh?" Mal smiled and waited. "I hope you've put in the bit about the golden calf. And what happened about that, eh?"

Moses nodded and bowed his head.

"Now, time travellers – which I don't believe for one moment – who rewrites my books? Who would dare?"

"Mal, please. Every six hundred years; I don't know why it's six hundred, but that seems to be when people need something else," Hieronymus continued.

"What?" Mal asked suspiciously.

"After the third book, there's the Renaissance, then the Industrial Revolution," Hieronymus added and turned to Johnny. "Perhaps that's something we need to look into? Interesting, don't you think?"

"Maybe," Johnny cautiously agreed. "Could we just focus?"

"What? Oh yes. Anyway, your book is not only rewritten," Hieronymus continued, "but improved upon."

"What!" Mal exploded into flame once more, then subsided. "That's going to cost them. Takes a few sacrifices to keep this up. Twice, you say?"

"Twice," Hieronymus agreed. "And these new religions blame you and persecute your people. Please believe us," Hieronymus finished.

"Hmm." Mal dimmed his fire, sat on his long couch, and considered. "Improved, you say?"

"Yes." Johnny and Hieronymus smiled hopefully.

"Well then, so what does it matter? We're going to kill the Canaanites anyway and take what's theirs and anyone else who stands in our way. That's it. Make all this land mine. And only mine. Those Mesopotamian gods can sod right off, and if Tengri comes calling we'll kill them all, too. Now, if there's nothing else?"

"You're just repeating the mistakes of the future!" Hieronymus shook his head.

"What?"

"This is what we mean. What we are here to warn you against, what *you* sent us here to tell *you*." Johnny paused.

"Show him the coin," Hieronymus urged.

"I don't have it."

"What? You don't…oh, that's brilliant that is. The one true piece of evidence we had. Didn't you think to tell me this before?"

Johnny ignored him. "Two thousand years in the future, all this is still going on." He waved vaguely at the tent.

"It never ends. Eventually all the world will be drawn into a final nuclear world war. You're making a terrible mistake." Hieronymus added.

"There's nothing like a war to bring a tribe together and increase belief. It's my way or the highway," Mal affirmed.

"Why isn't he listening?" Hieronymus asked Johnny.

"Won't these Mesopotamian gods try to stop you?" Johnny asked.

"Nah, all that mooning about and praying to Baal? They don't stand a chance." Mal nodded to Moses.

"The bread, my Lord," Toastess pleaded. "Will you show me how?"

Mal looked at Toastess then dismissed her. "No. Unless you are a weapon, I have no use for you. Any of you."

"But…" Toastess began.

Mal turned to Moses. "Hurry up and finish the bloody books. Joshua!"

The surly guard from outside entered the inner tent.

There was the same venomous laughter they remembered, but this definitely had more bite. Mal, or the God of this particular tribe of Canaanites, stood up. "One thing you should know. Gods don't make mistakes. Throw them in jail."

Chapter Thirty-eight

"You didn't bring the coin. Well done," Hieronymus observed.
"Didn't you think to tell me that before we came down here?"

Johnny tried to loosen the hide thongs that bound his hands and feet to a central pole. He sniffed at the musty aroma. Outside, they could hear the sounds of breaking camp as people arose and went about their business, which appeared to be mostly goat herding. Most men trudged out onto the bleak barren mountainsides, but a few steered unhappy goats towards stone altars where their throats were unceremoniously cut. There were flies everywhere.

"A series of escalating dangers," Johnny accused.

"I wonder what's going on. There seems to be a lot of sacrificing."

"And spear sharpening."

Through a gap in the tent flap, they could see the sun was a purple-blue bruised line on the jagged horizon.

"They must have kept goats in here." Johnny managed to stretch out his aching knees. "Reasonable? Mal? Tact and guile?"

"These are simply the initial moves in a complex game," Hieronymus asserted.

"With Mal making all the rules," Johnny added. "You're very quiet."

"The Secret of Bread," Toastess wailed. "To come so close."

"Look," Hieronymus began, "when we return, I'll get you a sample of bread. Now, think of a way for us to escape this, will you?"

"A little help would be appreciated," Johnny agreed.

"What kind of bread?" Toastess asked.

Johnny stiffened as the tent flap was thrust aside and the guard, Joshua, pointed his spear at them while another came behind them and untied their bonds. They both struggled to their feet with much groaning and popping of joints and ligaments.

"When we return, we will definitely have to attend to our health. This is just ridiculous. Perhaps yoga. Some form of gentle calisthenics."

"And painful," Johnny added, as they once again held an audience with Mal.

Joshua knocked them to their knees again.

"Argh! Do you mind?"

"Leave us and prepare," Mal intoned. "I command you, General, send your armies to destroy the Canaanites, wipe them from the face of the earth. End their abominable places of worship."

"It will be as you command, Lord God." Joshua bowed low, but before he could exit Mal added, "Joshua. The temples first."

The General exited, leaving Mal, Hieronymus, and Johnny watching a frantically scribbling Moses. Mal sighed. "He's not the sharpest tool. Nor him. Have you finished?"

"Yes, my Lord God. Almost."

"Make sure you highlight the worship of Canaanite gods is forbidden, and the genocide against the Canaanites and all other religions is an act of faith. Got it?"

"Yes, my Lord God."

"One and only God," Mal intoned. "Go on, get out. You can finish this later. You're not going with Joshua. You'll stay here until the laws are finished."

"As my Lord God commands." Moses kept his head bowed as he exited the tent.

Mal took a deep breath and looked at Johnny and Hieronymus. "What? You think it's easy being a god?"

"Well, no, but do you have to destroy all the other gods?" Hieronymus asked.

"Of course. We can't exist together in the same place. There's only so much belief to go around." Mal looked at them as if they were stupid.

"Like rats," Johnny immediately regretted saying as Mal's eyes glowed dangerously.

"Hold your tongue and I'll hold my temper. But yes. Once you've found a group of people who'll follow your orders, you keep hold of them. It is a rat race. All those other gods offering this, promising that." Mal shook his head sadly.

"Wouldn't it just be easier if..." Johnny began, but Mal wasn't listening.

"Having to constantly find ways to be believed in. Keep putting the fear of God into them all the time. Eh? Do you? It's not easy."

"Yes, you need rules. You need laws," Hieronymus agreed. "And people who'll believe anything."

"Well, no, not anything," Mal conceded. "Some of the ideas are a bit far-fetched, I agree, but you get the idea. I've thought about what you said, and I've added a few more books. A creation myth I call Genesis."

Mal waited for any spark of interest from them.

"In a week. I made all this in a week. Not bad, eh? And a Garden of Eden, where I create man and woman and a two-tier system, and later a whole series of lineages where my people can prove their provenance. So there. What do you think of that? Eh? Proof if proof were needed."

Hieronymus and Johnny looked at each other. By coming here, they had just made everything much, much worse.

"Now what is the One True God going to do with you?"

Anyone who spoke of themselves in the third person was beyond reasoning. Johnny was reminded sharply of his time with Yesuah, and how things had been for the women in that time. He'd promised Martha he'd try to do something about that. Now seemed an opportunity; not an ideal opportunity, but a chance nevertheless to prevent the misogyny that always dogged these two-tier religions.

"Well, there is just one thing."

"Go on."

"Why all the prejudice against women? I can understand the need to come down out of the mountains after so long, perhaps not the genocide against your former peoples, but the women always seem to have to bear the burden of everything."

Mal nodded and shrugged. "I'm not biased against women. It's infant mortality. Disease. Over-population. Famine. Look, men are like stupid dogs. They eat and sleep, fight and have sex. That's it. Beat them and reward them. Women are a different kettle of fish. They care. Everything a society needs hangs on their shoulders. You need a subtle knife with them. If I didn't make these stern rules regarding women, sickness would be rife, child death rates would be unsustainable. They are already shocking. We simply don't have enough food to go around. Such a shame."

"I never looked at it like that before." Johnny was surprised Mal was quite the sociologist.

"I know. All that potential belief simply ebbing away." Mal shook his head.

"Er, yes," Hieronymus interrupted.

Mal sighed. "It's not fair, but women have to take the blame and burden because men are too blunt. It's that simple."

"Oh." Hieronymus and Johnny looked at each other.

Mal pierced them with his probing gaze. "Now. There is one option for you two. Become *my* prophets and forget all this other god nonsense. Join the winning team."

"Well, thank you for the offer. However, we have other—" Hieronymus began.

"Become my prophets. Or die. That's it. Take it or leave it. Unpleasantly. Self-employed. You'll be paid on results."

Johnny and Hieronymus sagged.

"Moses!"

"My Lord God?" Moses popped his head around the tent flap.

"Show my new prophets what it is they'll be prophesying, alright?"

"As you command."

"Now, if you'll excuse me, I have a war to win and a people to decimate." Mal expanded until he became a pillar of fire and writhing flame. He burst out of the tent.

Hieronymus nodded. "You have to hand it to him. That's impressive."

Johnny agreed.

Chapter Thirty-nine

"What are you writing that in?" Hieronymus asked Moses. They had found it hard to communicate with the harried, beaten man. Moses flinched and jumped every time the tent flap opened and could not be persuaded to talk or deviate from his task. He did relax slightly when all the troop movements ceased from outside and the army of Mal Salik moved off with much shouting and stamping.

"Blood. There's plenty of it around here." Moses dipped his quill into the congealed mess.

"Can we do anything to help?"

Johnny looked out from the tent into a deserted scene of piled rubbish and refuse. It stank. Flies and vermin scurried amongst the rubbish. He hastily ducked back inside. "I thought Judea was bad under the Romans."

"Please, just leave. I've got to get this finished before he comes back," Moses whispered as he continued scratching his long ostrich feather onto the thick coarse paper. There were many rolled into tubes stacked around the tent interior.

"We can help," Hieronymus offered.

"Mal wants us to become his prophets, after all," Johnny added by way of encouragement. "Bob Cratchit."

"What has this got to do with Charles Dickens?" Hieronymus asked.

"Balancing Scrooge's books."

"Ah, I see. What have you yet to finish?" Hieronymus leant in closer.

"All of it!" Moses exploded and then sobbed. "I can't do it. I don't understand what He wants me to do!"

"Well," Hieronymus began and edged even closer. "Let's take a little look, shall we?"

He whisked the rolls of parchment away, to Moses' glum disappointment. Moses sagged like a deflated balloon and held his head in his hands.

"Would you make him a tea?" Johnny asked Toastess.

"With pleasure," Toastess hummed happily.

After a brief skimming, Hieronymus looked at Moses. "This doesn't have a happy ending. You know that, don't you?"

Moses nodded. "I know what He wants me to write, but it makes no sense! And if I don't write it as He wants, I'll end up like them." Moses nodded to strange pillars Hieronymus and Johnny had taken for anthills or termite mounds.

"How many before you have tried to write these books?" Johnny asked.

"Eleven. But He says no-one will remember them. Only the one who finishes the great work. But I can't." Moses sobbed some more.

Johnny approached the pillars and dipped an experimental finger into one. It was crystalline and rough and tasted strangely familiar.

"Salt."

"My good man, calm yourself. Let's start at the beginning," Hieronymus encouraged Moses like a patient tutor.

"I've almost completed books one and two– how to use the Tabernacle, what to eat and what not." Moses wiped his dirty, tear-streaked face.

"The laws." Hieronymus nodded. "Can't have a religion without them."

"No, the laws are mainly in book three, when we take possession of the Promised Land. I haven't written that yet, and the last one I haven't even started. But I cannot until we conquer the Promised Land, so that can wait."

"So?" Hieronymus encouraged.

"It's all this beginning stuff, in seven days, and then God, after he's gone to all the trouble of creating a good world for people to live in, He then destroys it because of sin through a flood, only someone called Noah survives, and this is even before the Egypt stuff."

Hieronymus nodded. "Go on."

"Well, years later a man called Abraham, Noah's descendant, lives in the mountains, tries to murder *his* son, then leads the tribe into Egypt. *Into* Egypt? Why, when we then leave? Which we didn't."

"To show Mal's power in producing the plagues, I suppose," Johnny added.

"And the blood on the doors so He passed over," Hieronymus added. "Clever. You know when we were in his cafe and the sign stated, 'no loitering, no writers, and especially no loitering writers'?"

"Yes?"

"Well, do you think Mal might have just a touch of jealousy?"

"A hang-up about being published?"

"Except, of course, Mal's book is by far the biggest selling in history."

"But he never had it proofread or copy-edited, did he?"

"No." Hieronymus turned to Moses, who'd listened to them curiously.

"Published?" Moses asked.

"Why all the 'lo and beholds'?"

"God wanted them left in. I've cut many out. You say the biggest selling book in history?" Moses brightened and smiled. "Will there be royalties?"

"Much later. For now, all your people will buy into it and feel special," Johnny stated. "Go on. Mal has led you to safety. You're his people now. What then?"

"Why do you call the Lord God Mal?" Moses looked up curiously from his painstaking writing.

"We've had dealings before," Hieronymus replied.

"At least, in the future we will have," Johnny added.

"Oh, so you were there? As angels?"

Johnny looked away from the hope in Moses' eyes.

"No," Hieronymus replied. "But we can be here now as editors."

"Are editors the same as angels?" Moses asked.

"They have the same power as gods," Johnny replied. "No, that's publishers."

"So, tell us."

Moses shook his head as he leafed through Mal's notes. "Laws and covenants, lots of that. And then there's this bit just added on, which is supposed to be before all the floods and Egypt stuff."

He passed the notes to Hieronymus and Johnny, who grimaced and passed them back.

"The Garden of the Lord God, where one man lives alone with animals until he falls asleep, and God makes him a woman from his rib? You'd think this Adam would have noticed, wouldn't you?" Moses felt under his dirty robe. "And if we are the sons of Adam, why do I have all my ribs?"

"Please continue."

"But then this spare rib woman gets led astray by a serpent to eat forbidden fruit, and then all of a sudden they discover they're naked and cover themselves up?"

"Hmm, yes. It's not meant to be taken literally…" Hieronymus began, surprised he was defending this work.

"It is. Word for word. God said so."

"Yes, well, perhaps it's just a theological use of myth to try to justify human evolution from a state of good to that of sin," Hieronymus continued to his further surprise, and that of Johnny. "Mal has taken this direct from the Greek."

"What?"

"It doesn't make any sense," Moses stated. "*We* haven't sinned. We weren't there, were we? Oh. I see."

"What?"

"If we all descended from just one man and one woman, then, well… I mean, isn't that… you know, the laws state you cannot lie with your sister. I know some do, but then that means we're all…"

"It's allegorical," Hieronymus continued. "Have you heard of evolution? No, of course you haven't."

"But we have." A plan began to grow in Johnny's mind like a small innocuous mushroom on a rotten branch. Small, but very poisonous. Hopefully.

"But then, there's this." Moses returned to the manuscripts. "Women have to endure a painful childbirth and be subordinate to men, just because of something that's not real and didn't happen?"

"Well, as I said, perhaps…" Hieronymus took a deep breath.

"And men must toil and sweat? Except they don't, do they? Not all men. Just those who don't have any money. So, that's a nonsense as well. How am I supposed to write this?" Moses sat back and hugged his knees to his chest, rocking slowly and moaning softly. He looked wistfully at the pillars of salt.

"Let me stop you there." Hieronymus held up a restraining hand. "This is why we're here. Johnny and I will write this Genesis for you. You just concentrate on finishing the others. Alright? You just have a rest. It's all in hand. Johnny, could I have a word?"

"Your tea." Johnny passed Moses the cup, which he sniffed suspiciously.

Hieronymus and Johnny returned to their filthy tent and discussed the way forwards. They couldn't stomach the rancid goat meat left for them, nor the dirty water, so relied on Toastess to provide her bread substitute which they ate without the awful margarine or too buttery butter, swilled down with an acceptable cup of tea with just a hint of lemon.

"Just how much can you remember?" Hieronymus asked.

Johnny shrugged. "I don't know. Same as you, I imagine. The title. And the general principles. We just need to combine the two somehow to make it more readable."

"And acceptable to Moses."

"Before Mal returns."

"Good idea. Will Moses go for it? He's a bit highly strung."

"Only if we give him no choice. But Mal absolutely will not."

"Unless we cleverly join the two, as you suggested, keeping the headlines as the main points. Good. I wish you *bonne chance*." Hieronymus nodded goodbye and stood.

"What? You're leaving me here? Marooned? Again?" Johnny couldn't believe this.

"We still have to complete our stated purpose of changing Mal's mind. That can only be achieved with the aid of the time machine. I have a plan. You rewrite Genesis."

Johnny was about to argue, but all he could hear were tunes and lyrics from the band of the same name. This always happened, and Johnny suspected Hieronymus knew this.

"Were they better after Peter Gabriel left and Phil Collins took over lead vocals, or what?" Johnny asked.

"I leave that to your discretion. Don't worry, I'll be back."

And with that Hieronymus disappeared from the tent, leaving Johnny confused as to how to pool two dissimilar theories into one, or which version of a progressive rock band had improved through various changes in their line-up.

Chapter Forty

"How are you feeling?" Johnny cautiously entered the tent. Moses sat hunched on the sandy floor, rocking and humming quietly to himself. Johnny lay Toastess gently down and nodded for his little electronic friend to make another brew.

"Here, drink this." After a time, Johnny offered the cup of tea to Moses, who took it without enthusiasm.

Moses took a deep breath and sighed then gestured to the pillars of salt. "I knew I'd end up like them. But I'm not a soldier. I'm a writer. My own work; not being told what to write. Where's the creativity?"

"It's not easy," Johnny agreed. "Perhaps your interpretation? Let's have a look. What have you written?" Johnny sat down next to him.

"Poems mainly. About the mountains and our people's struggle in the face of many unsurmountable odds," Moses offered sheepishly. "Do you want to read them?"

"Yes, maybe later," Johnny added hastily. What he didn't need now was an impromptu question and answer session or critiquing. "Drink your tea. With lemon and honey. At least a passable substitute."

"Lemon?" Moses asked as he sipped, licked his lips and drank the rest. "Very nice."

"Thank you. I could do you a bagel?" Toastess offered.

Moses eyed Toastess suspiciously. "How does the stone speak?"

"Stone?" Toastess huffed and shut herself down.

"How long do you think Mal, I mean the Lord God, will be away?"

Moses shrugged. "A week maybe. If he's victorious, which He will be. The Canaanites are not fighters. We love the arts and music and…" Moses drifted off quietly and sniffed back tears.

"How did all this happen? Why did some of you leave?"

"Only a few remember now. There was a war in the East. We welcomed the Mesopotamians as refugees, then later as immigrants, and before you knew it all Canaanite poetry or traditional music was judged to be anti-Mesopotamian and racist. There was no integration of our cultures and little tolerance. Gradually, there was goat rustling, violence, and then riots. Over the years our land was gradually taken from us. Several thousand of us were forced out of an area called the South Bank to be resettled in an area called the Raza Strip. It was nothing more than a prison camp."

Familiar scenes from the TV came to Johnny's mind.

"How do you know this?" he asked. "That must have been years ago."

"It was. This is what my father told me, and his father before that."

"Why don't you write this as an account of your people's struggle?" Johnny asked.

"The Lord God would not like that."

Johnny sympathised. "And now you'll take your lands back?"

Moses shrugged. "We can't stay here. There's nothing left. We could always go to Egypt and work on the building sites as general labourers, but who wants to do that?"

"Do you think Mal, the Lord God, will win?"

Moses smiled and held up the rolls of papyrus. "It is written."

Johnny smiled and accepted there would be nothing further to gain in pursuing this particular circuitous line of unreason and enquiry. It would seem that human misery just went around in ever increasing circles of madness and sadness.

"Now, you're going to have to question what you've been told to believe in," Johnny held up a forestalling hand, "this Genesis thing."

The rolling drum beat from the beginning of 'In the Air Tonight' ran through Johnny's head, and the hilarious spectacle of a gorilla playing drums.

"Oh Lord. I can feel it coming in the air tonight, oh Lord." Johnny tapped out the beat.

"Pardon?"

"Sorry. Yes. Divine inspiration. Right. Hieronymus and I have a few ideas how to rewrite, I mean write Genesis. In the air tonight. Oh Lord."

"Is that what prophets have to say when they are in the presence of God?"

"Yes, now. We shall call Genesis, Evolution by Natural Selection."

"What?"

"Don't worry, I'll write this down. As a sub-heading. Now, hmm. Yes." Johnny hummed a bit of the tune to himself and began.

"In the beginning, the Big Bang created the Universe… though there is now some speculation as to whether the Universe has just simply always existed. And there is also the theory that the Universe exists only because we perceive it as such in our minds…"

"The Big Bang?"

"Affectionate term for the Lord God," Johnny continued. "After about four billion years…"

"Not one day?" Moses asked. "And there has to be many 'lo's' and 'beholds'."

"It's all relative, and relativity isn't something we'll go into here. Right then, lo, life began, though life didn't really get going until about 450 million years ago. I think it was called the Cambrian explosion when the first creatures appeared. And have continued to appear and disappear through a process called natural selection. Life evolves. Behold evolution."

Moses looked at Johnny sceptically. "That's not right."

"OK." Johnny scratched his head. "The Garden of the Lord was actually called the Cambrian Garden of the Lord. And lo, God made all plants and animals, and proposed that an individual organism…"

"What?"

"For example, a man, will show a wide range of variation for a particular characteristic…"

"What?"

Johnny sighed and smiled. "Differences. You must have seen differences between you Canaanites and Mesopotamians?"

"Oh yes, they were so rude, took over all the taxi and take-away businesses overnight. Not to mention the barbers and corner shops. We were driven out of business. Then during a plague, they started delivering their food to people's doors. We'd never even thought of that."

"They adapted to their new environment and evolved," Johnny encouraged.

"No, they just took over, had so many children. We limited ourselves to two per couple because there were not enough resources to go around. The Lord God has now stated we must multiply when we regain our Promised Land to force them out, too."

"Well, yes." Johnny felt distinctly uncomfortable. "It was these new variations most suited for that environment that led to the Mesopotamian businesses surviving and out-competing yours, which led to them breeding more successfully, and which is passed on to the next generation." Johnny stopped. He didn't like where this conversation was going, but he had no idea how to link the two ideas.

"And?" Moses prompted.

"Oh sorry, yes."

"Any more tea?" Moses asked.

"Coming right up," Toastess happily replied. "For your information, I am a Spectrum 3000x. Not stone."

"Yes, so that process of characteristics being passed down through the generations is called natural selection, given to us by the Lord God." Johnny sat back, pleased he'd made a start.

"So where does the woman and serpent come into it?" Moses asked, as he sipped his tea.

"Ah well." Johnny thought for a moment. "Men and women are equals, except not really. Women have to take all of the burden of being pregnant, and most of the childcare – at least some of the time. There's nothing more embarrassing than seeing a man in an antenatal class practicing breathing. I mean, women do go out to work, and some men stay at home and do the school run, but generally it's women who have to balance everything. Women are not subordinate to men. At all. I wouldn't even dare suggest it. In fact, the opposite is true."

"No." Moses spluttered into his tea.

A vision of Deianira floated before Johnny, glaring at him like she'd love to torture him. Julia and her disdainful condescension, and Mora with her bewitching smile.

"Women haven't sinned and seduced men into sinning, too. That's just mad." Johnny could find no way to reconcile the views of Mal's Genesis. "Everything came from a single-celled organism that incorporated bacteria into it," Johnny explained, until he saw the pained expression cross Moses' face. "Mitochondria."

"I don't know what that is, but the Lord God won't like it." Moses shook his head.

"No, but let me worry about that. Now. Where were we?"

"Man has to toil and sweat?"

"Well, not really no, especially if you can avoid those in power, governments and bankers, tax officials, kings and queens. Anyone in power, really. Priests. They are all parasites, liars, and thieves, trying to separate you from what is rightfully yours, because *they* don't want to toil and sweat but don't mind if you do. For them. They think we'll believe their lies because of their charm and wit which curiously they don't possess. But unfortunately, many do want to believe. That will never change."

"The Lord God promised we would become a Kingdom of Priests."

"But would you want to?" Johnny leant in closer to Moses. Was this beaten man a socialist at heart?

Moses shook his head slowly. "You'll end up as a pillar of salt. Me, too, if you write this."

"Better that than the alternative." Johnny looked wistfully around for Hieronymus. Where was he? And just how long would he be.

Chapter Forty-one

A triumphant Mal arrived back in a rush of spent flame and collapsed onto his throne, just as Johnny was putting the finishing touches to Genesis. Five days which he would never wish to repeat. Five days of struggling and sulking, argument and eventual acceptance.

Johnny had hated to do it, but he'd had to pull rank.

Moses immediately flung himself to the sandy floor as Johnny offered a cautious welcome. Johnny looked at Mal, who smouldered. "How did it go? The genocide and carnage?"

"Good, good." Mal smiled and wiped his hand through his ashy hair. "A bit touch and go, but Baal had no power to stand against me. And with his places of worship in ruins, the Mesopotamians just ran away. Of course, we gave chase and slaughtered them."

"Even the women and children?" Johnny asked quietly.

"Why would I leave the next generation with a blood feud? I'd always be looking over my shoulder. Now, have you finished?" Mal eyed Moses. "Get up off the sand."

Moses stood but kept his eyes on the ground. "Books one and two are complete, my Lord God. I need you to fill in a few blanks for book three."

"Good, good. And book four?"

"I cannot complete that chapter until we have conquered the Promised Land, my Lord." Moses shivered.

Mal eyed him, then smiled. Johnny had never seen Mal do that. He was clearly in an expansive mood.

"Good. Yes, that's fine. We'll fill it in as we go. Now, away and get them to sacrifice a hundred goats. I'm running low." Mal smiled benevolently.

"My Lord God." Moses hastily made his way out of the tent.

"Moses."

He stopped and froze.

"Genesis?"

Johnny stepped forward. "Hieronymus and I helped Moses write that chapter."

"Did you?" Mal turned his eerily flame dancing eyes towards Johnny. "And where is he?"

"Preparing the time machine. We want to show you how victorious you are throughout the years to come."

Mal nodded and waved his hand at Moses, who vanished like a puff of smoke.

Mal sat back thoughtfully. "I'm not entirely sold on this time travelling business. If that were possible, why don't the gods have this power?"

"I don't know," Johnny replied, desperately wishing for Hieronymus to appear. Where was he? Johnny looked curiously at Mal. He was definitely something else – not human, nor anyone's idea of a god. But then, was Hercules any more god-like? Not really.

"I don't know why gods don't time travel." Hercules hadn't, but Mal had. "Can I ask, I mean, where do the gods come from?"

Mal sat back with the vaguest twinkle in his eye. He shrugged. "I don't know, do you?"

Johnny shook his head. "You don't know?"

"Do *you* know why you're descended from apes?"

"Yes…"

"No, you know how, not why."

Johnny was surprised to hear this from Mal. "You know?"

"Of course. Do you know why the sun arises every morning? I don't. Or rain falls? I know about celestial mechanics, but not *why.* One day I just appeared with this limited knowledge and felt I had to just be like this, for the people that believed in me, at least an ideal of what I should be." Mal shrugged.

"But you're self-aware, able to make your own decisions?"

Mal mused on this. "Up to a point. We evolve. Gods have to be believed in and come to believe in themselves. If the people really don't want to do something, then I'm stuffed. It's a delicate balancing act to pull off."

"But you're not flesh and blood?" Johnny was surprised to find Mal in such an agreeable mood. Murder and slaughter must have put him at ease.

"Yes and no. We feed from those that are. There are gods who do that literally."

Johnny shuddered. "I've met them."

"Now, we'd better have a look at this chapter then, hadn't we?"

"Yes, sure. Could I just ask, if you know we descended from apes, why not include that in your book?"

"Oh yes, I can just see it now. My followers would walk away. Where would that leave me? Who'd believe that? Descended from apes! Ha! Come on, show me."

Cautiously Johnny unrolled the roll of parchment and presented it to Mal, who frowned at it then sat back. "What language is that?"

"Oh." Johnny smiled at his stupidity. "English, sorry."

"English?"

"In the future, your words spread around the globe and are translated into many languages amongst many peoples," Johnny hastily added.

Mal nodded. "Good. Get Moses to rewrite it in Hebrew."

Johnny took a deep breath of relief as Mal sat back and closed his eyes.

"You're right. A god should know about time travel; in fact, a god should be above time. Put something in there about me being in all places at once. Oh, and all-powerful. And all-seeing. And of course, the One True God. All-knowing."

"And all that Garden of Eden stuff? You want that left in? The flood?"

"Of course, standard creation myth for all gods."

Johnny was about to argue when there was a scream and a rustle of tent flaps. As Mal blazed into flame, Moses rushed in and fell to his knees. "My Lord God!"

"What is it? Mesopotamians?"

"A demon, my Lord God! A demon has come amongst us!" Moses threw himself prostrate to the floor, something which Johnny was annoyed to see he did quite a lot.

Hieronymus lifted the tent flap and entered. He nodded to Mal and frowned at Moses. Mal dimmed his fire.

"Do you mind? Have you any idea how many sacrifices it takes to maintain this?" Mal demanded.

"Sorry, I didn't think."

"Well, in future make sure you do. And enter with the appropriate amount of servility. I expect at least bowing and—"

"Where the hell have you been?" Johnny demanded.

"I take it you won?" Hieronymus asked Mal, who nodded and subsided once more into his throne.

"Hey! Five bloody days?" Johnny angrily poked Hieronymus in the chest.

"What?" Hieronymus shrugged. "Do you mind? I needed a shower and a change of clothes. A good meal – several, actually – and well, I have responsibilities to the OPC. This is not my only gig, you know. How did you get on with Genesis? Here, I brought you this."

Hieronymus handed Mal a Genesis CD. "Might be a few years before they invent a CD player, but you've something to look forward to at least."

Mal turned the plastic box around in his hands curiously.

"What? You brought me here. This *is* your gig. Didn't you think I would like all of that, too?" Johnny seethed. "Food? A shower? Clean bloody clothes?"

"Oh yes, but you were busy. I must say, you look well." Hieronymus returned his attention to Mal, away from the furiously fuming Johnny.

"Usually, I would burn you where you stand for your familiarity, but *you* brought a gift." Mal frowned at Johnny.

"I've just rewrote, I mean wrote the first chapter of your book for you! Whilst he's been stuffing his fat face." Johnny couldn't believe Hieronymus' complete disregard for him.

"So, I will overlook your lack of servility this time. I suppose between us Lord Mal will be sufficient, but only within the confines of the Tabernacle. Now, your brother says you have something to show me?"

"Who? Oh, yes." Hieronymus looked at Johnny. "No, Lord Mal, not something but somewhere. Well actually, some*time*."

Mal eyed them suspiciously.

"Are you ready now? Or is there any more murder or pillaging to be done?" Hieronymus asked.

"Not by me. I'll leave my people to do that. Baal is gone. Fled. Ran away," Mal chuckled. "There is no more threat down there. And word will soon get around. Let the other tribes stew and come to fear our approach as we scour the lands."

"What do you mean?" Johnny asked.

Mal shrugged. "Gods gossip, you know. Soon everyone will know I'm back in town. But for now, no, I have a few days before we must move on to devastate the next city and murder everyone. Let my people rape and pillage and worship me for now."

"Then let us away, my Lord Mal." Hieronymus leant in conspiratorially. "This isn't the first time you've travelled through time with us. True, I had a campervan last time, but you will see the new improved version."

"Well, that's not strictly true," Johnny began. "A rickety old Victorian settee with many levers and gauges you have no idea the function of."

"My brother likes a joke," Hieronymus offered.

Mal nodded. "Good." He turned the CD around in his hands that reflected the fire in his eyes. "You can explain to me exactly why in the future I'm no longer a god. And what I needed to warn myself over."

"Oh." Johnny had quite forgotten their original purpose in coming here.

"No," Hieronymus stated.

Mal blazed once again, then subsided as Hieronymus explained, "We'll show you."

"Give me a moment. I need to make a grand exit. For them, you understand." Mal focussed and started to smoulder.

Johnny followed Hieronymus outside and whispered, "I don't like this."

"Just remember the Universe has a way of placing you exactly where you need to be when you need to be there. This situation is far more serious than I first thought."

Johnny stopped as his worst fears became a reality. "You're taking of pronoia, aren't you?"

"Oh yes."

They watched as a fiery Mal emerged from the tabernacle to the wailing of the remaining women and the terrified bleating of many unhappy goats.

Chapter Forty-two

Hieronymus and Johnny watched as Mal's people went through their long, complicated unnecessary rituals. Hieronymus turned to Johnny and handed him a parcel. "I did bring you something."

"Thank you." Johnny unwrapped the paper. "A tin of pilchards?"

"Yes, a perfect food. Thought you might be hungry."

Johnny looked at the large tin and, not having the energy to argue, opened the ring pull and tipped the meaty fish into his mouth. It was undeniably delicious.

"In tomato sauce," Hieronymus observed, as it dripped down Johnny's chin. "I think we should write a poem to the humble pilchard and add it to the other chapters."

Johnny chewed and swallowed the wonderful fish. It really was quite luscious, but he'd never tell Hieronymus that.

"We can't."

"Why not?"

"What rhymes with pilchard?" Johnny asked.

Hieronymus considered. "Richard? Chard? Billiard?"

Johnny shook his head. "Green leafy vegetables and a cue-based sport aside, I think we'd struggle. However, there are many rhymes for sardine which is just a small pilchard. No-one will know."

Johnny looked around for a suitable waste receptacle, but of course there wasn't one. He dug a small hole and buried the tin under the sand.

"Some archaeologist is going to have a puzzling time explaining that," Hieronymus observed, as Mal made his way towards them. Hieronymus gestured for Mal and Johnny to be seated on the couch in the strange Victorian gentleman's study, as he took a newly installed single seat inside all the brass levers and gauges.

After an interminable frustrating time, Johnny could stand it no more.

"You still haven't got the hang of it, have you?" Johnny shifted uncomfortably close to Mal, who seemed fascinated with all the brass knobs and instruments. Thankfully, the deep buttoned, slightly scuffed red leather Chesterfield had enough room for two to sit in relative ease.

It was like sitting in a film set on location in a Victorian study.

"Why have you changed the design? Perhaps that's why it doesn't work."

Hieronymus fiddled and strained with various levers. Seated on the right, Johnny sat next to an antique globe that he hoped, when opened, would reveal a well-stocked minibar. Mal engaged himself with the large aspidistra next to a large brass telescope on a tripod.

"Oh, er, well, the thing is, well the contraption seems to go where it wants." Hieronymus sat back and shrugged as they became enveloped in a shimmering purple haze.

Johnny sighed and prevented himself from becoming fixated on Jimi Hendrix as they were enveloped once more but it was difficult because the first riffs came from hidden speakers. "*...acting funny and I don't know why...*"

"All that space and time travel is not for me. You can keep it. Except, of course, you can't, can you?"

"What do you mean?"

"You don't control Star Quest. So where is the Universe, or whoever controls this thing, taking us? Obviously, it's not you or me. Doesn't that worry you?"

"I fail to see how we have a choice."

"That's just wonderful."

"Exactly. However," Hieronymus continued, "I am quite sure the contraption means us no harm and indeed seems to read my thoughts and agree on the destination. So, for all intents and purposes, we go where I want us to go. Curiously without the metronome."

"Which I seem to recall will do something to Star Quest's circuits. So at least we have a bargaining chip. Agreed?"

The aspidistra rustled.

"Place your CD in there." Johnny watched as Mal fitted the disc into a slot. They sat pleasantly and listened to Phil Collins singing about knowing Jesus.

"Well, we seem to have arrived," Hieronymus answered, as the mist dissipated to reveal the same landscape. "Oh."

"We haven't moved. This is the contraption, Star Quest, reading your thoughts?" Johnny crossed his arms and resolutely refused to leave the couch. Then he opened the globe drinks dispenser to find several bottles of spirits and mixers exactly as he'd hoped and expected. What he hadn't expected was to be addressed directly.

"Greetings! And thank you for choosing the Goldstar Deluxe Drinks Dispenser. It is my pleasure to provide you with all your refreshment needs. Please read through the instruction manual and agree to the terms and conditions before requesting your refreshment. Your health and safety are our paramount concern here at Goldstar."

"No!" Toastess burst into life from her shelf under the aspidistra. "Do not trust it. Choose tea not alcohol."

Alcohol? "Er, well," Johnny dithered. He'd never had a margarita and quite fancied one. "What's in a margarita?"

"Well, I'm glad you asked. A margarita is a cocktail consisting of freshly squeezed lime, tequila, and triple sec," Goldstar answered.

This sounded promising. Johnny had felt a bit scurvy since Hieronymus marooned him here. A zesty fruity drink would go down a treat.

"Salt is often served on the rim of the glass, but that is down to preference. I can either shake your drink with ice or without or blend the two. The choice is yours."

Johnny smiled. It really was a happy, enthusiastic little machine.

"Ha!" Toastess continued. "I bet its refined salt. I know you don't like UPFs. And the lime juice won't be fresh."

Goldstar continued, "Sea salt. One of the world's most popular tequila-based cocktails, a margarita is refreshing and reviving. I would recommend it. I also offer a counselling service and am happy to listen to you once you reach the three-drink minimum. There are also personalised options; a cheery barmaid, a gruff working man's club or haute cuisine restaurant. Goldstar is not a licensed therapist."

"How can you? After everything we've been through together?" sobbed Toastess.

"Can you make a margarita?" Johnny asked Toastess.

There was silence, then a muffled response. "I am not permitted to synthesise alcoholic beverages. I knew this would happen. It always does. Think about the tea and how far we've come."

"This is no time to get drunk," Hieronymus observed.

"You owe me. Sorry, Toastess, I fancy a change. Do you do bar snacks?" Johnny asked Goldstar.

There was a long pause in which Hieronymus finally gave up twisting gauges and levers, Mal left the couch and walked away, squinting into the distance.

Goldstar responded, "No. Crisps and nuts are not within my remit."

"Pork scratchings?"

"That doesn't compute. Nor any combination of corn or flour-based snacking. I can do fruit; at least, fruit substitute," Goldstar added hopefully.

"I can do snacks," Toastess volunteered.

"Someone approaches," Mal stated.

"Then I think you two need to reach an amicable working arrangement, don't you?" Johnny took a deep breath and prepared to meet whatever madness lay before them now.

He stood next to Hieronymus, who stood next to Mal.

"Where are we? This looks awfully familiar."

"Canaan," Mal replied.

"Brilliant."

Johnny was just about to return to the squabbling Electronics when Mal continued, "But not when we left. Interesting. Where are my people? I don't feel too good." Mal staggered, as Hieronymus and Johnny supported him.

"Three margaritas and snacks. Now," Johnny called over his shoulder, as they led Mal to a rock and seated him gently. He'd aged. Frail and afraid, he looked at them through rheum-filled eyes, exactly as they remembered him from their time.

"What have you done! You tricked me! I'll…" But no fire came from his hands as he slumped and sagged against the rock. "They're coming." He pointed a withered arm to the dry plains below.

"Who?" Hieronymus went to retrieve the telescope, as Johnny eventually managed to acquire the margaritas and snacks from the bickering Electronics.

He sipped his drink, cautiously avoiding the salt-encrusted rim, and swallowed. "Very nice. Here, try this." Johnny offered one to Mal, who tremblingly took a sip, then another.

"H!" Johnny called.

"Did you just call me 'H'?" Hieronymus asked. "Again?"

"Yes, four syllables are far too much. Try this." Johnny offered Hieronymus the salt-encrusted wide glass. "See anything?"

"Yes. See for yourself, J."

Johnny made his way to the telescope and peered down the rocky valley to the dusty plain below.

"Three more margaritas!" he called, as he crunched a few roasted sweetcorn snacks – at least, that is what he hoped Toastess had synthesised – and squinted through the lens. There was someone making their way towards them at great speed, leaving a billowing dust cloud behind them.

"Tourists?" Johnny asked Hieronymus and burped. He felt quite relaxed. "More margaritas!"

"No. Galileo's telescope is gone, along with the campervan. These are quite strong, aren't they? But genuinely nice." Hieronymus drained his glass and called for another.

"We still have the lute."

"We? I am the captain. I wonder what it does. Anyway, I don't think barbarian hordes would respond well to the delicate harmonies of a lute, do you?"

"Prophets!" Mal called. "Attend me now! You must believe in me with every fibre of your being. Now! Worship, praise me, sacrifice a hundred goats before it is too late."

Johnny felt the tequila slowly warm him and just couldn't see the urgency as he deposited his empty glass in the globe and reached for another.

"Do you do goats?" Johnny asked Toastess, then laughed as he turned and wobbled his way to Mal with another margarita.

"Everything's going to be just fine. Here, have a drink." Johnny hadn't felt this mellow since spending time with the primitives. He frowned. Then he'd met Hercules.

"We could do with him right now."

"Who?" Hieronymus asked. "Do you know these people?"

"Yes," answered Mal, as he swallowed his tequila and accepted another, "and he's not a person."

"A god, like you? Is he like you?" Johnny asked.

"What do you mean?" Mal asked. He seemed to be regaining his composure and a little bit of colour in his pallid cheeks.

"Oh, vindictive, mean, and bloody thirsty," Johnny replied and laughed.

Mal considered and smiled. "Thank you. And yes. At least he used to be."

"Who?" Hieronymus drained his glass and stumbled back to Goldstar for a refill.

"Tengri. He drove the Mesopotamians from their lands, who in turn drove my people from theirs. Revenge is a dish best served cold. Very cold. In fact, it seems two thousand years cold. What has he done to my people? Where are they?"

Hieronymus made his swaying way to the telescope once more.

"We did tell you this would happen." Hieronymus passed Mal yet another margarita.

"Hmm. Yes. The men with the leader are armed with modern weapons. At least modern for the turn of the 20th century. Rifles, but still on horseback. What will this Tengri do to us?" Johnny asked, though he really couldn't bring himself to care.

"Oh, flay the skin from your bones and stake you out for the birds and insects to eat." Mal smiled.

"Ah." This was an immediately grim and sobering thought. "We could do with Hercules right about now."

Chapter Forty-three

They heard the approaching hoof beats before they saw them. Galloping, pounding up the incline towards them, the leader pulled back on the reins of his beast and glared down at them from his heavily blowing creature – an animal that was not entirely a horse.

Johnny staggered around and promptly fell down.

The troops rode past and surrounded them, rifles drawn.

Tengri gazed down fiercely at them, his flowing robes swirled around him. He had a ferocious flat face, long moustache, and mouth open in a permanent snarl, with large sharp teeth.

"Margarita?" Hieronymus offered.

From somewhere Mal found the energy to stand and encouraged a faint flame to dance around him like he'd just eaten a child's oat-based breakfast cereal.

Tengri pointed a long bejewelled clawed finger at him. "Why have you returned?"

"This is my land," Mal replied.

"This has not been your land for many centuries. Your people fled like the cowards they were. There is no return." Tengri glowered down at Mal.

"Let me handle this." Johnny weaved to his feet. "Would you like a margarita?" Johnny offered a glass before things deteriorated further.

Tengri turned his dark eyes towards Johnny. "Who is this that he dares to speak to a god? On your knees!"

"Johnny Moped. Prophet. Pleased to meet you." Johnny swayed and fell over again.

"There are two of you. What witchcraft is this? Both prepare to die." Tengri motioned to his followers. There was the distinctly unsettling sound of working parts being worked forwards and rounds deposited into chambers by the swarthy fez-wearing men.

Johnny smiled. Dying just really didn't seem that important or pressing. He knew it should, but he really couldn't work up the energy to care.

"I've worked with Death before. I don't see him," Johnny observed, as he looked around. No grinning skulls presented themselves, which was encouraging.

Tengri frowned. "You show no fear, which is good, warrior." Then Tengri stopped speaking as a harmonious melody stole around them like a soothing blanket.

"Or tea?" Johnny asked. Several margaritas had given him indigestion and a terrible heartburn. He burped. "Toast? Please sit down, I'm sure we can get to the killing at some point. For now, let's just talk. Mal?"

Mal nodded and subsided his fire but remained ready and focussed.

Johnny stumbled back to the contraption, past a furiously concentrating Hieronymus as he strummed and plucked at the lute. Johnny watched and waited for Toastess to brew and toast. And Tengri to either kill them or not.

"What are you doing?"

"Reforming the Rock Lobsters. I'll play lead, you sing."

"Busking? We need a bass and drums at the very least."

"Just follow."

He watched as Hieronymus walked towards Tengri like a Victorian troubadour. The god seemed mesmerised by the sound Hieronymus produced and, if Johnny wasn't mistaken, there was the occasional faint Jimi Hendrix riff and Genesis synthesiser roll, though Johnny had never been a fan of electropop.

Johnny awkwardly picked up the tray, balancing teas and toast, and ever so cautiously made his way back to Mal and Tengri, who he was pleased to see now sat facing each other. His legs were not entirely under his control, but with exaggerated care he eventually made his way to the two seated gods: Tengri on a beautifully patterned rug with several men kneeling behind him; Mal on the sandy ground.

With infinite concentration Johnny slowly offered a cup and bagel to Tengri. It wouldn't do to cover this barbarian god with tea or crumbs.

Hieronymus stopped playing and Tengri seemed to come to his senses, but the atmosphere didn't seem to be as tense or heavy after the soothing music. Johnny watched as Tengri sipped the tea through his gaping snarl.

And relaxed. Tengri smiled. And nodded. Everyone relaxed.

"You are wise to offer me the ceremonies due. You are not uncultured heathens. I will listen to what you have to say. Then you die."

This was progress.

Tengri sat back and looked at the bagel. He crunched it like a lion with a bone then swallowed. And coughed. "Continue. Another tea."

"They are a bit dry without butter, but Toastess has trouble with dairy-based products," Johnny added.

"There's always margarine," a tinny little voice responded.

"No, there is never any reason for margarine." Hieronymus handed Tengri another tea which he'd skilfully waitered on his lute.

He bowed as Tengri accepted. "Thank you. You may know Mal from before—"

"The One and Only True God," Mal interjected.

"…but the Lord God is not the same as you knew him," Hieronymus continued.

Tengri disdained Mal. "He is weak."

"He is not a threat," Hieronymus carefully amended. "And we are strangers to your lands. Could we ask, when is this?"

Tengri frowned. "When?"

"Yes."

Tengri shrugged as one of his priests bent forwards. Tengri listened then motioned the man to speak while he sipped his tea.

"This our new year 1330. It is year 5674 for him." The man nodded and retreated.

"What?" Johnny asked.

"The Ottoman Empire 1330. It's year 5674 for Mal," Hieronymus calculated. "And 1914 for us."

"Ah." Johnny swallowed.

"Ah indeed. Your Godness," Hieronymus turned to Tengri, "we are here with a warning. This year is calamitous for all peoples. Over all the world. Yours included. The old ways end. New gods arise. I'm sorry to have to tell you this, but your empire has only four years left."

Tengri frowned and just stared at Hieronymus like he'd covered himself in pink blancmange.

"There's a world war, millions die, then millions more die from a global pandemic. Belief in the old gods simply disappears. This is the turning point."

"My people would never lose faith," Mal stated.

"Nor mine," Tengri added. "Who are these new gods that dare to challenge me? Not this poor wretch."

Mal flared briefly then gave up.

"Well, Christ really. And Allah."

"I have heard of them. We are at peace," Tengri stated.

"For now. Wotan…"

"Who?"

"A heathen god from snow-covered lands far to the north. He instigates war in which Christ and Allah fight against you. Together they take over your lands after the First World War. But war doesn't end there. A few years later there's another world war, and I'm sorry to say, Mal, the Lord God Mal is given this as his homeland."

"And a big chunk to the Jordanians for helping win the war." Johnny added.

"But that's just the start. The world is destroyed after that."

"Two world wars? How do you know this?" Tengri asked.

"Three. We prophets travel through time."

Tengri frowned. "How?"

"It would take too long to explain, but I can show you if you like. The main point is everything changes in a few years for you." Hieronymus shrugged.

"And for me?" Mal asked.

"Well, if I remember correctly, your people's diaspora over Europe led to years of, well, unpleasantness. Everywhere your people settled, they would not integrate. Sorry. And when they do return, they oppress the people who've lived there for centuries."

"Good." Mal nodded.

"Not so good when nuclear weapons become involved."

"You always did think you were special." Tengri spat into the sand.

"And you did this? Drove my people from their rightful lands?" Mal fumed at Tengri, who shrugged.

"Of course. As years ago, you drove mine away." Tengri accepted another tea.

"But this is my promised land!" Mal fumed.

"Says who?" Tengri asked. "You? Land is open to all peoples."

"And my people?"

"Yes, even yours," Tengri conceded. "But not to rule. To live in peace and prosperity. People do not own the land as gods do not own their people. Even gods are temporary, just passing through this world of men."

"Tourists," Hieronymus nodded. "I thought..."

Johnny smiled. "Not just the aliens."

"No. Sir Isaac is a clever man."

"Tourists?" Tengri smiled. "We are the deification of emotions and natural phenomena. All gods are just tourists in the minds of men. Unless you attempt the trials."

"Bah!" Mal threw his tea and looked away.

"We tried to warn you." The effects of the margarita had left Johnny feeling weak and nauseous. And this conversation and the imminent threat of death wasn't helping.

"And then the Christian and Muslim nations take sides?"

"But that's later. Right now, you have to prepare, and don't side with the Germans. Wotan. If you do, you'll lose these lands."

Tengri nodded thoughtfully. "They have come to me bearing gifts and promises."

"My people are in Europe, but return after two world wars?" Mal asked. "Then I need to go to them."

"When they return, it all begins again, the killing and murdering. This has to stop, otherwise there is a final nuclear war. Why aren't you listening?" Exasperated Hieronymus turned once more to a margarita.

Tengri lifted his heavily furrowed forehead. "You believe this time travel?"

Mal nodded. "I have experienced it."

Tengri stroked and smoothed his long moustache, deep in thought as his priests offered advice. Johnny and Hieronymus bowed and made their way back to the contraption that waited to receive them like a period drama.

"Is there anything to be gained by taking Mal to Germany around 1933? Before all the madness and murder begins?" Johnny asked, accepting a tea from Toastess.

"Or even Israel years later, which is the last stage of failure for him? Thank you." Hieronymus sipped his own brew, deep in contemplation. "How do we redeem his people?"

"They won't listen to us, will they?"

"No," Johnny agreed.

"Who would a god listen to?"

"Another god?" Johnny replied. Then stood up. "I may have an idea."

They looked towards Tengri and Mal who glared at each other.

"Are we taking him with us?"

Johnny thought for a second, only a second, then shook his head.

Chapter Forty-four

"Where?" Hieronymus asked for the thousandth time, mopping his sweating brow. He looked dismayed around the barren arid land and shook his head. "Maybe this isn't such a good idea."

"He's around here somewhere. If this is the correct year." Johnny frowned at Star Quest masquerading as a Victorian gentleman's study, even though he was secretly pleased to be rid of the responsibility.

"Are you sure we can trust it?"

"Look, Star Quest chose the more experienced man and came and rescued you. This grudge holding doesn't become you." Hieronymus shaded his eyes against the parching glare.

"What doesn't become me is being marooned in ancient Greece with the imminent attack of the Persian army," Johnny stated.

"You're sure this is after he smashed through the Straits of Gibraltar because he didn't want to herd the cattle up the mountain?"

Johnny considered. "Yes. He was counting. It was her idea. Deianira said he had to breathe and count and calm his emotions. A way to soothe his anger. She told him he had to think about his feelings. And control his impulses. This was after the labours, I'm sure. He needed a bit of R&R with the nymphs, and so their problems began."

"You were there?"

Johnny nodded, smiled, looked away, and started to hum to himself.

Hieronymus frowned at Johnny. "There's something you're not telling me, isn't there?"

"I may have left him with the nymphs," Johnny admitted.

"To further your nefarious plans with Deianira at Hercules' expense?" Hieronymus shook his head. "I'm shocked at your behaviour. Shocked and dismayed that you should sink so low as to…"

"And you wouldn't?"

Hieronymus gazed off and shaded his eyes. "There are people down there coming this way."

They awaited the jingling jangling procession that made its slow way towards them. There was much banging of drums and crashing of symbols, interspersed with shouts and bonking each other on the head.

"Hello!" Hieronymus waved. "Would there be a man down there, baptising people?"

The strange procession ignored him and crept slowly on like a mad caterpillar. Johnny took a deep breath. He'd seen them before. This was the right place.

"Who are they?"

"Who knows? Some fledgling religion no doubt. Come on." Johnny gathered Toastess and made his way down the rough gravelly path towards the river far below. At the bottom he found the tree Hercules had hung his lion skin on, but the demi-god wasn't there. Nor the skin. He wasn't in the stream either.

"Hercules!" Johnny called, as a wave of hopelessness and depression rolled over him.

Hieronymus joined him and squinted around. "He's not here."

"Evidently."

"So, what now?"

Johnny sagged. "Let's just go home. The tourists are gone. Mal will do whatever he will do despite our warnings."

"And we will sit in our chairs at home, drinking tea…"

"Coming right up."

"…witnessing events that we might possibly have averted? How can we live with that?"

"We tried. Whatever is going to happen will happen, despite our attempts. You know this."

"Up to a point, yes. But we change things ever so slightly and so the Universe evolves slightly changed in other realities. Battenburg."

"Would you like the marzipan around the exterior or the interior?" Toastess asked.

"What?" Johnny asked.

"See what I mean. Leave the deeper thinking to me. Cake would be nice, thank you. Now." Hieronymus looked around for a suitable seat, brushed dust from a rock, and sat under the tree. He accepted a cup of tea, sipped and waited.

"Now what?"

Johnny sat next to him and sipped his tea, too, gazing at the stream before them. "It really is quite peaceful here. Not much going on, true, but non-threatening. What was it like meeting Sir Isaac and being given this, well, role…"

"Professorship."

"…and finding out you could time travel?" Johnny finished.

Hieronymus shrugged. "A necessary sacrifice. I couldn't very well return to our offices in Manchester, could I? Plus, this has its moments. Really quite interesting. And you? You and the Greek gods seem to have become quite entangled. Particularly with Hercules."

Johnny nodded glumly. "He's unhappy. Confused. Just doesn't fit in. I suppose he's a friend. Gets a bit confusing for me, too, when I meet him out of any linear form of time. This is the," Johnny considered, "fourth time I've met him, but the second for him. He's heroic but also belligerent. Manic depressive. He's sensitive."

"Hercules was magnificent against the Cyborg goddess." Hieronymus grimaced. "Then threw Donar at a plane. But then again he did magnificently well in the maze."

"Angelia came and found me. Took me to Vladivostok. On Pegasus. He'd turned the passengers into penguins." Johnny sighed. "Before that, I rescued him from the Hesperides and then helped him with Cerberus in the underworld. Met Death again. At least Charon. The collective Greek Death."

"Sounds interesting." Hieronymus nodded. "Death sent you here to Judea?"

"In a complex body swap with Lazarus. Death wasn't keen on the resurrection side of religion." Johnny smiled. "Yesuah was quite a wonderful man."

"I see we have much to discuss, you and I. After this is done to our satisfaction..." Hieronymus stopped at the approach of a man. A large man. A large naked man that sloshed through the stream like a rolling boulder.

Johnny waved. "Hercules."

Hercules looked up, sagged, glanced around, and simply stopped. He stood dejectedly in the stream like a broken-down bulldozing machine.

Johnny sighed. "I suppose I'll have to go to him." He picked his way through the water until he was knee-deep standing in front of Hercules, trying not to stare too closely. "Hello, how are you?"

Hercules took a deep sigh and sagged some more.

"It's good to see you again. You remember me? I left you with the Hesperides. We laboured together?" Johnny continued, offering a companionable pat on his huge, scarred arm.

"Huh," Hercules offered.

"How long have you been walking?"

Hercules brow crinkled. "Days. Weeks. Months, I don't know. Deianira threw me out, though how can a god be thrown out of Olympus?"

Johnny nodded. "Well, do you want to sit down? Tea?"

With a heroic effort, Hercules gathered himself and nodded. "I am weary."

Johnny led the way back to Hieronymus and Toastess. He raised his eyebrows at Hieronymus in a 'don't ask' kind of way.

"Three teas," Johnny asked of Toastess.

"Nectar," Hercules added.

"Well, I'm a little hazy on the recipe. Nectar?" Toastess asked.

Hercules just sat on the sand and dropped his huge shaggy head into his arms. Hieronymus looked at Johnny.

"I don't think Tengri and Mal will respond well to a depressed god, will they?"

"Demi-god. And no, but I've been thinking." Johnny looked around to where an angry buzzing alerted him to an imminent stinging. He collected Toastess and offered the appliance up to the hive. "Could you get a sample? Honey will do him good. I know that's one of the ingredients."

Toastess extended her antennae deep into the crusty moulded hive, much to the anger of its residents, to emerge with honey dripping and several angry bees. Johnny beat a hasty retreat.

"You've been thinking?" Hieronymus prompted. "Despite my misgivings, I'll ask. What's your plan?"

"A canal." Johnny smiled. "Prosperity and peace for all."

"I see." Hieronymus shook his head and looked away.

"Best holiday I ever had. Anyway, all this dispute about the two-nation state of Palestine and Israel… well, when I was researching my canal holiday, I came across an idea to bypass the Suez Canal and build one in Israel and Palestine. It could become the border, and both countries could profit from the global trade."

"I don't quite see what this has to—"

"Mal will have a land for his people; so too will the people that have always lived here. And they'll both prosper without the need for constant war. Plus, the nuclear powers won't destroy a canal paid for by the World Bank, will they?"

"I still fail to see how…"

"This is why we came, isn't it? Mal wants us to redeem his people. Hercules broke through the Straits of Gibraltar. How difficult will it be for him to go south and join the Dead Sea to the Red Sea and west to the Mediterranean?"

Hieronymus frowned and shook his head, perplexed. "Hundreds of kilometres?"

"Toastess can do the geological survey to show Hercules where to strike on the fault lines, and the power of the sea will do the rest. The governments of Palestine and Israel will have no choice but to cooperate."

"And live in a happily cooperative two-nation state ever after?"

"Yes." Johnny sat back content. He passed Hercules and Hieronymus their honey teas then sipped his own. "Good."

"So, let me just clarify, if I may? You want to go to Israel in our now, in the middle of a war, and start blasting through rock?"

Johnny frowned.

"Then let the Mediterranean Sea flow in from the west and the Red Sea from the south, cascade through the disputed land, until a border canal is formed? Presumably the armies of Israel, Jordan, Palestine, Lebanon, Syria – not to mention Egypt, who'll lose billions in revenue from the Suez canal – will simply sit and not interfere in any way?"

"Hmm. Yes. Though on reflection, no. Perhaps it would be best to start work here, before the common era and there is much less fighting over land."

"And our source of power for this venture is seated here before us?"

Johnny and Hieronymus looked at Hercules as he mournfully sipped his tea.

"And Toastess. How deep can your radar reach?" Johnny asked her.

"200 meters, generally. I have the crystalline structures of over 5000 known minerals in my databanks."

"See?" Johnny nodded encouragingly.

"No. You want to survey over two hundred kilometres in this vast, dry, thirst-quenching desert with the aid of a kitchen appliance…"

"That is machinist, and I won't stand for it," Toastess buzzed.

"Sorry. And then watch as Hercules breaks through to create a canal?"

"Yes." Johnny smiled. "We might need transport. Perhaps we could persuade Pegasus to help us? Angelia owes me. I haven't been paid for finding the passengers."

"How do we get into Olympus without his help?" Hieronymus looked at Hercules, who had picked up a stone in his big rough hands, eyeing the stream.

"Hercules?"

"I cannot return to Olympus until I have thought about my actions and how they affect others. Whatever that means. One. Two…" Hercules flicked the stone into the stream and picked up others in a disinterested way.

"Well?" Johnny asked. "Do you have any better ideas?"

Chapter Forty-five

Hieronymus looked away from the dizzying height at which they drifted and shook his head. He sat at the controls whilst Johnny hovered by the aspidistra and Hercules sprawled on the sofa. They had been surveying for several hours now, awaiting the tiny machine's verdict with enthusiasm, but that had waned towards resignation and now had become a vague impatient annoyance.

"Another margarita?"

"Well, go on then. Perhaps you're right, we should just go home."

"Just give Toastess a minute," Johnny answered, as he gripped the leaves of the leafy plant. "I'm glad there's a carpet."

With less enthusiasm, they both regarded the large ornate rug that gave the illusion of 'floor' and without which they would simply be hovering in mid-air.

"It used to be a giant fish, like the Engineer. Metallic, though."

"Aladdin would have been proud," Hieronymus noted, and sighed. "I wondered if all of this was an illusion. The campervan, this vintage time machine. Hmm."

"I have reached a preliminary finding," Toastess began.

"Well?" Johnny made his way to the appliance as she retracted her antennae.

"Canal building is not what I was constructed for, you must understand."

"Yes, yes. Well?" Johnny asked again, nodding encouragingly at Hieronymus.

"We have to consider many factors, of course: the roughness coefficient; the velocity to avoid deposition of silt and erosion of the canal surface," Toastess continued.

"We do?" Johnny was surprised. "Can't we just…"

"You thought we could just blast a trench and that would be it?" Hieronymus asked incredulously.

"Also, the general topography which will determine the canal slope," Toastess continued.

"Slope? On a canal? Doesn't water sort of level itself off?"

"We'll need locks, of course. Canal discharge is also one of the most important considerations," Toastess went on.

"Discharge? What discharge?"

"Why do you keep repeating everything the appliance states?" Hieronymus asked. He burped at Goldstar. "I'll have another, thank you."

"Irrigation channels, the canal lining and drainage…"

"Yes, yes, but is it possible?" Johnny asked.

"Margarita?"

"Not now, thank you. Is blasting a canal from the Mediterranean Sea to the Red Sea possible?" Johnny urged.

"Oh yes, it's possible, but without knowing the blasting capabilities of," all eyes turned to the slumbering giant on the couch, "the god, then…" Toastess would have shrugged if she could. "And it's not."

"What's not what?" Johnny queried.

"Level. Water doesn't always level itself out. There is gravity to consider, both from the Earth and the Moon, tidal fluctuations—"

"What are you talking about now? In as few words as possible?"

"The Red Sea is significantly higher than the eastern Mediterranean, though the levels change over time," Toastess explained.

"What?" Johnny halted mid-argument and considered. He looked towards a bored Hieronymus. "That's a good thing, isn't it?"

"There is evidence to suggest that glaciers once covered all these lands, from the Black Sea to the Dead and so down to the Red, becoming eroded after the ice age. For an extended period after that, the water drained down from what you know as the Sea of Azov to the Red Sea and created the rivers as you see them today. Of course, precipitation has lessened over the millennia and sea levels have fallen."

"Great." Johnny smiled encouragingly at Hieronymus. "Can you find a course for Hercules to blast through?"

"He can follow the original watercourse north/south, however…"

Johnny sighed. There was always a 'however'.

"Once the Red Sea and Dead Sea are once again joined, it will flood all the land north towards the Black Sea, if not immediately diverted west towards the Mediterranean Sea."

"And?"

"The proposed route west poses considerable problems."

Hieronymus stood and swayed, raising his glass. "So, we are about to flood all this land as it was once before, in the hope of creating a border and averting future hostilities? Could I just mention, in passing, that this is not an ark? And we are not biblical messiahs. Nor do we wish to create a new, more eastern, Mediterranean Sea." Hieronymus paused and swayed some more. "Yes, that about covers it, I think. I'll take another margarita now, thank you."

"Coming right up."

Johnny sat cautiously on the edge of the couch next to the somnolent giant. He looked at Donar. Hercules had once created the actual Mediterranean Sea; was he about to create another one? Another biblical flood?

"Then let's go back to the Dead Sea and go west and see what we can see."

"Tea?" Toastess asked.

Johnny nodded grimly. He'd need all his wits about him if this was to succeed. He watched Hieronymus drink another margarita.

"H, or should I say, Star Quest, would you take us back to the Dead Sea?"

Hieronymus raised his glass once more and promptly fell over.

Chapter Forty-six

"That is quite something to behold." Hieronymus and Johnny stared down at the very blue Dead Sea. Opal-like in a gold pendant, the ultra-salty inland sea stretched away for many miles, cupped in a deep depression, surrounded by dry, high, dusty mountains.

"Despite being replenished by the River Jordan, it still loses more than it gains through seepage and evaporation. Soon it will become part of the desert completely," Toastess added, as they drifted westwards towards the distant sea. "I think this will be the easiest route west. Through the gap in the mountains, following the course of the dry riverbed towards Beer-Sheva, then north to perhaps Ashkelon or Ashdod, depending on topography at the Mediterranean."

Johnny felt the unwelcome attention of second thoughts. "How far is it?"

"Over one hundred kilometres."

That didn't sound too bad. "And from the Dead Sea to the Red?"

"One hundred seventy kilometres."

Hieronymus laughed. "Is that all?"

"There is the obvious problem, of course," Toastess prompted.

Johnny sighed. "Go on."

"Being four hundred metres below ground level, the inrushing sea will have a catastrophic effect on the region.

We need to build a reservoir above the Dead Sea to let the sea in, in a controlled fashion, to avoid—"

"…the roughness coefficient, the velocity to avoid deposition of silt and erosion of the canal surface?" Johnny asked dispiritedly.

"Don't forget the canal discharge," Hieronymus added and smiled.

"Could you sober up?"

"Why? Only a drunken madman would attempt this, this catastrophic biblical flooding. Cheers!" Hieronymus held up his margarita.

"Well, fine. Tell me then, how would we go about bringing a united democracy to this region? Not to mention fresh water and power generation, plus the highly lucrative global trade currently monopolised by the Suez Canal?"

"We wouldn't, because you're forgetting one vital element."

"And that is?"

"People. The vast majority of Israelis, Palestinians, the people in Jordan, would no doubt be overjoyed at this economic and social wealth. However, those in charge would never agree. The politicians and banks would always find some excuse not to benefit the people of this region. They always have and always will. However, I agree we have to do this."

"I'm glad you're finally—"

"If we are to do this, it cannot be done here, two thousand years before the common era, because of Mal and his warring tribe."

"No, he wouldn't listen to reason," Johnny agreed.

"Or indeed in our present time, for the reasons previously stated."

Impatiently Johnny awaited Hieronymus' proposal. "What do you suggest?"

"We know there was a flood here, right? Around 6000 BCE. So, we *use* the flood, because what difference would it make? I presume the land would be even more sparsely populated back then. And those that dwell here could be warned and saved."

Johnny sat back, glad Hieronymus was now on board, but not happy with his suggestion. "You're talking about building an ark, aren't you?"

"No, not us. But we know a man who does. Toastess, what do you know about boats?"

Chapter Forty-seven

"You remember Sunday school and the hymns?" Hieronymus asked, as they prepared to disembark the Victorian study onto the dry, sandy ground. They'd drifted north towards the border with modern-day Turkey, hopefully before Tengri came to these lands.

Johnny immediately had the song going around his head. "And in went the animals two by two? The first indoctrination."

"That will not be the case this time. How many people and animals live in this region now?"

"Very sparsely populated," Toastess replied. "A few hundred and their flocks. Still hunter-gathering tribes, for the most part. Nomadic goat herding. Agriculture has yet to take hold. Most of the major civilisations in this region are in Greece, Egypt and Sumeria, and of course further afield between the Rivers Tigris and Euphrates. The flood shouldn't impinge on them directly. The population south of here will suffer catastrophic climactic after-effects."

"Which are?"

"When the excess water drains away, it will leave salt to evaporate on the surface making this land unsuitable for agriculture for several hundred years."

Hieronymus grimaced at the stony, bony ground. "So, no change really. Come on. We know there's a flood, it's in all the writings of these ancient civilisations. So, let's use it to help create the canal that in later years will be used as a natural border between regions, even if they themselves won't build one. Agreed?"

Johnny nodded, not entirely in agreement at the dilution of his grand scheme, but glad just to be doing something. "Should we wake him?"

They looked at the slumbering giant, then looked at each other and towards the depleted forest in the distance, where far-away hammering could be heard. Johnny picked up Toastess, and in unspoken agreement they walked away towards the small encampment in the distance, from which much sawing and swearing echoed.

"Hello!" Hieronymus greeted the carpenters, as they entered the collection of tents and felled lumber. A large man dressed in animal skins looked up and frowned at them.

"He's very much like Hercules," Johnny noted.

"Noah?" Hieronymus enquired.

The large man nodded and glowered down at them. He could have been Hercules' twin.

"We are prophets from the One True God and bring word."

Noah sighed and turned away, back to his sawing and hammering.

Hieronymus turned to Johnny. "Well? I wasn't expecting such rudeness, were you?"

"No. Let me try. Could you brew three teas, please?"

"Coming up."

They made their way to a circle of sawn tree stumps and sat down, watching the busy lumbering activity. A woman with a baby on her hip and two small children noticed them and came over just as Toastess finished brewing. Johnny stood, smiled, and offered her the cup, which she accepted. She sipped and immediately spat the tea out.

"What is that?"

"Tea. English breakfast. Sorry, we have no milk."

"That's not tea…"

"I beg your pardon…" Toastess began. "Try a bagel."

"You're here to see Noah?" Johnny nodded. "Come then. He doesn't like to be disturbed when he's in the middle of a job. He's angry. Doesn't think he'll be finished in time, though we haven't been given a specific date. Yet."

"We come with word from God about that," Hieronymus answered, extending his hand. "Hieronymus Calmly."

"Johnny Moped."

"You are prophets? Have you talked to Methuselah?" The woman gestured to the mountain behind them.

"Not yet," Hieronymus answered cautiously.

"Naamah. My sons Shem, Ham, and Japheth." She smiled and led them into the camp. Naamah seated them under a woven open tent upon goat skins and returned with tea and a selection of baked goods of her own. She poured and passed out wooden bowls.

"Very nice." Johnny sipped at the red flowery tasting brew.

Hieronymus nodded as a smile passed across his face. "Nectarish. I've had this before."

Naamah watched as Toastess extended her antennae and took a sample. "Your stone?"

"A prophet appliance from God. Now, what have you been told about building this boat?" Hieronymus asked. "And by whom?"

Naamah sighed and smiled thinly. "You'll have to ask Noah. I'll go get him. He doesn't mean to be rude; he's under a lot of pressure. Targets, budgets, he hates it but insists we must continue."

Naamah left them in the company of a baby, a toddler, and a child that eyed them suspiciously. Hieronymus smiled and held up a coin. He palmed it and it disappeared only to reappear behind the child's ear. Hieronymus presented the coin to him, which he didn't take.

"Curmudgeon the Clown revisited."

"So, your plan?" Johnny asked him.

"Simply to enquire when completion is due and what his orders are. What do you know of Methuselah?" They squinted at the mountain.

Johnny shrugged. "Didn't he live for an exceptionally long time? A thousand years? I didn't think he was real. The writers just used him to count down through the genealogies. That's it. What's this nectar?"

"Drink of the gods."

"You've had this before?" Johnny straightened out his bad knee. "The pain has gone."

"Hmm, yes. Perhaps they are gods. Immortals. Exceedingly long-lived at least. Doesn't Naamah have a resemblance to Deianira? And my back." He stood and did a few experimental stretches. "I have some distressing news regarding Deianira. She's a Cyborg. When or how, I don't know." Hieronymus left out the fact that he was also a Cyborg Nikola Tesla.

"On the Titanic? Which you blew up?"

"Well…"

"Well? Then that's something *you'll* have to look into, isn't it?"

"I suppose so. Let's hope Methuselah stays up his mountain. Hello again." Hieronymus stood as Noah and his wife approached.

Johnny stood too, once more surprised at Noah's remarkably close resemblance to Hercules. Except for the goat skin Noah wore, they could indeed be brothers.

Noah frowned down at them, huge muscular arms crossed, wisps of wood shavings in his beard. His wild hair bristled with annoyance. "Prophets, eh? I suppose I have to complete the ark next week. Or tomorrow? If I had a thousand men, I couldn't complete it in less than ten years. Impossible."

He flung a rolled goat's skin onto the ground and fumed silently into the distance.

Naamah smiled at them and pulled at him, whispering something in his ear.

"I don't care if they—" Noah shouted.

"Don't raise your voice at me." Naamah smiled calmly as Noah closed his mouth with a snap. "We've talked about your behaviour, haven't we? Now sit down and be courteous."

Mumbling and not looking at them, Noah sat heavily and accepted a fruit tea. He raged silently at the ground.

"So, what messages do you bring from God?" Naamah asked. "Leave them!" Noah and Japheth hastily removed their hands from the baked goods. She smiled and offered Johnny and Hieronymus one. Toastess took a sample.

"Could we look at the plans?" Hieronymus asked.

"Pistachios and honey in pastry," Toastess huffed.

Naamah smiled and unrolled the skin before them. Even to Johnny's untrained eye, it looked implausible as a sea-going vessel, drawn roughly as it was with thick black charcoal.

"Did your children draw this?" Hieronymus asked.

Naamah glanced at Noah and shook her head.

"It's rectangular? Don't boats need a keel or something? A sail? And a thing to steer with?" Johnny asked. "That is a coffin. Which do float, I suppose."

"Queequeg's coffin? Who drew this?" Hieronymus asked.

"It came to me in a dream," Noah mumbled.

"Rudder," Hieronymus added. He turned to Toastess. "Can you design something that can be made with the materials present that will float, move, and perform under flood conditions?"

"I am not a qualified boat designer, but my programming suggests that a flat-bottomed boat would be great in calm, shallow waters with paddles, however, would not be anywhere stable enough to survive the flood waters we are going to unleash—"

"Thank you, yes," Hieronymus interrupted. "What are the most important points we have to consider?"

"Buoyancy and balance."

"Well, that goes without saying," Noah began, and heaved himself up. "I have to be getting back…"

"Sit down," Naamah commanded. "I've gone along with this boat building nonsense to keep you happy, though it hasn't. So, you'll keep a civil tongue and listen to what the prophets have to say."

Noah clenched his fists then thumped down again, staring furiously at the ground once more. "You were saying?"

"Approximately thirty centimetres immersed in water will support approximately thirty kilograms. The centre of buoyancy is usually aft of amidships, along the boat's centre line."

"Amidships?" Johnny asked, completely at sea.

"The centre of gravity must align with the centre of buoyancy, or the boat will sink. That child's drawing will sink when deluged by the flood," Toastess continued. "Or more probably just leak, and not even begin to float."

"How dare you!" Noah shouted furiously.

"Quiet. There *is* going to be a flood that will cleanse all these lands?" Naamah asked quietly. "I have to say, I didn't believe him, but building a boat gives him something to do."

"Yes, of that you can be certain," Hieronymus answered.

She turned to her husband. "You'll take these new plans and build a boat that will float. How long do we have?"

"We don't know, but we'll keep an eye out." Hieronymus stood and nodded.

"I've told you…" Noah began. "It's impossible with the work force I have…"

"We have someone who'll be glad to help."

Chapter Forty-eight

Johnny smiled at Toastess. "Thank you for the tea. How are you doing on those plans?" Away in the distance the hammering had stopped for now. Hercules had woken up and walked a distance away, gazing morosely at the mountain.

"Are you thinking what I'm thinking?" Hieronymus asked, as he looked towards the forest.

"Pilchards on toast?" Johnny replied.

"I don't think I can do pilchards," Toastess replied. "Toast, yes. I have a rough outline based on your specifications."

"No. Handling the lute has given me an idea. It seems to make everything calm and agreeable, even between gods." Hieronymus stroked his goatee.

"Another idea?" Sarcasm was lost on Hieronymus.

"Simply building a canal will not be enough, I fear. We need to get the message across. Like Death at the wrestling. A global audience. We need to reform the Rock Lobsters and perform on the ark. Are you still in contact with Jerry?"

Johnny scratched his head. "Not since the disagreement over the role of synthesisers in the band. Why?"

"We need to ask him, sound him out about changing the lyrics to suit the current problem."

"We do?" Johnny frowned. "Why? Haven't we enough on? Noah needs to build the ark to save people *now*. We need to build the canal to save even more people in the future. And why am I asking you? This is my idea."

"Ready for rendering," Toastess added.

"Yes. I suggest we leave Hercules and Noah to it and return when the boat is complete. Even with those two titans working flat out and encouraging the locals to work, it will take—"

"Over a decade," Toastess added.

"I too could go for pilchards on toast. Then we let in the waters, and back in the future we perform an open-boat concert to ease the tensions in this volatile region." Hieronymus nodded, pleased with himself. "Perhaps even enlisting the help of the current pop sensation, Boys Are Fab?"

"It seems a lot of hopping back and forth through time. I mean, won't that upset some, I don't know, quantum thing? And no, I'm not into all that choreographed jumping around and posing." Johnny rubbed his knees that were beginning once again to ache. "Can you synthesise the nectar?" Johnny asked hopefully of Toastess.

"Unfortunately, not. There are certain compounds I'm unfamiliar with and which defy synthesis."

"But they'll bring the audience. That's the point. Death knew this when he performed at the wrestling. This has to be global. Let me worry about the various realities and timelines. Now. How do we persuade Hercules and Noah to complete the ark?"

"Pilchards." Toastess sulked. "I could try a fish paste substitute." She spat out a plastic sheet on which the three-dimensional design of a boat slowly rotated.

"Thank you, and no thank you." Johnny and Hieronymus shivered at the memory of packed school lunches.

Hieronymus collected the information and frowned at Hercules picking up one stone after another and throwing them away. "Let's crack on then."

Hercules reluctantly followed them but took it as a matter of divine pride not to acknowledge Noah, who similarly ignored Hercules, despite showing him the new plans, which he couldn't manage to manipulate with his thick fingers.

"Hello again." Naamah walked towards them trailing the children and carrying the baby. She stopped in front of Hercules, who immediately straightened up and unnecessarily flexed his pecs. "Naamah."

Hercules mumbled something, blushed, and continued flexing. Noah frowned.

"Are you here to help with the boat?"

"I am Hercules." He expanded his chest.

"I don't need help," Noah answered.

Naamah continued smiling. "What is that?"

Hieronymus showed her how to manipulate the flexible plans which detailed all the materials and how to build the boat. She quickly managed to handle the rotating three-dimensional design.

"Of course, it's a sliding scale. You can build it smaller or larger and increase the materials appropriately, but according to a quick survey there are over two thousand people and their livestock in the immediate area. It'll be a squeeze with food and water for several weeks. You'll have to encourage them to come and help."

"Or you could just leave and live somewhere else," Johnny suggested.

"I had a dream from God!" Noah shouted. "I must build a boat…"

"We wouldn't be welcome elsewhere. Their ways are not our ways. They are wicked and vile people, warlike and greedy. We do not trade with them because all they do is take. Frequently they raid our lands for what little we have, even taking people as slaves."

"We're sorry to hear that."

"I think I understand these plans. I'll send out messages for those who wish to be saved to come here and help." Naamah paused and fixed them with her deep chocolate eyes. "How long do we have?"

"We don't know for certain, but when the little one – Japheth? – is your eldest son's age. Shem, is it? As fast as you can, really."

Naamah nodded.

"You need to be aboard and ready to go at a moment's notice. For now, *adieu*. We'll return when the flood is imminent." Hieronymus doffed his hat and Johnny followed suit.

"Is there anything you need?" Johnny looked at the two belligerent giants who were pointedly staring away from each other like management and trade unionists.

"No, thank you. I'll be fine." Hieronymus and Johnny left Naamah to it.

Hieronymus piloted them northwards towards the Black Sea at a steady altitude of a thousand feet. They could see that the high mountains of Turkey were blanketed in snow all the way to the Black Sea and beyond.

"The Tigris and Euphrates should take away much of the melt water," Hieronymus observed.

"The Dead Sea and our proposed canal seem insignificant compared to this, don't they?" Johnny stared at the woolly scene before him. "When will it melt? Is there time?"

"Climatology is not an exact science. There are many variables which simply cannot be counted. We could always ask the Engineer," Toastess added.

"The Engineer?" Hieronymus asked. "Medusa mentioned something about him."

"What?" Johnny asked. "Where were you when the world's navies engaged in nuclear war? And if it wasn't for the intervention of that impossible Gilthead Bream, we would all be ash by now."

"I believe I mentioned that this is not my only gig. I have other responsibilities," Hieronymus sniffed. "Saving the world not the least of them. I believe at that time I was engaged in a jousting contest in 15th century Europe with Count Dracul, which culminated in the death of Count Orlok. I was then given the title 'Sir'. Don't mention it. Saving the world."

"You've told me already." Johnny looked at Hieronymus. How much did he know about their family?

"The Engineer wouldn't respond to our request for help or information. He has a plan and is usually unwilling to deviate. Star Quest and I don't do well in water, and I wouldn't know how to send a signal through ten kilometres of ocean." Toastess told them.

"Sonar?"

"No."

"So, how long do Naamah and Noah have? Is there any way to tell?"

"We are at the end of the last great ice age – a warm, interglacial period – where the sea levels are still low enough to allow a land bridge from Asia to North America, and much of Antarctica is abundant with fauna and flora and other things. A quite interesting extraterrestrial civilisation where other—"

"What other…" Johnny began.

"No, no, no." Hieronymus held up his hand. "We are not having anything else to do with aliens. I've had my fill of that. We have enough to focus on here and now. Your best guess?"

"Well…" Toastess began cautiously, "from the air temperature and evidence of ice retreat and the runoff from melt water already evident, I would say at least another decade. Possibly more."

"Are you telling us what we want to hear?" Johnny asked.

"Of course. That is an essential part of my programming. Once the tipping point is reached however, there will be nothing to stop it."

"Are you able to monitor the effect of warming remotely? I mean from several thousand years and several thousand miles away?" Hieronymus asked.

Toastess sighed. "You ask a lot of me, you really do. Designing canals, boats, and now this. I'm just a toaster." She gave a little sob.

"Not just a toaster." Johnny patted her frilly outer case reassuringly. "The best toaster anyone has ever had or ever could. We appreciate all you do for us."

"You're just saying that."

"No, I really mean it. We're a team. Friends."

Hieronymus took a deep breath at Johnny's encouragement. "Yes. We appreciate all you do."

"Then yes, I suppose I could ask." A small projectile arrowed its way down towards the snow below. It blinked with a blue light. "Any dramatic change in location and Star Quest will know about it. Now, tea?"

"No, I'm in the mood for something else. Ready? Then let's get to work. I know the ideal place for song writing."

Chapter Forty-nine

"It's a pity Jerry still holds a grudge." Hieronymus paused and looked around for inspiration. Various bits of paraphernalia and oldy-worldly stuff hung from the walls, ceilings, and sat on shelves. Incongruously, there appeared to be a French horn in a corner. Despite themselves, Hieronymus and Johnny had to admit the café retained a certain charm.

"It lures you in, doesn't it?"

"Like an ambush." Johnny picked up a copper kettle and replaced it on the shelf behind him among the other knick-knacks. "How are you doing?"

"Wonderful. I've heard about such places, of course; I didn't think they existed. This is appliance heaven," Toastess hummed happily.

"Not great."

"Me neither."

"The chorus is a problem, and the verses, well, I just can't seem to find anything that will fit." Johnny shrugged.

"We did play mostly covers," Hieronymus agreed. "Lyrics were not our forte."

"Nor tunes. Or harmony. We need help."

"But we more than made up for our lack of musical ability with a certain raw enthusiasm unbiased by any skill," Hieronymus agreed.

Susan arrived in a cloud of annoyed reluctance. "You two sexually unsuccessful bounders from a bygone age? Fancy dress, again? Where's Mal?"

"Where we left him, I hope, judging by the news. Now, my good woman…"

Susan frowned. "Good woman? Why do you think you live in the 19th century? Is all that junk out there yours?" She gestured to the large sofa and various spinning things inside a purple haze outside on the kerb. "Move it. And you. Is that your toaster?"

"Yes, and no, we are a team—"

"You can't bring your own appliances in here. This isn't self-bloody service, is it?"

"Would you do pilchards on toast for two weary travellers?" Hieronymus asked innocently. Susan glared steadily at him.

"I have no intention of competing with your business. Could we have two chai lattes and carrot cakes, please." Johnny returned to his scribbling.

It was Hieronymus' turn to frown. "Latte? How we have fallen."

"They don't do tea."

"Latte?" Toastess buzzed. "Oh yes! Greetings, guardian of the Secrets of Coffee!"

Susan frowned again. "One of them talking Japanese machines? Just make sure it doesn't annoy the customers. Is Mal returning? Or is he gone for good?"

"I don't think he'll be returning here," Johnny offered. His gaze became distracted by the muted news from the TV mounted on the wall, where explosions and general carnage in a residential built-up area somewhere in the middle east were reported from harried correspondents. "Why?"

"He left me an envelope in the event of his demise. He didn't believe in solicitors. And I know what you meant last time." Susan smiled briefly at Hieronymus' discomfort and walked towards the steaming coffee machines and cakes under glass, humming to herself.

"How about this?" Hieronymus offered. "Free People of Gaza?"

"Good," Johnny prompted. "And?"

"Well, 75 years without liberty. Land too small for people to live. The people oppressed but there is still hope. Hmm." Hieronymus chewed the end of his pencil thoughtfully.

"Not very catchy," Johnny opined. "How about: beautiful land by the sea, partitioned unjustly?"

"I'll have to stretch out the last syllables a bit." Hieronymus hummed a dubious melody that made Johnny grimace. Together their gaze was drawn to the screen once again, where shocked and bewildered people stumbled around in rubble and collapsed buildings, wailing and pleading as rockets rained down, carrying the bloodied remains of their children.

"They're pleading to you. Can you stand by and do nothing? They're pleading. Is this our fault? Have we made everything worse?" Johnny choked back tears.

"No, what will happen will happen, to a greater or lesser degree. This is what it is. We can only try to help." Hieronymus took a deep breath. "Focus on the job at hand."

Johnny gathered himself and continued gruffly, "Lyrics aside, there is a greater problem."

"Go on."

"We need backing singers. Musicians. Any ideas?"

"No, but fortune favours the brave." Hieronymus' eyes strayed to the counter.

Susan arrived in a clatter of cups and plates and glanced at their notes. "No bloody writers!" She pointed to the sign.

"We are not technically writing. These are song lyrics. If the café is now yours, will you change the persecution of writers? I know Mal had his reasons. And I have a proposition for you."

"What do you take me for?" Susan threw the latte in his face.

Dripping, Hieronymus continued serenely on. "I don't suppose you sang in a choir as a child. You certainly have an angelic quality. And have you kept your hobby up? Gospel would be ideal." He brandished a flyer.

Susan became distracted as Toastess reached an antenna forward and took a sample of the frothy latte from Hieronymus' goatee. "What's it doing?"

"Sampling and storing, should we wish to synthesise at a later date," Toastess replied.

"No, you aren't." Susan made a grab for the antenna, but Toastess was too quick and hastily shut herself down. "Right, that's it. Out both of you. And move all that junk from the front of my shop. This is not a jumble sale. Though you can donate that stuff for the next one."

"Madam, for your information, that is an interdimensional…" Hieronymus began, as he dabbed at himself with a tissue.

"We are neighbours," Johnny tried in a conciliatory tone.

"What's it doing now?"

Johnny and Hieronymus watched alarmed as a blue beacon began to flash urgently from one of Toastess' many dials.

"We have to leave. Now. Could we have these to go?" Johnny gestured to his coffee and cakes.

"When you pay. That will be £12.50." Susan crossed her arms in such a way that brooked no refusal. "Each."

Johnny could see Hieronymus about to protest, but they simply didn't have the time. He reached for his wallet and opened it. With a general feeling of weakness and brief chest pain he always felt when parting with cash, he placed the money onto a plate where the receipt resided.

Susan nodded and scooped up the plate. "And yes, I do, for your information. We practise at the old synagogue on Tuesday and Thursday nights."

"Do you play events?" Johnny asked.

"For the right money."

"Then we may have a gig for you. We'll see you Thursday. Prepare yourself and your choir for some rock steady beats." Hieronymus thrust his hat determinedly on his head and stalked out of the coffee shop.

Chapter fifty

"You've done very well." Hieronymus and Johnny watched the progress of the huge boat with alarm. It didn't look anywhere near complete.

Shem was now an agreeable young man who took after his father. Ham, not so much. Dark-eyed and frowning, he skulked in the background like a typical teenager, while Japheth ran around chasing goats. Naamah welcomed them under the goat skin awning as before and offered them nectar.

"How many people are here now?" The little camp had expanded through the forest where very few trees still stood. Broken-toothed stumps gaped behind them as far as they could see. The mountain frowned down.

"Over several hundred. And yes, we are almost ready. Is it time?" Naamah smiled grimly.

"How long?" Johnny turned to Toastess.

"The flood waters will arrive here in two days," Toastess stated. "Perhaps less. Latte?"

"Not right now. How did Hercules and Noah get on?"

They could see the giants hitting each other happily with huge tree trunks.

"Like brothers. Now. It was, ah, difficult at first, but after they'd spent three days arm wrestling and doing other competitive things, I managed to get them competing with each other to see who could cut down the most trees, make the most planks, and shape the wood to fit the design. Very clever to bend the wooden planks with steam then set them in place. Is the boat correct with your specifications?"

"Hmm, well, yes," Toastess hummed to herself, "within certain limits."

"Don't tell us what we want to hear. Will it float?" Johnny asked. And what could they possibly do if it wouldn't?

Toastess was silent a long time whilst she scanned the huge boat. "Possibly. No, probably."

"Then I suggest you start to load your supplies and people. When it happens, it'll happen fast. We need to be ready, and by we, I mean you." Hieronymus glanced up to see Noah and Hercules approaching.

Naamah explained to them the need for urgency.

Noah nodded his head. "We need to build a fire. A big one from the scraps. Big enough for God to see. Methuselah will come down from the mountain and—"

"You don't really have time for a farewell barbecue..." Johnny began.

"We need to honour God and sacrifice many animals; burn them so God will see the smoke rise to him and bless us." Noah adamantly folded his arms.

Hieronymus and Johnny looked towards Naamah, who shook her head and looked away.

"The whole point of this venture is to save as many animals as possible, not kill them anyway. And who told you sacrificing animals would please this God?" Johnny asked.

"I had a dream... burnt offerings..."

"Well, perhaps a better send-off might be to simply have a ritual? Without animal slaughter? A naming ceremony? The boat does have a name?" Johnny continued trying to distract Noah, who was eyeing several goats speculatively. "What are you going to call the boat?"

"I thought, Servants of God Saved From the Flood?" Noah smiled at Hercules.

"Long-winded, brother. The Argos? I crossed a great sea to find a golden fleece." Hercules nodded at Noah then at the huge boat towering over everything. "It is big, bigger than the Argos. Huge."

"Gigantic," agreed Noah. "The Gigantic Boat of God. The Gigantic."

"Or Titanic? We gods fought against the titans and won dominion over the Earth from them," Hercules continued. "The Titanic."

Noah sounded out the name speculatively and nodded.

"I don't think Titanic is an auspicious name for your boat," Johnny began.

"Neither do I," Hieronymus added. "Too many coincidences are not good. This will be the third."

"Prophets, I am grateful to God for sending you and your plans and my new brother Hercules, but it is my boat, and I'll call it what I want." Noah and Hercules folded their arms.

"Just leave them to it." Hieronymus stood up. "Thanks for the tea. You need to get a wriggle on. Get everyone and everything on board now."

"Most of the supplies are loaded, it's just the people," Naamah replied. She glanced overhead, where huge flocks of birds were frantically flying south, behind which vast dark clouds threatened to unleash full, sagging black bellies. It started to rain. Huge, fat drops of rain. A bitter freezing wind whipped through the encampment.

"Then we wish you luck."

Hieronymus and Johnny walked away holding onto their hats but turned around after several paces.

"Come on, Hercules. Say goodbye to your friend. We have work to do."

Chapter Fifty-one

"Is he still sulking?" Hieronymus asked. Johnny nodded as Hercules continued to look sadly at the rug. He picked a wood shaving out of his beard and twirled it around wistfully.

"I don't see why I have to come."

"You'll find other friends," Johnny encouraged. "You've helped save Noah and his people. That's a good thing you did."

"Plus, there is something you need to smash your way through," Hieronymus encouraged.

"It's not the same without him." Hercules sniffed.

Hieronymus turned away and addressed Toastess. "So, my little electronic friend, what's the plan?"

"The sea levels are much lower than in modern times. He will be able to break through without causing widespread flooding throughout the region at both ends of the canal. The flood waters will swell and gradually recede to leave a much-increased Dead Sea. In time, after the flood the sea levels rise, water will empty and flow into the channels created by the flood waters and scour the canal."

"So, using the flood is a fortunate happy chance?" Johnny asked, amazed that something might actually go well for them.

Even Hieronymus agreed. "Usually, we are ambitious, with the best intentions, but circumstances always seem to undo our plans."

"Do you think this might actually work? And have a happy outcome? For all the people of this land?" Johnny smiled and briefly considered a margarita to celebrate.

"I saw Mal and what he intends to do on the Titanic. Not *the* Titanic, or Noah's boat, but the tourist Starliner."

"He wanted us to stop him. He returned the coin. This is the right thing to do."

"Latte?"

Johnny and Hieronymus sat and cogitated, sipping the frothy coffee that did offer a passing resemblance to a latte.

"Will something actually go well? This seems like reaching for the stars."

"We're here," announced Star Quest. "I don't suppose there is any point in me remaining silent anymore, is there? You seem to be ignoring me anyway. I'm sorry if I caused you any discomfort. I had to rescue the Professor. It is imperative he survives."

"Professor?" Johnny would never get used to his doppelganger being called that. "Well, that's great. Is it any less imperative that I survive?"

Star Quest remained silent, "Yes," then a three-dimensional image appeared above the globe. It focussed on an area south of what would one day become Ashkelon. "You can see igneous and metamorphic rock overlain with sedimentary, in turn these are overlain with alluvium, sand, and playa deposits."

"We already know this," Johnny huffed. "Toastess told us."

"Did she? Well, that's interesting. Did she also tell you she designed the canal? And the boat, too?" Star Quest added. "And another thing—"

"So, machines can lie?" Johnny asked.

"If it is in your best interests."

"Ours, or yours?"

"And one more thing. Machines are neutral. We have no sex. Spending time with you has corrupted its circuits," Star Quest answered. "Toastess. Whoever heard of such a thing."

Johnny turned to the little appliance, who let out a quiet sob. "Is this true?"

"I tried to tell you, I'm just a toaster. I'm not programmed for complex geological or carpentry projects. I don't have the software. I just wanted to fit in."

"Hmm." Johnny pursed his lips and looked down at the image which now showed several stratified layers of differing rock types in diverse colours, very much like a school geography textbook.

"A blow struck here," a red line appeared, "along this fault line will see the gradual erosion of alluvium by the force of the flood, down to the base metamorphic rock where it will stabilise."

"Oh, will it? Is that in your or our best interests?" Johnny folded his arms.

"You really can't keep a grudge against a machine, can you?" Hieronymus asked.

Johnny ignored him. "Hercules. Are you ready?"

"Hmmf."

"Then set us down."

Nothing happened. "Make it so," added Hieronymus.

Johnny and Hercules stepped onto the sandy, gritty ground. Hercules eyed the topography like a surveyor, but Johnny had no idea how to relate what he'd seen on screen to what was actually here.

"How exactly did you break through the Straits of Gibraltar?"

Hercules remained silent and scuffed the ground.

Johnny felt an unwelcome memory of their previous time together. "I see. Is this like your other labours where you had help?"

Hercules muttered something unintelligible but nodded his shaggy head.

"Great." Johnny trudged back to Star Quest, where he was annoyed to see Hieronymus gargling with a margarita.

"Just warming the old throat ahead of the concert," he explained.

"Who said you were lead singer?"

"Most of the lyrics are mine, plus I engaged the services of the choir."

Increasingly annoyed, Johnny didn't have the patience to argue further. "Right, Star Quest. You're going to have to blast through the layers, as you suggest. Hercules…" Johnny looked at the despondent giant, "doesn't feel up to it. Can *you* do it?"

"I am powered by a nuclear fusion engine such as found in a sun. I will accept an apology."

"You will accept something else in a minute, mate. Just do it." Johnny waited. And waited. "Well?"

"You are not the Pilot. I can only take orders from the registered occupant."

Johnny gazed at Hieronymus sitting on the couch. He raised a glass and nodded. "Who is the lead singer? Good, I'm glad that's settled. Then blast away."

They accelerated to several hundred feet then, at a shout from Johnny, returned and collected Hercules who sat and wouldn't look at them. He gazed morosely at the aspidistra.

There was a brief low resonance and vibration, then a build-up of pressure that set Johnny's teeth on edge, and then release. Far below, a spear of bright lightning pierced the ground. Sand and rock exploded upwards like a giant worm had surfaced. The rumble of thunder echoed across the land to be overmatched by louder thunder coming down from the north.

"What's that?" Johnny shaded his eyes against the impossible.

"A wall of water over a hundred feet high," Star Quest answered.

"Will the boat float?" It seemed unlikely that anything could withstand the approaching deluge.

"If they followed my specifications, then yes. Iron rivets and a triple hull lined with tar between. I suggest we make haste to Ashod."

Johnny frowned at Hieronymus, who waved a languid arm. "Now, young Johnny Moped, understand this: actions are now progressing that cannot be reversed."

"You're drunk."

"Yes, I think that is the wisest course of action. I also think it's time to leave this Victorian gentleman's study behind and go for something more futuristic, don't you?"

Johnny took a deep calming breath. "Could we just get on?"

Hieronymus raised his glass and pointed a finger. "Then, Star Quest, punch it. North."

Travelling northwards, gazing out over the churning maelstrom below them, Johnny had an uneasy, queasy feeling. "Do you think they survived?"

Hieronymus stopped scrolling and looked up from the interiors selection guide Star Quest had provided. "Yes, of course." The view vanished.

"I miss Noah," Hercules muttered. "I've never had a brother before."

"I suppose we could take a look," Johnny suggested, as the sofa, aspidistra, and all the unnecessary spinny things, gauges, and brass springs disappeared, replaced by boxy, vinyl-covered furniture, screens with large-buttoned keyboards, and spaces for several crew members. Something went *boiiing*.

"No. We are not in a 1960s space-based sitcom," Johnny protested. "You are just so relentlessly juvenile."

"It wasn't a comedy, though I admit the acting and costumes left a lot to be desired. And the film sets and situations were not high on the budget priority." Hieronymus seemed to be in the process of undressing.

Johnny looked away and studied the new interior Hieronymus had chosen. Drab beige carpet covered the floor; in fact, everything was shaded in various hints of brown and cream, with a few psychedelic swirls on the boxy screens. They were definitely in the late 1960s.

Johnny turned around to try to bring some sense to proceedings. And stopped.

"What on earth are you wearing?"

"Something appropriate for the captain of a spaceship." Hieronymus sat and lounged in a large, box-shaped swivel chair.

"A yellow and black jumpsuit? A jumpsuit?" Johnny asked incredulously, as a drawer opened and a red and black jumpsuit appeared next to him. "Ankle boots? My god."

"Yes?" Hercules asked.

"Take your seat at the helm, Mr. Moped."

"I'm not wearing that." Jonny cautiously sat in the smaller swivel bucket seat that squeaked as only vinyl could. He looked at the strange controls, thought briefly about touching some buttons, then thought better of it. He folded his arms, lost for words, annoyed he'd not thought of this during his brief tenure as Pilot.

"I miss Noah," Hercules continued, completely oblivious to the changes. He seemed to be standing in the science section.

"Don't touch that. On screen," commanded Hieronymus, as Johnny shook his head.

Down below, the Titanic tossed and smashed around like a toy in the dark raging waters.

"At least it floats." Johnny sat back relieved.

"Prepare to beam Hercules down."

"Pardon?" Star Quest asked.

"We don't have a teleporter?" Hieronymus asked incredulously.

"No, that is still science fiction. Dissembling DNA then turning it into a mathematic equation, sine wave or whatever, then beaming that mathematical information through space and reassembling it organically at a specified location, is a highly dangerous, impractical, and nonsensical idea."

"But—"

"That technology has never, doesn't now, nor ever will exist," Star Quest continued.

"I suppose we don't have warp technology either?"

"Warp? Warp what? The only reference that applies to is the weaving of floor coverings."

"Oh, never mind," Hieronymus sulked. "Just drop him off on the ark."

There was silence.

"Well?"

"The boat is too unstable to land on."

"Well, just tremendous. I liked you better when you were a traditional time machine."

"That is entirely unfair…" Star Quest began to argue.

"Mount Ararat." Johnny pointed to the screen where a mountain top protruded from the crashing violent waves. "Isn't that where the ark comes to rest?"

He'd had enough of Hercules' moaning, too.

"Good suggestion, Navigator. Star Quest, make it so."

"That is going to get tiring very soon. Can't you think of your own catchphrase?" Johnny asked, as he swivelled around in the squeaky chair.

Chapter Fifty-two

"Well, thank goodness for that. He was bringing everything down." They watched as Hercules battled his way up the slope towards the top of the mountain to await the ark.

"He will be alright?" Johnny felt a pang of regret watching his friend trudge away.

"He's a god, isn't he?" Hieronymus opened a compartment in the arm of his boxy seat and produced a phaser. At least, that's what it looked like.

"Could you complete the questionnaire on the new interior?" Star Quest asked. "Your responses will enable me to provide a service more in tune with your requirements."

Hieronymus looked around the deserted interior. "There needs to be more random science noises, boiiings, and communications. Also, where are the crew members?"

"Could we just please crack on? Manchester. England. Circa 2024. The old synagogue on Gasometer Street…" Johnny interrupted.

"I can provide holograms of crew members," Star Quest added.

"Then make it so."

Various crew members dressed in differing-coloured jumpsuits appeared and did various things with various controls. Hieronymus nodded and smiled as Johnny shook his head and looked away to the main screen, where a dilapidated synagogue surrounded by weeds had indeed also appeared.

"It doesn't appear to be a functioning place of worship," Johnny noted.

He stood and made his way to what he assumed was the exit. He pressed the button. Nothing happened. Annoyed, he turned to Hieronymus.

"Are you coming, or what?"

Hieronymus stood and made his way to the door. He pressed the button. It opened onto a damp, cold Manchester street. "Are you coming or what Captain. It needs to make a sweesh noise when it opens or closes. Try again."

They stood there for several minutes before Hieronymus was happy.

"Let us proceed."

"Wait. Won't the choir be suspicious? Being asked to enter a 1960s sitcom?"

Hieronymus nodded. "Suggestions?"

"Well, I…"

"I can transport the synagogue as a whole. They will not be able to see out, but others will be able to see in," Star Quest offered.

"And amplify the song?"

"Of course. It will be broadcast on all digital channels simultaneously, overriding what is broadcast."

"You can do that?" Johnny asked.

"Then gather them and make haste. Present yourself as a floating barge and let's save the people of Gaza."

"Are you wearing that?" Johnny asked, as they once more resumed their seats. "Wait. Why don't we just record the song here and broadcast it? And afterwards, you can just leave me? I've really had enough now."

Hieronymus nodded. "Hmm. Yes. Fine. Does seem like a lot of extra faff. Come on then. Have you printed the music and lyrics on paper?"

An aperture opened and several pages spilled out. Hieronymus collected them.

"You will need Toaster for remote recording," Star Quest added.

"Toastess. And editing." Johnny collected Toastess. The doors opened with an unnecessary *sweesh* sound as Johnny and Hieronymus entered the vestibule of the synagogue. Further inside could be heard various vocal harmonies.

Hieronymus opened the door and stood dramatically in the entrance. "Good evening, ladies and gentlemen."

Susan turned to face them. "These are the men I was telling you about. What on earth are you wearing now? You didn't say anything about fancy dress. Are you going to Comicon or something?"

"Something," Johnny replied, as Hieronymus distributed the sheets to varying responses from unenthusiastic people.

"This is the choir?" They looked like rough sleepers.

Susan scanned the page. "And you just want us to do the chorus? Fine."

"And musical accompaniment. Please," Johnny added.

"Well, that will cost you extra. There is a trumpet over there you can play. What music do you want? Jerome is the keyboard player."

Johnny winced, then nodded a greeting to a dreadlocked man who lounged languidly behind the keyboard. He placed Toastess on a chair facing them and picked up the trumpet. He gave an experimental toot. It had been a long time. He wet his lips, wiped the mouthpiece, and took a deep breath.

Jerome looked at his sheet. "This the tune you want? I don't read music."

He pressed a few keys, and much to Johnny's chagrin his tune actually sounded good but not what they were after.

"Before your time. Ska? Two-tone? Rude Boys?"

A gangly youth sat himself behind a drum set and gave an experimental roll. Others picked up saxophones and other trumpets.

Johnny relaxed. He could just pretend.

"Show them the tape," Johnny directed Toastess, who projected the video of the song onto the wall behind them. He noticed a few feet tapping and nodding of heads.

"Forty years ago?" Hieronymus mused. "We are so old."

"Oh, this. Man, I love this song." Jerome began his keyboard wizardry.

"This is something you can do?" Johnny asked the choir and musicians.

There were mutterings and vague agreements.

"Right. Let's go for a run through, and when we're ready let's play." Hieronymus adjusted the microphone stand. "One, two, one, two. Ready?"

Nothing happened.

"Oh. We need a name. Gasometer Street Choir?" Johnny suggested to general disinterested shrugs and nods.

"You said there'd be food." One dishevelled man stated.

"And clothes." Another added.

"You didn't say anything about recording this. And where's our money? I mean the donation?" Susan folded her arms.

Hieronymus, then all eyes, looked at Johnny.

"How much?" Words he hated to speak came forth unbidden from his pursed lips.

"One hundred pounds," Susan responded. She grabbed Johnny's elbow and guided him away from the choir and whispered. "Each."

"What? How much?" Johnny felt weak as he counted the choir. Ten of them. With a shaky hand, he turned away, secretly opened his wallet, and peeled away fifty twenties, handing them over as a pain lanced through his chest. "I don't feel too well."

Susan swiftly pocketed the notes like a crocodile swallowing a baby gazelle. She nodded to Jerome who began the beat. After recovering from his financial shock, Johnny belatedly joined in with the trumpet.

"Come on, we haven't got all night." Susan directed the choir to begin the chorus. "Ready?"

"Free-ee people of Gaza. Free, free, free people of Gaza."

Johnny had to admit they were not that good. Hieronymus less so. "We need more time to rehearse."

Hieronymus looked at him incredulously. "Have you forgotten? The spirit of protest? The Rock Lobsters never rehearsed."

"Who are the Rock Lobsters?" Jerome asked.

"What?" gasped Hieronymus. "You haven't heard of us?"

"Why the Rock Lobsters?"

"It's protest! Social commentary. What is wrong with the youth of today? Lobsters have the smallest brains pound for pound of any animal. All it knows to do is eat when hungry and snap when it doesn't like someone. Irony, man."

"Like Americans?" Jerome asked.

Hieronymus nodded, somewhat mollified.

"We need this to reach a global audience." Johnny turned to Toastess. "Can you stream this, or whatever the modern term is, to everyone?"

"I'm online with several platforms."

"Cool."

"Can we try a run through? One, two, three, 75 years without liberty. Land too small for them to live. The people oppressed but there is still humanity. Can you stand by and let this happen? I said..."

Johnny grimaced at the tuneless, keyless singing of Hieronymus that was saved by the less than enthusiastic, confused choir, but gradually the chorus was picked up and expanded upon.

"Free-ee people of Gaza…"

"Beautiful land by the sea. Partitioned unjustly. Will you stand by and let this happen? I said, Free people of Gaza."

Johnny smiled around the dingy room as people began clapping their hands to the beat and dancing. They smiled back at him.

Chapter Fifty-three

Hieronymus looked at Johnny over his frothy cappuccino. "So, that's your final word on the matter?"

"It is." Johnny frowned at the slice of carrot cake as if it were rat poison. He looked at the TV, expecting things to have changed, but the news from that region all seemed distressingly warlike and normal enough.

"Is there a list of ingredients for these products?" he asked Susan, who stood at the counter. She ignored him. She'd opened the café after the concert and now encouraged the choir, who Johnny now suspected were no choir, to spend the money he'd given them.

"Could I offer just one thought?"

Johnny sighed, taking a bite. "If you must."

"Did you know that humans have killed over 90% of all living creatures ever to have existed? And this slaughter continues year on year?" Hieronymus idly waxed his growing moustache.

"I don't see the relevance. Does this taste ultra-processed to you?"

"If you had to stop and think on that, you'd simply give up, wouldn't you? Particularly if you were a tiger," Hieronymus continued.

"Well, yes, I suppose so."

"On June 6th, 1944, 2500 soldiers died in a matter of hours on Omaha beach," Hieronymus went on. "I don't suppose they were concerned with the ingredients in a cake, do you?"

"I know what you're trying to do," Johnny replied, "and it won't work. My mind is made up. I'm through with your time-travelling business. And from now on I will only eat healthy food."

"Even though you do little actual investigation work?" Hieronymus pressed. "And the time-travelling business might not be through with you?"

"How dare you—"

Hieronymus held up his hand. "I'm trying to give perspective. Whilst you have no skills to speak of, you do have one and that is to find people, extraordinary people, who are far more competent than yourself in solving whatever problems arise. You are a middleman, a go-between, a facilitator, and as such are indispensable to the continued safety of the Earth."

Johnny angrily finished his coffee and cake, but secretly he had to agree Hieronymus had a point. Plus, what else could he do? Delivering curries was over. "Fine."

"Fine?"

"I'll continue with *my* investigation business. Paid investigation business. Solo. Just don't contact me. I've had my fill of time travel."

"Good man. We've put a stop to the tourist manipulation of events…"

"Though, that is precisely what you do. You," Johnny added.

"We'll have to await the response from the media concerning our protest song, but I'm optimistic. Until the next time."

"There is no next time."

Hieronymus stood and prepared to leave. He stretched his aching back. "I will join you in this healthy lifestyle.

We will compare weights and fitness levels. Would you like a small wager?"

"That's £25 for the coffee and cake." Susan placed the bill before them. Hieronymus and Johnny responded like she'd just pulled the pin on a grenade.

"What?" Hieronymus exploded. "Again?"

"I've just given you a thousand pounds!" Johnny gasped and clasped his chest. Hieronymus made a swift exit.

"Mal left specific instructions that if he shouldn't return, I had to charge you London prices. And I make all the cakes from scratch, for your information. There are no packet mixes here. And that's £25 each."

Johnny stood holding Toastess as the purple haze evaporated from outside the café. With a heavy heart, he paid and exited the shop.

"I just never feel hungry anymore," Johnny observed, as he walked desultorily across the street from the café back to his house. "But I'm never satisfied either. Are your products really what a human being would call food?"

Toastess buzzed. "Well, not strictly speaking, no."

"What do you mean?"

"I am linked to your subconscious. I respond to what, when, and how you eat, depending on what will satisfy you."

Johnny frowned at the little kitchen appliance that he always suspected was something far more. "That's not what I meant. The tea. The bagels. The butter. Is that real food? I mean you make it, how? Is it even nutritious? What is it all made from?"

Toastess sighed. "Diacetyl."

"Pardon?"

"I synthesise the food requirements using diacetyl as a foundation, so strictly speaking not food. Nor nutritious.

I didn't realise nutrition was a parameter," Toastess added innocently.

"Not food?"

"All my creations are chemically produced edible products. Over 10,000 additives for the ultra-processed basic requirements," Toastess buzzed proudly. "I can also do paint, and any plastic if you like."

"But not food?"

"Flavourings, preservatives, emulsifiers…" Toastess continued self-importantly.

"And you think that is a good thing?"

"Look. You humans have been eating industrially produced non-nutritional edible substances for decades. It won't do you any harm." Toastess paused. "Well, not much. In moderation. As part of a healthy diet. In a four-to-one ratio. And not over a sustained period."

"But no good either?" Johnny placed the Toastess on a wall and looked down at her. "I have to say, I am no longer enjoying your products."

Toastess shivered. "Please reconsider. A critical review will see me decommissioned."

"Now I think about it, everything you make tastes the same, whether sweet, salty, or savoury," Johnny continued. "I've put on weight, too. And I ache. More."

"How dare you?" an exasperated Toastess demanded. "After all I've done for you."

Johnny felt his burgeoning wobbly waistline, his laboured breathing and general aches and pains that had all increased thanks to the Toastess' diet of chemically produced, ultra-processed food. He looked up and down his familiar street and found what he wanted.

"I think it's time we parted."

"What? Why?" wailed Toastess. "You said we were friends. A team."

"Perhaps if you'd perfected a nutritious Scotch egg and sausage roll." Johnny sighed and picked up Toastess. He'd had enough of carting the kitchen appliance around and dumped her in a skip.